MISSIONS

A NOVEL

MARC MCGUIRE

Black Rose Writing | Texas

ISBN: 978-1-68433-460-5
PUBLISHED BY BLACK ROSE WRITING
www.blackrosewriting.com

Printed in the United States of America
Suggested Retail Price (SRP) $18.95

Missions is printed in Baskerville

*As a planet-friendly publisher, Black Rose Writing does its best to eliminate unnecessary waste to reduce paper usage and energy costs, while never compromising the reading experience. As a result, the final word count vs. page count may not meet common expectations.

For Karina

MISSIONS

CHAPTER 1

When her car reached the restaurant, she saw that the destruction was far worse than she feared. Crumpled human forms lay everywhere among the smoking rubble. Rescue workers dug noisily among the debris, some carrying survivors toward ambulances that lined the street. The entire front of the restaurant was blasted away, leaving a smoldering cavern. Firemen pumped water through the smoke toward flames deep inside the ruin. Over the wail of sirens and clang of shovels, she heard someone scream.

Christine Dupont had seen attacks before, but never of this magnitude. Two explosions, several minutes apart, was the report she had heard on the police radio as they rushed over. It was a short drive, but long enough for her boss, Dominique Carpentier, to call her twice with instructions. The strain in his voice was understandable, but she wondered about the other voices she heard in the background, voices she had not yet identified.

Dupont turned toward the area where the second explosion had occurred a dozen meters down the avenue. The space was strangely empty except for a massive pile of fuming debris pressed up against the building, evidently blasted there by the savage explosion. A car door lay incongruously atop the pile. Police had formed themselves into a human barricade to prevent crowds from pressing closer, their fear of another explosion having apparently passed. Ambulances and fire trucks continued to arrive in front of the restaurant.

Where to start? DST had long prepared for an attack, but this was worse than most of the scenarios Dupont had studied. She would have to improvise, to coordinate as best she could the conflicting imperatives of getting medical attention for the survivors and collecting evidence of the crime.

Turning back toward the restaurant, she saw that mounds of rubble had formed on the sidewalk where the explosions had driven together shattered glass, twisted metal and chunks of concrete. Rescue workers probed a nearby mound. A rivulet of blood flowed through the rubble into a dark pool near her feet. Raising her eyes, Dupont saw the rescuers pull from the mound the headless corpse of a child. "Stop them," she ordered Giles Lambert beside her. "I want the bodies tagged by location before they remove any more." Several DST officers standing behind Lambert departed. "We'll need more investigators," Dupont continued. "Three forensic teams for the restaurant and four more teams for the street."

She watched firemen pull a hose out of the restaurant and back their way across the sidewalk, weaving carefully among the smoldering rubble and the bodies. There was no way to prevent them from contaminating the crime scene. "If the fire is out and they have all the survivors, get them out of the way so we can photograph everything." Two more DST officers departed. "Everything," Dupont shouted after them. She could not predict what would be important.

Looking toward the restaurant, she studied the yawning cavern left by the blast. *First priority is to figure out if the bomber stayed around for the explosion.* He would be more torn up than the others. *Same procedure over there.* She looked back down the avenue to the location of the second explosion. Once she had identified the bombers, even one of them, she would be on their trail. But would Dominique Carpentier allow her to hold on to the case that long? True, it was hers by right of her recent promotion at *Direction de la Surveillance du Territoire*, but she was only thirty-four years old and this was far bigger than the last two cases she had led, an embassy kidnapping and a drive-by assassination. She recalled the frantic voices behind Dominique's on the phone. *But who else can they find at DST who is better prepared than I am?*

Her gaze fell upon the pool of blood near her feet and then rose to view the rubble mound. The child had been removed, but the image of its small body, broken and headless, returned to her mind. She breathed deeply to compose herself. Before she realized her mistake, a whiff of acrid smoke entered her nostrils. Fighting back the urge to gag, she forced herself to concentrate on the scene before her. What was it trying to tell her? Someone had planned this carefully, she knew. Someone had deliberately chosen the *Avenue des Champs-Élysées.* They knew that lots of people would be here, people from all over the world. They knew there would be children. Staring into the glistening pool of blood, Christine Dupont strained to catch a glimpse of the still faceless evil. *Who out there is celebrating?*

"They gave us no warning," Giles Lambert said, as if following Dupont's thoughts.

"It could be someone we haven't been watching."

Special forensic units began to arrive. After giving them instructions, Dupont watched the new teams fan out, some gathering information from the police, firemen and paramedics already at work, others photographing the restaurant, sidewalk and street in preparation for the collection of evidence. "Get the names of all the bystanders before they get away." She pointed down the sidewalk where the crowd outside the police cordon seemed to be growing. "Some of them must have seen something before the explosions."

The chopping sound of a helicopter circling overhead reminded her that the scene was already being broadcast throughout Europe. Even before authorities announced their suspicions, journalists would be declaring this to be the worst café bombing in Paris since the Algerian War of Independence four decades earlier. Within hours the entire world would be demanding answers.

She caught up with one of the forensic teams at work inside the restaurant. A detective directed her through the interior rubble, his pointing hand protected by a red rubber glove. Then she saw it, deep inside the kitchen, obscured by smoke and steam, a wounded monster brandishing jaws of jagged steel. Dupont stepped toward it, the gaping hulk of blasted metal looking as though it were about to devour her.

"It's a car," explained a voice behind her. "What's left of it, at least."

CHAPTER 2

Six Months before the Paris Attack

The fields along Richmond Highway were covered with snow the morning Doyle O'Gara took a taxi from Ronald Reagan airport to begin his new assignment. The snow looked fresh and white, not yet sullied by mud or exhaust. The taxi driver said something over his shoulder, but Doyle was not listening. He was staring at the Pentagon as it passed by like a glacier in the distance. The ugly chasm in its southern wall scowled down impatiently at the multitude of reconstruction workers swarming below. Doyle felt good to be joining the war, no matter how small or peripheral his role might turn out to be.

The Washington office of Sentinel Systems Corporation was located in Tyson's Corner, about three miles from Langley. Doyle's new boss, Suresh Kumar, had said he would meet him in the lobby. Instead, he was greeted by a security officer, most of whose questions he had already answered during the previous weeks of clearances. The officer typed his latest answers into a computer and then took him into another room where he was photographed, fingerprinted and asked to place his right hand over a scanner. The process took nearly an hour. In the end, Doyle received a thin plastic card that bore his name and a computer chip.

"It's about time, man!" Suresh Kumar stepped into the room, raising his hand in a high-five salute before slapping it against Doyle's. "Was your flight delayed by the storm?" Despite the weather, Suresh wore a bright Hawaiian shirt that suggested he had just walked in from a beach. Doyle glanced down to see if he might be wearing sandals. "Don't worry." Suresh said, motioning with his cell phone for Doyle to follow. "We'll make up the lost time." Struggling to keep up as they crossed the lobby, Doyle discretely buttoned his coat for the next meeting. *Too many expense-account dinners with Ann Arbor clients.* He planned to join a gym in Washington to get back into shape. "We can go right up," Suresh said. "Howie has some time now."

Howard Silver, Suresh's boss, was vice-president for government services. The title seemed a bit lofty for a software salesman, but Doyle knew Silver was considered a heavy hitter thanks to the government contracts he had recently won for Sentinel. Doyle had met him once when he visited the Ann Arbor office, but he doubted Silver would remember him, a mere software developer.

"Our security system is different here." Suresh pointed his phone toward a glowing screen next to the elevator.

"What does it do?" Doyle asked as he placed his hand on the screen.

"The human hand contains twenty-seven bones and a complex web of interconnected joints, muscles and tendons," Suresh explained, "so each person's hand is unique enough to confirm his identity." He paused until the mechanism signaled the elevator door to open. "Hand geometry!" he exclaimed triumphantly.

Offices of the big shots, Doyle thought as they stepped out on the fourth floor, *wood paneling and fancy paintings all around*. He followed Suresh across the thick carpet until they reached the desk of a stout secretary with a serious demeanor. She eyed Doyle doubtfully, her expression reminding him of a bulldog, and then nodded consent to pass. Evidently her job was to guard, not to greet. When they entered his office, Howard Silver was already on his feet, striding toward them with one hand extended like a basketball player and a smile nearly as large as a basketball hoop. "Doyle O'Gara, I'm delighted Suresh persuaded you to come down to Washington to help us."

"Despite your degree from the University of Michigan," Suresh said with a wry smile.

Silver rolled his eyes. "I'm sure Suresh has told you, Doyle, that he came to us with a seal of approval from the Massachusetts Institute of Technology." He polished his fingernails on his lapel in satirical admiration.

"Don't believe him, Doyle," Suresh shot back. "I learned everything I know about computers from Lahore Elementary School and Popular Mechanics."

"We've always doubted the MIT part," said Silver, throwing his arm playfully over Suresh's shoulders, "but he makes up for his poor education by working long hours." Silver motioned his visitors toward a leather sofa and in the same fluid gesture dropped into a chair facing them across a wide coffee table. "So much work is flowing into this office, Doyle, that we're drowning in it. I hear you're a fast swimmer."

"Yes, sir," Doyle replied, thinking it best not to address Silver by name, yet. He turned toward Suresh to accept a cup of coffee, but when he turned back, Silver had vanished from his chair. His voice could be heard whispering to the bulldog somewhere behind their sofa. Doyle studied the coffee table, resisting the temptation to turn around, until Silver dropped back into his chair as suddenly as he had left it. He looked puzzled, as though he had momentarily forgotten the purpose of their meeting.

"Suresh, I'll need an update on DCS right after we finish with Doyle. I have a call with Grebb this afternoon."

"I told him yesterday," said Suresh, sounding a bit peeved. "We've run into problems."

"Grebb doesn't give an owl's hoot, Suresh. He's going crazy over there."

"Okay," Suresh sighed, "we'll put together a show for him, but it may delay things."

Silver turned his attention back to Doyle, explaining that his Ann Arbor experience with Market Eye was going to be very useful to them in Washington. "Of course you guys had one big advantage over us."

"What was that?" Doyle asked.

"You were tracking consumers with e-mail addresses and Internet accounts. Our client may have nothing more than a pseudonym or an old photograph." Silver's gaze lifted to some place above Doyle's shoulder; the bulldog was evidently signaling him from the doorway. "Excuse me again, Doyle; I need to take this call."

Doyle started to rise, but Suresh motioned for him to remain seated. "While we're waiting for Howie, let me tell you about your first project. It involves DCS-1000, better known as Carnivore." Doyle leaned forward to hear the briefing over Silver's animated telephone conversation a few feet away. "The client expects to use Carnivore far more extensively in the future," Suresh explained in his choppy Pakistan accent, "so they've awarded us a contract to develop more powerful versions." *The client.* The thin disguise seemed to Doyle like a secret handshake among children; everyone knew the nature of Sentinel's work in the nation's capital, but no one seemed willing to break the ritual.

"A lot of critics say the client did a bad job connecting certain dots," Howard Silver said as he returned to his chair. "They imagine it was a simple task, like looking out into a starry sky and figuring out which stars form the Big Dipper." He poked his finger into the air touching several imaginary stars. "Well, the critics don't understand the problem. The real challenge is not to connect the dots but to recognize what the heck qualifies as a dot in the first place." Silver spread his hands wide as though to impress Doyle with the vast number of potential dots to connect. "Every day the client receives huge amounts of information from all over the world, some of which is relevant but most of which is not. Photographs, travel records, intercepted calls, tips and rumors. Their problem is to decide which bits may be worth following." Silver pinched an imaginary bit of information out of the air between his thumb and forefinger. "But those important bits are mixed in with all the other stuff. It's like trying to pick out a few odd-shaped snowflakes in the middle of a Boston blizzard. Am I right, Suresh?"

"Absolutely. What makes it worse is that the blizzard changes from one day to the next."

"Well put," said Silver, jumping to his feet. He eyed his telephone, perhaps anticipating another urgent call, and then thrust his hand toward Doyle across the table. "I'm sure Suresh is in a hurry to put you to work solving these little problems for us. Good luck young man!"

Doyle followed Suresh to their next destination, passing unavoidably before the desk of Silver's secretary. The bulldog nodded at Doyle after glancing at her watch, evidently relieved that his welcome meeting had been brief. "So it sounds like I'll be mostly rewriting the Carnivore software," Doyle remarked when they reached the elevator. "The same sort of work I was doing with Market Eye."

"But here you'll be leading the team," Suresh corrected. He studied Doyle a moment. "Don't worry, man. You just turned twenty-nine, didn't you? If you perform the way we expect, you could become a manager before your thirtieth birthday." He spread his arms to display the full splendor of his flowered shirt. "Just like me," he added with a smile.

CHAPTER 3

Four Months before the Paris Attack

Joseph Morgan sat alone at the window end of the reading room waiting for his guest. If he did not arrive within a few minutes, Morgan decided, he would leave. Even if he had been on time, Morgan still had serious reservations about working with him, qualms he had shared often enough with his clients. He had authorized the receptionist of the University Club to send his guest up to the reading room—Morgan felt it was more dignified than waiting for him in the lobby—but now he hoped she had found some excuse to bar the man from entering the club.

Just as he rose to depart, Morgan heard the sharp clacking of footsteps and looked up to see Mohammed Jamal approaching across the walnut parquet floor. Morgan felt a lump in his stomach, as though he had swallowed too much spaghetti at lunch.

"Sorry, I'm a bit late, Joseph," Jamal apologized as he arrived.

"No trouble at all. Traffic from the airport?"

"Yes, indeed. London seems more crowded each time I visit. You English are allowing far too many foreigners into the country." Joseph Morgan smiled politely and gestured toward a leather chair across from him. He started to remove something from his jacket pocket, but hesitated at the sound of more footsteps.

"The weather in Damascus was hot this morning," Mohammed Jamal offered, fanning himself with both hands. "Unbearably hot." Morgan guessed as much from his guest's attire. Jamal wore a tan suit of a silk-wool blend, ideal for springtime in the Middle East, but a bit out-of-season for

London. Something else was odd about Jamal's appearance, but Morgan could not yet identify it.

The footsteps ceased as the waiter arrived before them. "Is it too early for a gin and tonic?" Morgan asked.

"Of course not, sir."

"I'll just have water," Jamal interjected.

"How clumsy of me," Morgan said.

"It's more a matter of personal habit than belief in the ancient traditions. *Allah* has bigger concerns these days than what we eat and drink."

"Two bottles of Perrier for now," Morgan instructed the waiter. He watched the man depart and then slipped his hand beneath his jacket to remove a large envelope. The jacket was a single-breasted, chalk-striped model purchased at Doves & Green. It conveyed his professional status, Morgan felt, without overstating it. A solicitor by training, Morgan had been born in Amman, Jordan, but sent to London after high school to study business, his father expecting the young man—his name was Youssef Moqued back then—to return home to manage the family's Mercedes dealership. Morgan soon realized that life in London and a career in the banking law offered him more opportunities for wealth and even a bit of power. "The transfers will be complete by the end of the day," he said as he passed the large envelope to Mohammed Jamal.

Opening the envelope, Jamal read the numbers written inside. "Very generous," he said with a smile. "I assume these are Euros? I'm not yet used to the new currency."

"Don't worry. They are British pounds sterling."

"Most generous, indeed," Jamal said, raising his eyebrows and nodding his head in an amiable salute. He slipped the envelope into his aluminum briefcase and snapped it shut. "Your clients have surely satisfied their *zakat* duties for the rest of their lives."

Morgan had little interest in Muslim traditions, but he did appreciate the value of *zakat,* one of the Five Pillars of Islam. The duty to donate one-fortieth of one's income was originally intended to support widows, orphans and the poor; but a flood of petrodollars had transformed *zakat* into an inexhaustible source of funds for mosques, schools and libraries around the world. A few of the benefitting charities promoted the spread of Islam by more aggressive means.

The waiter returned with a tray bearing two bottles, a pair of glasses and a plate of salted almonds. Morgan studied his guest while the waiter poured the drinks. Jamal wore round rimless glasses above a small mustache. His olive-brown complexion was neatly framed by jet-black hair, his features rising in sharp angles, as though they had been chiseled from tinted marble. Morgan's gaze returned to the mustache that crossed Jamal's upper lip like a thin black caterpillar. Then he realized what was odd in Jamal's appearance: the same lip had been clean-shaven when they had met a few months earlier.

Jamal lifted his glass first. "To France."

"Why France?" Morgan asked before he caught himself.

"Because it is the source of this fine water," Jamal replied. After the waiter departed, he lifted his glass again. "Besides, we may send you good news from Paris in a few months."

"Paris," repeated Morgan, placing his glass back on the table.

"Would your clients prefer a different location?" Jamal asked. "Does their gift have any attached strings, as our American friends would say?"

"No, the charities I represent have no wish to influence your group." Morgan passed his hand over the leg of his trousers several times. The rich fabric reassured him. "But they trust their generosity will be put to effective use."

"What do they consider effective? Speaking hypothetically, of course."

"Yes, hypothetically," Morgan replied, lowering his voice. "The recent events have brought to the Muslim world a new sense of confidence. Our people feel surer following their leaders along the Straight Path."

"There can be no surer path than Islam," Jamal observed.

"Yes, of course, but unfortunately some Muslims have grown impatient with their leaders. A few radicals seek to exploit this discontent. They demand change regardless of the consequences."

"There can be no change except what *Allah* wills. And what *Allah* wills, no man can change."

Morgan smiled at the verse from the *Qur'an*, though he detected a note of sarcasm in Jamal's recitation. "Yes, so it is written. We all understand that change must come eventually, but my clients believe it is dangerous to change too quickly." He wondered if the younger man understood Middle East politics well enough to appreciate that danger. "Imagine the common people trying to elect the Commander of the Faithful."

"So, what precisely do your clients want?" Jamal asked, his voice sounding sharper.

Morgan spotted something on his trouser leg and dusted it away while he composed his thoughts. "The events and locations are entirely up to you. The growing popularity of Islam will give my clients valuable influence in the future. After all, the oil may run out some day." The two men gazed out the reading room window at the lush greenery of St. James Park, as though they were trying to peer into that distant day.

"I think I understand," Jamal said after a moment.

"But don't go too far," the older man said quietly. "The reactions must be controlled."

"Reactions?" Jamal asked, as though the possibility surprised him.

Morgan stared into Jamal's rimless glasses, trying to read his dark eyes. "They will go after your group, of course. We assume you are well prepared for that. But they may also oppress Muslims in general. You know: arrests and surveillance, immigration restrictions, employment discrimination; things like that."

"Such oppression may serve your purposes," Jamal observed. "Anger and resentment will only bring our people closer to Islam."

"You may be right," Morgan conceded after a moment. "But be careful." He stood to signal that the meeting was at an end. After his guest departed, Joseph Morgan walked back to his chair by the window. His shoes felt plush under his feet. He had worn tasseled loafers of deep burgundy leather to lend the meeting a casual air: a small sign to remind Jamal of his place. An hour remained before dinner. He called the waiter and ordered a gin and tonic.

———

One of the passengers on the British Air flight from London to Cairo that night carried an Egyptian passport bearing the name Hosni al-Sheriff. In the days to follow, the man would visit several Middle East capitals using the same false identity. As he flew from city to city, the money from Joseph

Morgan would also travel through the Middle East, making its way from one bank account to another, each opened by a different corporation that disappeared shortly thereafter. The trail of money would be impossible to trace. Impossible, that is, unless one had the envelope of banking instructions that the man calling himself Hosni al-Sheriff carried in his aluminum briefcase.

During his stop in Abu Dhabi, Mohammed Jamal visited *Société Générale*, one of the largest French banks, at its office perched atop a skyscraper still under construction. Stepping from the elevator into the reception area, he felt the swelling of an erection against his trousers. He had felt such excitement during past operations, just before the explosions and the escapes, but his present state of arousal was more intense. *A great battle is about to begin,* he thought, *a battle that will shake the world. When the foundations stop shuddering, the power and wealth of the Middle East will have fallen into the hands of new leaders.*

One of the bank's officers, a young woman assigned to high-net-worth clients, inspected Jamal's credentials, including the false Egyptian passport he had presented to her weeks earlier, and informed him that a deposit in pounds sterling had been credited overnight to one of his recently opened accounts. Yes, the funds were already available for further transfer. Her tone was businesslike, but Jamal detected a discreet invitation in her smile. After requesting a Euro transfer to a branch of *Société Générale* in Paris, Jamal wrote out a withdrawal slip for US dollars in cash. The young woman delivered the money a short time later in an attractive attaché case bearing the bank's logo. Shaking her hand to depart, Jamal allowed his eyes to be drawn momentarily into hers. It would be delightful to enjoy the aphrodisiacal qualities of money in Abu Dhabi, he imagined, but he had more pressing business.

Waiting for the elevator, Jamal admired the view from thirty stories above the Persian Gulf. It was time to pay another visit to certain Islamist militants, members of the shadowy *shura*. Hiding in half a dozen countries, they had already approved Jamal's plans, but it was prudent to brief them again face-to-face. Their continuing support was the seal of approval that would help maintain financing from the oil-rich tyrants represented by Joseph Morgan. He just needed to remind them that exporting jihad to Europe would help them attract support for their own fanatical causes.

The elevator finally arrived. *What are their causes, exactly?* Jamal sometimes had trouble remembering. Some wanted only to convince a monarch or two to impose *Shari'ah* law; others wished to return the entire Muslim world to the medieval age of the Prophet; still others dreamed of provoking the Shi'ite and Sunni branches into a final confrontation to resolve religious questions dating back fourteen centuries, as though they still mattered to anyone. *No wonder the rulers want to get rid of them, the demented old goats.* Entering the elevator, Jamal spotted his image in the mirrored wall and noticed, not for the first time, how much his appearance had changed since his youthful days as a computer scientist at Damascus University. His well-trimmed hair was still black, but now it was marred by gray patches at the temples. The eyes behind his neat glasses looked a bit too tired for a man of only thirty-five years. He felt momentarily weightless as the elevator dropped toward the lobby. *Don't go too far.* Jamal smiled when he recalled Joseph Morgan's timid warnings. *The reactions must be controlled.* The operations that Jamal planned would provoke reactions far more horrendous than anything the effete solicitor could imagine.

The elevator door opened. Stepping out, Jamal encountered puzzled glances in the lobby. *Was I laughing to myself again?* His emotions sometimes ran ahead of him, he had noticed, but that was because his plan was so inspiring. *But I must control my excitement.* Maybe he should relax a few days before the first operation. Visit his older brother Hassan at his big summer home in the Bekaa Valley. They could walk together among the vineyards; even go hiking in the Chouf Mountains like they used to do as boys. No, he decided; there was too much left to do. Besides, his brother had never invited him to his Bekaa Valley palace. *He hasn't talked to me in years,* Jamal remembered. *He'll never stop blaming me for killing the old man.*

CHAPTER 4

First Day of the Investigation

Bodies began arriving at *Hôtel-Dieu*, the oldest hospital in Paris, an hour after the bombings. They would continue to arrive all afternoon and late into the night. Christine Dupont had two reasons for selecting *Hôtel-Dieu*. The ancient hospital, constructed over the course of a millennium between the seventh and seventeenth centuries, had a state-of-the art forensic medicine department ideal for criminal investigations. Located on the *Ile de la Cite* next to the *Cathédral Notre Dame de Paris*, the modernized *Hôtel-Dieu* was also the closest hospital to the bombing scene. She had asked Dr. Hakim Abalian, the head of the medical-legal department, to call in extra doctors and medical technicians as soon as she realized how many bodies would require examination. They would need to come in immediately, she had explained. Yes, tonight and they should be prepared for several long days of work. It would be best to cancel evening plans, too.

When Dupont arrived with Giles Lambert around 10 p.m., Dr. Abalian said he had encountered no excuses. Every specialist in the city was eager to be part of the investigation. After the calls, he had reserved all the autopsy rooms available in *Hôtel-Dieu* and then contacted other departments to requisition still more space. As the doctor led them into a large examination room, Dupont saw rows of stainless steel tables surrounded by masked technicians. Approaching one group, she watched them sort through human remains, evidently trying to reunite missing parts with their former bodies. The matching would be necessary for proper funerals, Dr. Abalian explained, but the more urgent goal was to find which parts belonged to the suicide bombers. He led them to a table where some kind of surgical procedure was underway.

"An autopsy?" Lambert asked. "The cause of death seems pretty obvious."

"We're looking for objects and chemicals that may have penetrated the tissue. They may be calling cards from your bombers."

Dupont walked down the center aisle, looking right and left under the bright lights, until she reached a technician who was working with a scalpel and forceps as deftly as a sushi chef. Stopping to watch, she turned her thoughts to the meeting that was taking place at the *Élysée Palace*, less than three kilometers away. The country's top ministers were discussing how to manage the crisis. The scalpel sliced across an abdomen, widening a gash. Rumor had it that Dominique Carpentier was nearing retirement. *Does he still have the clout to back me up?* The forceps probed one way, then another, digging for something. Carpentier had sounded confident during their last call, but he had seemed unusually interested in the composition of her team. The scalpel returned to slice deeper. Still, she had persuaded him to approve her preferred candidates. Some of them probably resented her promotion, but she trusted their professional dedication. The nausea hit her just when she thought she had overcome it. She turned abruptly from the operation and walked back down the aisle, avoiding eye contact with Dr. Abalian and Giles Lambert.

She made it to the toilet just in time. When she finished vomiting, she rinsed her mouth in the sink. Breathing deeply several times, she studied her pale face in the mirror. *Still looking decent, all things considered*. She adjusted the collar of her white blouse, confirming it went well with her powder blue suit, sober but stylish. Checking her eyes, she recalled a remark Lambert had once made about them and smiled. *Back to work, Christine*. Walking back up the hospital corridor, she recalled more of Carpentier's nervous instructions over the phone. Members of the opposition political parties had to be assigned prominent roles in the team. *You know, Christine, the usual gang of idiots*. Carpentier was being much more hands on than usual. She ignored Lambert's concerned gaze as she reentered the examination room. "Do you have any idea which body parts belonged to the bombers?" she asked Dr. Abalian.

"Yes, although it would be more correct to call them body *fragments* at this stage."

"Where are they?"

"Are you sure you want to see them?"

Dupont nodded. The doctor led her and Lambert to a stainless steel table at the end of the room where the examiners had placed the most severely burned and blasted remains. Dupont studied them intently. "What do they tell us?"

"All the pieces were very close to the explosion inside the restaurant," Dr. Abalian replied. "We assume they came from the first bomber or from the nearest victims, but we'll know more after we compare the DNA from the blood and tissue found inside the car."

"What about the second bomber?" Lambert asked.

"We're still trying to collect body fragments outside the restaurant that might have belonged to him."

"We'll come back in an hour or two to see what more you've learned," Dupont said. She suddenly wondered if she harbored any doubts about the doctor's objectivity, recalling that he was probably Muslim. An unfair question, perhaps, but she was trained to be thorough. She turned to her second in command. "Let's see how the other teams are doing."

Known at DST as "the bloodhound," Giles Lambert had a reputation for sniffing clues out of the most unpromising tangles of evidence. It was coincidence, perhaps, that he also had an oversized nose which he tried to offset by growing his curly hair unfashionably long. With his customary diligence, the bloodhound had asked Dr. Abalian for space in *Hôtel-Dieu* where DST technicians were already analyzing objects coming from the bombing scene. Wrist watches, car keys, eyeglasses, wedding rings. Anything that could be linked to the victims or by process of elimination linked to the bombers.

It was still the first day of the investigation, a few minutes before midnight, when Dupont returned to *Direction de la Surveillance du Territoire*, the French version of the FBI and CIA combined. From its headquarters at *7 rue Nélaton*—not far from the Eiffel Tower—she placed a secure telephone call to Langley, Virginia.

"Good evening, Christine. You people are working late tonight. I thought France had a thirty-five hour work-week."

Dupont had heard the same quip several times from Burt Brown, the Deputy Director for Counterterrorism. Laugh at his jokes, Carpentier had once advised her, but never forget who he represents. "We'll have to investigate that, Burt, to see if anyone is breaking the law. I hear you people are busy, too, reorganizing yourselves under that new Homeland Security Act."

She heard Brown chuckle painfully at the other end of the line, then his voice turned serious. "Any idea who did it?"

"Not yet. How about you?" She knew her American colleagues had leaped onto the case as soon as the nature of the Paris attack had become apparent.

"Doug Grebb and his team have been going over the signal traffic before and after the incident. Have you been able to identify the bombers? That would help us a lot."

"We're still sorting through body parts. But we're calling one of the suspects Big Mac."

"Because of the restaurant they bombed?"

"No, because of the face."

"The face?" Brown asked.

"Yes, we found a face stuck to the wall. It looked like . . . how do you call that? A hamburger patty?" Brown's end of the line remained silent. Thinking he had not understood because of her accent, Dupont added, "It was flat, brown and somewhat burned."

"I got the picture, Christine. Maybe I should send over a couple of our people to help."

"No thanks, Burt. I don't think Dominique would like to read in tomorrow's papers that the Americans have taken over a French criminal investigation." She heard muffled voices on the line as she awaited Brown's reply. Probably the same cast of characters she knew, but she was not sure.

"We have an interest here too, Christine," said Brown. "We can stay in the background, but we would like to be closely involved. We have some ideas you may find helpful."

"Such as?"

More voices, low and inarticulate. "Considering the target," Brown resumed, "we looked at some of your anti-globalization extremists. But the signal traffic shows no unusual activity on that front. Some of your local jihadists have been quite chatty the past few weeks, but we've found nothing linked to today's attack, so far."

"You're not telling me the Central Intelligence Agency has been monitoring French telephones without our consent, are you?"

"Of course not, Christine. I'm sure that would be illegal."

"Look, Burt, we've been conducting some surveillance of our own, in accordance with French law—"

"Of course."

"—so it might be helpful to compare notes."

"Open book?" Brown asked.

"No, tit for tat," Dupont replied.

"Okay, tell me who we should contact. We can begin sharing files over the encrypted lines immediately. Tit for tat." She heard muted laughter in the background before Burt Brown hung up.

Christine Dupont had arrived at this point in her career by an unusual route, having spent her first six years as a corporate lawyer at one of the city's leading firms. She had just been promoted to partner and moved into a new office overlooking the Right Bank, when one of her colleagues mentioned that DST was hiring investigators. Dupont was intrigued. The more she thought about it, the more she realized it was exactly the career change she wanted. "It is an incredible opportunity," she had explained to her mother at the time.

"Working with spies and spy catchers?" her mother had asked. "Isn't DST something of a men's club?"

"Yes, but they are looking for women to placate the politicians. I could rise fast." And she had. As the terrorist threat grew, France responded with some of the strictest laws in Europe. With her legal training, Dupont quickly became an expert on the procedures for infiltrating and monitoring radical groups. Her boss, Dominique Carpentier, the head of DST's anti-terrorism unit, came to rely on Dupont to convince investigating magistrates to authorize wiretaps, preemptive arrests and custodial interrogation. She could weave the most circumstantial evidence into the tightest of arguments to justify suspicions that Carpentier sometimes only felt in his gut.

"Aren't you taking this crusade a bit too far?" her mother had asked recently.

"I find it fascinating," Dupont admitted. "Scary, but fascinating."

"They just want to change the world for the better," her mother observed from the living room sofa. "Perhaps their objectives justify some of their violence."

Dupont had invited her mother to move in a year earlier after her father had suddenly passed away—a fatal combination of heavy smoking and windsurfing on the *Cote d'Azur*—but the older woman was getting on her nerves. It was time to admit the mistake and find her a place of her own. "What do you mean, Mother?"

"All is not right in the world, Christine. Someone needs to shake things up sometimes."

"Like you did, back in 1968?" Dupont had replied. She found it best to humor the older woman whenever she reverted to her revolutionary youth.

Dupont made six more secure telephone calls to sister intelligence agencies that night. Despite the late hour in some capitals, she had no trouble getting through. Intelligence agencies around the world had cleared their schedules to pursue the implications of the incident on the *Avenue des Champs-Élysées*. Several commented on the date September 1. The attackers struck Paris just when everyone had been focused on New York in anticipation of the First Anniversary. Would the new enemy be celebrating earlier each year in different countries?

— — —

Around the time that Dupont completed her late-night calls, a red-haired technician was still working at the improvised investigation center at *Hôtel-Dieu*. The young woman opened a clear plastic bag marked "Restaurant, First Floor, Quadrant J-16" and dumped the contents onto a stainless steel tray. She straightened a moment to massage her lower back before leaning forward and to sort through the pieces. *Great for my spine, bent over for hours on this damned stool.* She came upon a small chip of plastic and metal about the size of her thumbnail. It appeared interesting but badly damaged, so she tossed the chip into a glass beaker marked "Unidentified Electronic Components."

CHAPTER 5

Three Months before the Paris Attack

It was Doyle O'Gara's first visit to the CIA. He and Suresh Kumar were greeted in the lobby by Ronnie Lapoint, a pale-faced man in his mid-forties, deprived of sunlight from too much computer work, Doyle surmised. As Suresh filled out the security log, Doyle paced around the perimeter of the CIA seal, a huge granite disc embedded in the lobby floor, and asked Lapoint how much it weighed. "At least a ton," Lapoint replied tonelessly, his eyes remaining on Suresh Kumar. Suresh had dressed up for the occasion, a magenta tie securing the collar of his black silk shirt, but Lapoint expressed no opinion about his attire. Evidently, the CIA was willing to relax its dress code to obtain the latest technology.

Lapoint tapped on his wristwatch. "Did Howard happen to say when he would be joining us?" Just as the question left his lips, Howard Silver appeared at the far end of the lobby and strode across the marble floor, offering the CIA man his athletic handshake and outsized smile. Lapoint hurried the group down a long, poorly lit corridor to a conference room reserved for outside vendors. Doyle expected a high-tech chamber lined with screens and consoles, but the room turned out to contain little more than a meeting table and some chairs. The government was apparently economizing on furniture as well as electricity.

While Lapoint offered them coffee, two more CIA staffers arrived at the entrance: a well-dressed young woman, followed by another pasty-faced man. Doyle turned to get a better look at the CIA woman just as Lapoint began to serve him, with the result that the hot coffee missed Doyle's cup and poured over his hand. The hand remained strangely immobile. The young woman strode into the room and delivered an affectionate embrace to her CIA colleague, allowing Doyle to appreciate at close range her striking figure sheathed in a beige knit dress. He tried in vain to remember her name. Lapoint had introduced the new arrivals too quickly.

"Good morning, Howard," boomed a voice. Douglas Grebb, a lanky man in his mid-50s came through the door. "We've been looking forward to hearing about your newest junk for weeks." Grebb pumped Silver's hand briefly before taking his seat at the head of the table. "You already know Ronnie Lapoint and Stan Stebbins." Grebb gestured toward the two CIA men. "They've cancelled their vacations in case you guys are ready to start work."

Silver smiled at Grebb's gibe. "I'm happy to say, Mr. Grebb, that all the delays are behind us." His tone was jovial, but Doyle thought he heard a defensive note.

"This is Leslie Jumana, our newest star." Grebb had turned toward the dark-eyed young woman. "She has degrees in International Relations and Middle East Studies from Stanford." Grebb drew out the university name in ironic veneration. "Leslie heads up a new unit to help us better understand Islamic terrorists." Leslie Jumana smiled skeptically at Grebb's introduction, her perfectly shaped eyebrows rising like twin exclamation points. Doyle imagined they gave a little salute in his direction. "As for me, all I need to understand is where they are hiding, so we can go there and kill them." Grebb winked at the young woman. "Shall we begin?"

"Thank-you Mr. Grebb," began Howard Silver, rising from his seat. "Sentinel Systems is eager to help the Agency confront the new challenges. It is an honor for us to be part of your team." Silver paused a moment, evidently to allow time for his message of enthusiasm and camaraderie to register. "We are here to tell you about our progress in improving Carnivore. As you know, the system was originally designed for Internet surveillance of domestic criminals. Our team has been working on four major improvements to combat the new global threat. The first improvement is speed." Doyle projected a slide on Silver's cue. "The number of messages you need to monitor is astronomical, simply mind boggling. Using the latest techniques for targeting, binning and parallel processing, we've developed algorithms that will allow you to mine the data you require much faster."

"Next is language." A new slide appeared on the screen. Although Doyle was playing a supporting role, he felt proud to be part of the meeting. After only a few months in Washington, he was already on the front line.

"We've heard this pitch before," Grebb interrupted Silver. "I want to see if your new technology works in the real world."

"We're prepared to begin the field tests, Mr. Grebb." Silver paused a fraction of a second. "This week, if you like." Doyle wondered if anyone else had detected Silver's slight hesitation. The aggressive testing schedule had been agreed upon before the meeting, but maybe Silver had private doubts. Doyle recalled his distracted behavior during their first-day meeting.

"What will that cost?" Grebb asked. "Burt won't authorize a dime until we're sure it works."

"Sentinel will bear the cost of field tests," Silver said. "No financial commitment from the Agency until you're satisfied our system helps you catch more bad guys. What's more, if the Carnivore upgrades perform as expected, we can apply them to Echelon at little extra cost."

Grebb smiled. "Okay, what else you got?" The presentation continued for another hour. Grebb seemed especially interested in Sentinel's progress with spyware.

"We can now upload spyware into a suspect's computer via wireless transmission," Silver explained as Doyle projected the corresponding slide.

"Without him knowing?" Grebb asked.

Silver nodded to Suresh Kumar. "That's right, Mr. Grebb. Our latest prototype is wireless and undetectable." Grebb studied Suresh quizzically as he spoke, as though noticing for the first time the outlandish colors of the Pakistani immigrant's shirt and tie. "Once inside," Suresh continued undeterred, "the spyware broadcasts the suspect's location and every keystroke he types."

Grebb looked down the table at the CIA team and saw Stan Stebbins pump his arm gamely in the air, his ghostly countenance offering a thin smile of approval. "Okay," Grebb said. "Give us some of that, too."

"If you still have room in your shopping cart, you'll want to test our profiling system. It's the cat's pajama." Silver turned to Suresh again.

"Yes, indeed, Mr. Grebb. We've worked with a team of psychologists to apply our pattern recognition software to analyze suspicious Internet activity. With enough data, the system can tell you if the guy is a leader or a follower, violent or passive, even gay or straight."

"Not that we intend to discriminate against gay terrorists," Silver interjected. Everyone smiled at the political correctness. It was hard to be sure under the dimmed light, but Doyle thought Leslie Jumana directed a smile to him as her adorable eyebrows rose in mock astonishment. When he looked back a moment later, he saw that her gaze had returned to Grebb, her lips standing at stiff attention as though awaited his orders.

"Okay, let's start the field tests," Grebb announced, pushing back his chair. "I hope your team brought their sleeping bags, Howard. We have no time to waste." As Grebb hoisted his angular frame from the table, Doyle noticed that the change of lighting exposed dark blotches under his eyes. Was he suffering from lack of sleep? Perhaps beneath his aggressive humor and crusty confidence he was gnawed by secret fears that the new defenses would not be ready in time.

"Are we also working on Echelon?" Doyle asked a few hours later, during the drive back to Sentinel. He knew a few things about the top-secret system, but today's meeting was the first time he had heard of Sentinel's involvement.

"I'll tell you what you need to know," Suresh said from the driver's side, "since you'll soon be working on the upgrade." Thanks to Echelon, a global system of antennae that monitored telecommunications outside the United States, the challenge was no longer to intercept messages—Echelon captured something like three billion every day—but rather to analyze them all. Sentinel was developing new Echelon software to detect word patterns that might disclose criminal activity, such as the word "bomb" in the same e-mail as "embassy." The latest versions could even learn code words; for example, detecting unusual uses of the word *gift* and then flagging that word in the proximity of *airplane*. "Our biggest barrier is language," Suresh said, turning briefly from the steering wheel. "Since terrorists rarely communicate in English, we have teams adapting search engines and voice recognition software for Arabic, Turkish, Farsi and other languages."

"One of the translators tried to explain the problems to me," Doyle said.

"Which one?" Suresh asked. "I'm delighted to learn you're interested in translations."

"It was Khalid Osman. We met several times for lunch."

"You mean Ozzie," Suresh said. "He was one of our best translators. I'm sorry he left."

"He left?" Doyle asked.

"Yeah, just a few weeks ago," Suresh replied. "Ozzie was a real patriot, too. He loved to rail against the jihadists, telling everyone how they've ruined the Middle East. You couldn't get him to stop. Ozzie made sure people knew which side he was on." They drove in silence until Suresh turned again to Doyle. "By the way, did you see what I saw?" His gaze remained on Doyle an uncomfortably long moment before returning to the steering wheel. "I think I'm in love," he said. Doyle guessed Suresh was referring to the young woman at the CIA meeting, Leslie Jumana, the same one he was thinking about. "What did they say her name was?" Suresh pressed.

Doyle said nothing, already feeling proprietary. When he got back to his sparsely furnished apartment late that evening, he turned on his computer to check his private e-mail account. A new message entitled *Hello Doyle* caught his eye. He opened the message and read: *Delete this. Reply from MouseTrap on Wilson Blvd any nite.* It was unsigned, but the sender's address was 22interested@netscape.net. Doyle was puzzled and intrigued. *Too, too interested.* Who could it be? He thought of girls he had recently met. Which ones might have access to his e-mail address? He read the dateline, *June 3 at 10:04 pm*, and realized it had been sent only an hour before. *What the hell*, he thought, looking around his undecorated room. He was not sleepy and the address was not far. He deleted the message.

Doyle saw only a few customers in the dim interior when he arrived at the MouseTrap internet café. Several looked up, as if hoping to see a familiar face, before falling back to their glowing screens. Doyle found an unoccupied computer near the back wall and logged onto his account, doyle999@aol.com, then he addressed a message to 22interested and clicked to send: *I'm here. Now what?* Almost instantly came back a reply entitled *Undeliverable* with a machine-generated message saying the destination address was unknown or invalid.

He laughed out loud. His eyes met those of a plump teenager across the room just as her surprised annoyance turned into an amused smile. This must be a practical joke, Doyle thought, probably by Suresh Kumar. He had both the technical knowledge and the malevolent sense of humor. Before he could log off, another message arrived from 22interested: *exit and go to your new mailbox, michiganman123@earthlink.com; password redE4u.* He smiled at the password. Maybe he was ready for her, too, but why all the cloak-and-dagger? Why had his mysterious friend gone to the trouble of creating a new mailbox and password for him?

He logged on and found another message, this one from 22excited@yahoo.com. He pondered the new name. Her interest had turned to excitement. Their relationship seemed to be progressing. What next? He opened the message and read: *like 2 chat with u. log on dateline chat room with username GIJOE444.*

"Shit," he muttered in a voice loud enough to cause a bearded customer to glare in his direction. *Why the hell is she changing addresses again?* Doyle wondered. He turned back to his screen and followed the instructions. A reply came in seconds: *hi. it's me.*

Who are you?

no identity yet. just want 2 chat.

He wondered again who it could be. He typed his reply and clicked to send: *OK, what would you like to talk about?*

what's your favorite sport? came the reply.

Isn't it too soon to discuss that? Doyle typed back.

actually it's a little late, replied 22excited. *nearly midnight and i have 2b up early 4 work. sorry. contact me here 2morrow around 9. sweet dreams.*

Half an hour later Doyle was back in his cheerless apartment furiously masturbating.

CHAPTER 6

Three Days before the Paris Attack

The taxi rocked violently across the rough paving stones of the *Place de la Concorde*, the largest square in the French capital. Inside, Mohammed Jamal held a sheet of paper up to his eyes, but the shaking of the taxi made it impossible to read what was written on it. Looking outside, he recalled that a thousand people had been guillotined upon this same square during the Reign of Terror, the high point of revolutionary exuberance during the summer of 1794. *The French are no strangers to bloodshed. The coming days will bring them a fresh taste of their glorious history.* Jamal glanced upward at the granite obelisk that dominated the center of the vast square. Three thousand years earlier, the same giant phallus had adorned the entrance to the Temple at Luxor in ancient Egypt. *Perhaps we will return it to its proper place after we correct our temporary reversal of fortune.*

Jamal caught the amused smile of the taxi driver in the rearview mirror. *I must have been laughing again.* It was normal, he assured himself, merely his excitement about the colossal rewards that lay ahead. Leaving the *Place de la Concorde*, the taxi headed north across Paris toward the *proche banlieue* of Saint-Denis. Jamal looked again at the paper, torn at the top and wrinkled with tea stains. It had required several meetings with Sheikh Musawi al-Amin to obtain the pitiful prize. A veteran of Lebanon's bloody civil war twenty years earlier, the old sheik now served as an *imam* in an obscure mosque on the periphery of Paris. Several members of the *shura* had urged Jamal to contact Sheik Musawi. Although his mind dwelt uselessly on his past battles in Beirut, his young followers could provide Jamal the help he required.

He had met the old sheik again that morning in the *Jardin des Plantes,* one of the city's great public parks. Musawi had worn a loose woolen robe, a *djellaba* of Moroccan origin, and a small fez-like *tarbouch*. Although his dress and untrimmed white beard distinguished him from most Parisians in the park that day, he had not looked out of place. One of the city's largest mosques, *la Mosquée de Paris*, stood near one end of the park. The Institute of the Arab World, reflecting France's historic links with North Africa and the Middle East, towered beside the river Seine a few blocks away. Restaurants offering *couscous* and *tajines* lined the streets between. They had sat together on an isolated bench, their conversation muffled by the laughter of children playing in the park. As during prior meetings, Musawi had insisted on offering his advice for the operation before he would lend his support. Jamal had pretended to listen but had almost lost patience before the old sheik finally produced the battered page on which he had scrawled the name of one of his followers and the address for their meeting.

The taxi stopped next to a small café behind a departing bus. Opening the door, Jamal stepped into a warm blast of gritty exhaust. Turning toward the café, he found a seat at one of the rusted metal tables that cluttered the sidewalk. Even before the waiter arrived, he spotted the short man—shorter than he had imagined from Sheik Musawi's description— approaching along the sidewalk.

"Are you the *monsieur* who wishes to buy some dogs?"

Jamal nodded. The short man took the seat across the table. *He may be a midget,* Jamal thought, *but he has muscles like a workman, or maybe a boxer.* The sheik had said he liked to fight. *Tae kwon do, wasn't it?* "Did Sheik Musawi tell you the kind of dogs I seek?" Jamal asked. It was a silly code the old man had suggested, but he found it amusing.

"You want clever dogs that can perform tricks in Paris." Waleed Yarkas was his name, Jamal recalled from the paper. Jamal's gaze shifted to the large crescent-shaped scar that bisected Yarkas's upper left cheek. *A souvenir from prison? It looks like the work of a broken bottle.* A waiter finally emerged from the café. Jamal ordered two coffees. As the waiter departed, Yarkas leaned forward so he could be heard over the traffic. "Why should I help you find such dogs?"

"For the glory of striking the first blow," Jamal replied. Waleed Yarkas smiled for the first time, but the effort caused the scar on his cheek to rise sharply into a livid peak, rendering his smile friendly and loathsome at the same time. "At least one of them must be prepared for martyrdom," Jamal continued. "Perhaps two."

"Are you serious?" Yarkas asked. Jamal said nothing, studying the short man's face to judge his reaction. *It will take time to get used to his scar*, he decided. Yarkas broke the silence. "We have a new recruit from Algiers, quite young. He might be suitable for your task."

"What about the others?"

"Not for that," Yarkas replied. "At least, not if we tell them in advance."

"Tell me about the young Algerian."

"His father sent him here to study," Yarkas began. "He was staying with a friend of the father, not far from here, but the guy kicked him out. I'm not sure why. Two of my friends met him in the park. He was sleeping there, I think."

"What is his name?"

"Ali Benhadj." Jamal closed his eyes, trying to picture the young man from the sound of his name. "He was unable to gain admittance to the school," Yarkas continued. "Problems with his papers, lack of money, something like that, I don't know. He kept going back to the school, five or six times I think, but they would not register him. He was sleeping in the park because he ran out of his father's money—most of it, anyway—and had no place to stay. My friends offered him a sofa in our apartment. They are training him to help in our religious work."

"Why hasn't he returned to his family in Algiers?" asked Jamal, his eyes still closed.

"We think he is afraid. He sends letters to his family about his progress in school. It appears he has something to prove."

Jamal opened his eyes. "We will give this Ali Benhadj a mission."

"Yes. He may want that. That is for you to judge. All I can tell you is he is very religious. He visits the mosque daily and prays at the appointed hours, even in the apartment. He says he wants to be closer to God."

"Does he have any friends?"

"Other than us?" Waleed Yarkas asked. "No, he seems alone here."

"When can I see him? I will need some time with him to be sure."

"He is with my friends at the apartment. We can go there now."

"I would prefer to meet him in the mosque where he prays," Jamal said. Yarkas unzipped his jacket and reached inside. "No, use this one," Jamal said, handing the short man a new cell phone. As Yarkas made the call, Jamal noticed a holster under his jacket. *Stupid of him to take such a risk, but good that he wishes to impress me.*

Three young men stood outside the Abu Bakr Mosque when Jamal and Yarkas arrived. Jamal would never have recognized the modest building as a place of worship except for its Arabic sign. *So this is where Sheik Musawi incites them with his thrilling sermons.* One of the three waiting youths, a slightly built teenager, regarded the two approaching men with an expression of aloof curiosity, then glanced at his watch. *That must be the new one from Algiers,* guessed Jamal. *He attaches some importance to his time.*

"How is my fat friend today?" Yarkas shouted to the largest of the three.

The fat friend was dressed in traditional Saudi garb, a *dishdasha* draped over his corpulent body and a *shumagg* covering his head. A pair of red Adidas shoes was visible below the white cotton robe. *He looks like a Saudi Arabian prince dressed for a track meet,* Jamal thought. He recalled the name Yarkas had mentioned at the café: *Hani al-Omari.* Overweight and dressed up like a prince, just as the scarred dwarf had described him. "If I am a bit fat," al-Omari replied, "it is because I possess a wife who cooks well. I can understand your jealousy." Next to him stood the third youth, but Jamal could not recall his name, only that he liked music and had been arrested for shoplifting. He seemed oblivious to the new arrivals thanks to the headphones clamped over his ears. *Or is he just pretending to ignore us?* Jamal wondered.

"Your wife causes me no jealousy," Yarkas replied, no longer smiling. "If I am jealous, it is because my father is not so rich that I can waste my days watching videos and discussing the *Qur'an*, as some people can."

"We should not waste our visitor's time with such chatter," al-Omari said. His pudgy face bore a bushy black beard and a pair of glasses with plastic rims, also black. "We are eager to hear about the project for which he requires our assistance."

Jamal ignored al-Omari's remark and addressed the thin Algerian youth: "*Salaam alaykum.*"

Ali Benhadj bowed slightly in response to the greeting. "*Salaam.*" Jamal studied the young man's face, his eyes sunk deep and surrounded by dark circles, his adolescent beard sprouting in irregular patches.

"I thought we came here to discuss an *alliance*," al-Omari pressed.

"Perhaps later," Yarkas interjected. "Mohammed Jamal wishes first to enter the mosque and pray with our young friend, Ali Benhadj."

"He may enter wherever or whomever he pleases," al-Omari said with a shrug of his broad shoulders. "If he wishes my advice, he should join us for the great battle in Afghanistan." Two women passed on the sidewalk as the fat Saudi Arabian prince spoke the last words. Jamal looked at him sharply. The eyes of the bearded man shifted within the black plastic frames, first following the two women suspiciously down the sidewalk, then leaping back to confront Jamal's gaze with a look of defiance.

He may not be a real prince, Jamal thought, *but he's a genuine fool.*

— — —

Ali Benhadj led the way into the lobby of the Abu Bakr Mosque, passing through a glass door between plywood-covered windows that had once displayed discount clothing. Although he had been praying here daily for several weeks, Benhadj always felt embarrassed when he entered the storefront mosque, as he did now with Mohammed Jamal following him. The building was so modest and improvised compared to the Great Mosque of Algiers. He suspected its humiliating condition, a virtual insult to God, was somehow imposed by the French. The lobby floor was covered with bright linoleum. Posters of Middle East tourist destinations hung from the walls. A young man sat behind a counter with a pile of red and green *Qur'ans* for sale. Benhadj led the way down the hall until they reached a lavatory equipped with extra sinks for ablutions. After washing, they removed their shoes and entered the dimly lit interior. Several men lay prostrate in prayer, while others sat quietly talking. Behind them the walls were adorned with verses from the *Qur'an* painted in graceful Arabic script, marred only by rough spots where holes had been repaired. The room had once been a dance studio for young ballerinas, Benhadj had been told, before the mirrors and handrails were removed. Crossing the carpeted floor, he stopped near the screen that separated the section for the women and girls. Turning to face the *quibla*, he raised both hands to his face and began to pray. *"Allahu Akbar."* God is great. *"Bismi-llahi rrahmani rrahim."* He bowed low, his hands touching his knees. *"Subhana Rabbi Al Adheem,"* he repeated three times.

At his side, Jamal joined in the prayers. Moments later, they rose together saying, *"Sami Allahu Liman Hamidah. Allahu Akbar."* God is great. Then they prostrated themselves and repeated another prayer three times. The ancient ritual continued, the standing and bowing and prostration, punctuated by cries of "God is great." When they finished, Benhadj felt the warm weight of Jamal's hand on his shoulder. The hand seemed to embrace his entire body, though it touched only his shoulder, imparting a sensation of security, like the half-forgotten embrace of his father. Jamal broke the silence. "I am pleased to be able to work with you and your friends."

Benhadj said nothing for a moment, then whispered, "I sometimes wonder if they are true Muslims. They say they are doing religious work, but their behavior . . ." He hesitated, recalling the shoplifting in *Galeries Lafayette*, the drugs in the apartment, the girl that Zacarias Essabar had bragged about. "They do not follow the Straight Path."

"You must be patient with them, Ali. They are the victims of this decadent society." Jamal paused and seemed to study his reaction. "I hear you are a religious man, learned beyond your years. What drew you to Islam?"

Benhadj looked back, wondering if the older man was mocking him. He was not yet sure if he trusted this well-dressed stranger. He seemed too Western. His round glasses and neat mustache gave him the appearance of order and clarity. So precise were the lines of his face that he might have been a drawing of himself. "The verses of the *Qur'an* make me feel pure and peaceful," he finally confided to Jamal. "As though God is speaking to me."

"Yes, I have heard that you have memorized the verses. That is remarkable. With a mind like yours, it is a disgrace they would not allow you to study in France."

"I confess I felt anger, but God may have something else planned for me. Perhaps it is decided that I should assist my new friends with their religious work."

"That may be God's will. It appears your friends would benefit from your guidance." The youth laughed briefly, pleased to discover that Jamal shared his low regard for the three men waiting outside. "But perhaps God is leading you toward a more important duty," Jamal continued. *Duty*, Benhadj thought. The word had special significance for a youth who had grown up surrounded by the Five Pillars of Islam, the spiritual edifice that molded his life and impressed his daily acts with meaning.

"What kind of duty?" Benhadj asked.

"As a religious scholar, you are familiar with the obligations of jihad, of course."

"Certainly. All Muslims must pursue both kinds of struggle."

"Some say there are three. Tell me your understanding."

"Most important is the believer's internal struggle," Benhadj began, "the struggle to live according to the Muslim faith and build a good Muslim society." Indeed, a life of religious purity was precisely what the young man had been striving to achieve for himself, although he doubted the rest of Muslim society could attain the same standards. He recalled with disdain the typical Muslims from Algiers, their mundane lives of no significance to anyone, forgotten quickly after death by everyone who knew them. Benhadj had long ago vowed to distinguish himself from the colorless mass of ordinary Muslims by adhering strictly to the teachings of Islam. "Next comes the external struggle to defend Islam against its enemies. It is written: *Fight in the cause of Allah those who fight you, but do not transgress limits; for Allah loves not transgressors.*"

"And the third type of jihad?" A light from somewhere within the Abu Bakr Mosque flashed across Jamal's glasses, preventing Benhadj from seeing into his eyes.

"Some scholars say we have a duty to attack our enemies first," Benhadj began slowly, "so as to prevent them from destroying Islam. The attacks of recent years have been of the third category. I confess I have rejoiced in them."

"We had plans for jihad long before you arrived," Hani al-Omari announced as the two men emerged from the storefront mosque. "I hope Ali Benhadj told you that."

"So I have heard," Mohammed Jamal replied. In fact, he had learned of the plans hours earlier from Waleed Yarkas at the sidewalk café. For months al-Omari had been promoting a scheme to send recruits to the Malakand training camp. The overweight Saudi warrior believed that Yarkas with his criminal past was the perfect partner to attract young jihadists.

"My well-fed friend watches too many of his videos," Yarkas explained. "They excite his imagination." He raised his hand for a playful slap, but al-Omari caught the short man's arm.

"Why do you mock our plans?" The third young man joined the debate, removing his headphones. "The recent attacks in New York have forced the Americans into Afghanistan where we can easily defeat them, just as we defeated the Russians a decade ago." With the headphones lifted, Jamal saw a diamond gleaming in the third youth's earlobe. *What did the midget gunman tell me about him at the café?* His name was Essabar, Jamal now recalled, Zacarias Essabar. "Americans are accustomed to relying on air strikes," he continued. "Such cowardly tactics reveal their lack of fighting spirit." Jamal smiled at the rhetoric. The young orator was of Algerian origin, he recalled, like Ali Benhadj. He loved music, that was obvious, but he also knew how to drive. That would make him useful. *What was it about Essabar that troubled Benhadj in the mosque?*

"Afghanistan, *ta gueule!*" Yarkas exclaimed as he grabbed Essabar around the neck and pretended to strangle him. "You would have trouble finding your way to the airport."

"Please, let him speak," Jamal said. "I am interested in the ambitions of Muslim youth. Come, let us walk together."

Al-Omari stepped forward, pressing his large body between Jamal and Ali Benhadj. "Zacarias is correct," he said from behind his black beard. "What the Americans fear most is hand-to-hand combat against us in Kabul because so many civilians will be killed."

"The reckless jihad of which you talk is no better than suicide," Benhadj interrupted.

Al-Omari started to reply, but Jamal spoke first. "You are correct, Ali. A soldier of Islam must be not only courageous, but also effective." Jamal was pleased to see that Benhadj was not too easily swayed by his friends; the task ahead required a youth who felt a degree of disdain for the imperfections of his fellow man.

CHAPTER 7

Second Day of the Investigation

"Let's start with the cars." Dupont had returned to DST headquarters after a few hours of sleep to begin the first of her early morning meetings. She asked the leaders of each specialized team to attend in person to assess progress and adjust priorities.

"We know the vehicle that exploded inside the restaurant was a Fiat Punto," reported Giles Lambert. "The one outside was a Renault Clio. We haven't found any numbers, yet. They removed the plates and filed the engine blocks."

"So this wasn't their first job," Dupont observed.

"Apparently not. But they may have overlooked some places; we're still looking."

"What about Big Mac?" Dupont asked, turning to Hakim Abalian, head of the forensic medicine team.

"We've found very little blood or tissue inside the Fiat. The blast was too intense. But the small amount of DNA we've recovered matches the face you peeled from the wall and several other body fragments. I'd say we have Big Mac one-third reassembled."

"Lovely," Dupont said. "Have you run his DNA through our database?"

"Since four this morning," Giles Lambert said. "No matches yet."

"What about the second bomber?" Dupont asked. "The one outside on the street."

"It's not clear he blew himself up," Lambert replied. "So far we've found no blood or tissue inside the Renault Clio. None of the bodies outside the restaurant is fragmented as much as the Big Mac remains."

"The driver was no longer in the Clio when it exploded," interjected Yves Bannelier, the leader of the electronic surveillance team. "One of the security cameras caught a few frames of the driver stepping out of the car and walking away."

"Have you identified him yet?" Lambert asked, swinging his large nose toward Bannelier. Dupont detected a note of irritation in Lambert's voice. Apparently he had not been informed of the discovery earlier.

"Not so far," Bannelier admitted. "The video shows only part of his backside." Bannelier's chin bore a slender black goatee, which he had a habit of stroking while delivering bad news. Dupont noticed he was stroking it now. "But we're still analyzing each frame for his clothing, hair color and body size."

"So they blew up the Renault by remote control," Dupont remarked. She glanced to the back of the room where two silent team members took notes. Ostensibly they were serving as liaisons to the cabinet, but Dupont could imagine what they were reporting back to their political masters in the opposition parties. "What about the other cameras?" she pressed Bannelier

"Only a few are installed on *Champs-Élysées* and connecting avenues. We can thank the civil libertarians for that." He glanced at the note takers in the rear. "We found one camera that panned both cars briefly as they approached the restaurant. Unfortunately, the camera angle was too high; it showed little more than the car roofs." Bannelier mounted his chair to demonstrate the overhead angle. "However, a camera on *Avenue Victor Hugo* near the *Arc de Triomphe* caught the Fiat earlier in heavy traffic." Stepping down from the chair he retrieved a large photo from the table. "The image is fuzzy, even after enhancement, but it looks like the Fiat contained three people at that time."

"Three people," Dupont repeated. She saw Giles Lambert shake his long hair, looking as if he was about to have a fit.

"We can't make out any faces," Bannelier added, "but we can discern three separate heads and torsos in several frames."

"That's it?" Dupont asked incredulously.

"I've got my team working around the clock. We're analyzing every camera in the city one frame at a time."

"Just get me one face, Yves. That's all I ask." She turned back to Giles Lambert. "Didn't anyone see the drivers or passengers? With all the people around that restaurant, someone must have seen at least one of them."

"We've interviewed over a hundred witnesses, but none of them could see inside the cars. Apparently, anyone close enough was killed by the explosions."

"What about the physical evidence?" Dupont asked, hearing a note of impatience in her own voice.

"We've collected almost everything from the bombing areas," Lambert replied, "but it's going to take a few more days to determine ownership of each item."

"We don't have that kind of time, Giles," Dupont said as she rose from the table. "Find me something that belonged to the bombers." The first morning meeting came to an uncomfortable close.

"Can we take a break and get something to eat?" It was two in the afternoon and Lambert's stomach grumbled. He had eaten nothing that day.

On the other side of the table Dupont reviewed a stack of witness interviews. "I can't go now, Giles. But be an angel and bring me back a sandwich. I'm starving." Dupont returned to her reading, but she sensed that Lambert was still watching her, as he often did. She was not surprised by his interest. At least a dozen men had confirmed her attractiveness since she had emerged from her awkward adolescence, although it had been another woman who had first identified her most alluring feature. *It's your lovely green eyes.* It was a mixed blessing, Dupont sometimes thought. At work, she sometimes wondered if her male colleagues were listening to her words as they gazed back.

"Let's go out for some air," Lambert persisted. "It's not healthy for you to eat alone at your desk. I found a new place nearby, good food and romantic atmosphere."

"No thanks, Giles." Dupont did not look up from her reading this time. It was not until she heard Lambert open the door to leave that she glanced over and saw him shaking his head, causing his long locks to swing regretfully back and forth. *Romantic atmosphere.* She smiled sympathetically at his slip of the tongue. Lambert's evident crush flattered her, but Dupont was already sufficiently occupied in the romance department. She was entering upon a second year of a liaison with a senior official at the Ministry of Foreign Affairs. Twenty years older, he was able to see her only once or twice a week, with occasional discreet rendezvous in foreign capitals. Like her, the official was quite occupied with his career, as well as with his wife, his children and their two dogs. The crowded relationship suited Dupont perfectly; the idea of marrying or even living with a man held no appeal for her. Ever since discovering her magnetic power over men, she had a mortal fear of being possessed.

After reviewing witness statements for several more hours, Dupont turned to a batch of technical reports. They had found more car parts, but still no identification numbers. Big Mac's DNA? Still no matches, but they were checking foreign databases. The CIA had not yet provided them anything of value. Dupont wondered if the Americans were holding something back: with their vaunted surveillance surely they had intercepted at least one message linked to the attack. Equally puzzling was the lack of results from Yves Bannelier's team. They had reviewed all the recent wiretaps, but could still find no forewarning of the attack. Even Giles Lambert, her reliable bloodhound, had turned up no new leads. When would they get a break?

It was ten o'clock, the second night of the investigation, when Dupont left DST headquarters. On her way home, she stopped by *Hôtel-Dieu* to check the latest results from the physical evidence team. "Any progress?" she asked hopefully as she entered one of the examination rooms.

A red-headed technician was bent over a metal table covered with small objects. "It's hopeless!" she shouted before looking up. "Sorry, I thought you were someone else." The technician sat upright and began rubbing her back. "I've been here almost two days going over bits and pieces. I can't even remember what I'm supposed to be looking for."

The young woman's fatigue and frustration struck a chord inside Dupont. *Hopeless.* How many times in her career had she felt that way? Those critical moments in law school when she doubted she was smart enough to succeed, the first year at DST when she feared her colleagues would discover her ignorance if she opened her mouth ... "Don't give up," Dupont heard herself order the startled technician. "Your work is going to help us solve this case." She started to leave, but turned back to ask her name.

"Angeline Odette," the red-haired woman replied, still massaging her back, but sitting up straighter.

CHAPTER 8

Two Days before the Paris Attack

"He may be the correct choice for the job," Mohammed Jamal said quietly. Seated across the table was Waleed Yarkas, looking uncomfortable in the lobby of the *Hôtel de Crillon*. Jamal handed him a business card. "Bring the boy here later today." As Yarkas read the address, Jamal glanced out the lobby window upon the sunlit splendor of the *Place de la Concorde*, the same vast square his taxi had crossed the previous morning on his way to meet the short man. Jamal placed three cell phones on the table. "These are clean ones for use in the operation." A waiter arrived. Jamal watched Yarkas pick up the phones as coffee and croissants took their places on the table. *Scars on his hands, just like on his face.* As the waiter adjusted the cups and spoons Jamal recalled the manicured hands of Hani al-Omari, the bearded Saudi clown whom he had met the day before. When he had shaken al-Omari's hand at the end of their walk, Jamal had felt its baby-like softness, as though al-Omari had never worked in his life. "When you deliver the boy," Jamal resumed after the waiter left, "buzz the apartment number on the card. My associate will come down to the lobby carrying a copy of *Al Anwar*, like this one." He laid a copy of the Arabic newspaper on the table. It was folded in half.

Jamal had spent the previous night with the same associate trying to decide if Ali Benhadj was the right choice. They had reviewed everything Jamal had learned about the young man. *Tell me again why he says he came to France. If he intended to pursue his education, then why did he arrive so ill prepared? He says he wanted to make the Hajj pilgrimage to Mecca, but claims that his father opposed it. Are you sure his religious zeal is genuine?*

He expresses contempt for his father at times, yet seems to fear disappointing him. What are his true feelings? Did he really strike the old man? He seems to admire his uncle because he had fought against the French in Algeria. That is important; tell me again exactly what he says about his uncle's role.

"After you drop off the boy, I will have another errand for you," Jamal continued. "Do you own a car?"

"Yes, of course."

"It must be a clean car, you understand? Everything must be legal."

"No problem. I know about cars."

"You must have a valid registration and driver's license."

"I told you not to worry." A weak smile lifted the scar on Yarkas's cheek.

"When you return from the errand we will need two more cars that cannot be traced back to your group. I suggest you acquire them outside Paris so the police here will not be looking for them."

"I know a guy who can supply cars without questions. Al-Omari and Essabar can get them while I'm running the errand."

"Good," Jamal said. "Now please repeat my instructions to make sure I have expressed myself correctly."

Yarkas lifted the coffee to his lips and regarded Jamal beyond the edge of the cup. "I understood everything."

"I asked you to repeat what I said, please." Mohammed Jamal removed his rimless glasses and placed them on the table. Yarkas repeated the instructions. "Excellent," said Jamal, replacing his glasses. He looked around the hotel lobby to verify no one was seated near their table. "Here are some funds for the operation." He opened the *Al Anwar* newspaper to reveal a thick envelope. "Twenty thousand Euros should be enough for what we have discussed. There will be more afterward." He refolded the paper and pushed it across the table. As he stood, Jamal spotted the holster under Yarkas's jacket again. "Don't carry that thing during your trip. It will only cause questions if you're stopped."

— — —

Waleed Yarkas remained at the table another fifteen minutes. It was his first time in the *Hôtel de Crillon*, so he intended to enjoy the rest of his coffee and another croissant. *High society,* he thought, recalling how the doorman had stopped him to verify he had been invited by a hotel guest. He felt a mixture of resentment and embarrassment about his clothes. He might have dressed better if Jamal had told him the place would be so fancy, although it was difficult to find fresh clothes now that Ghadah had left. Finishing the croissant, Yarkas wiped his fingers on the upholstered chair and then drew the envelope from inside the newspaper. He was pleased by the amount of money, but he resented Jamal's remark about his pistol. *Merde, travel without a gun, c'est des conneries! It's bullshit.* He doubted Jamal had ever spent a night being questioned about missing cars. All night long, the same questions, so close you could smell what the cops had eaten for dinner. *Fils de salopes,* he thought, *sons of whores. I don't plan getting caught again with nothing but my limp cock to point at the flics.*

By the way, Mr. Master Planner, I do know something about cars. Indeed, after completing a two-year program in auto mechanics, Yarkas had obtained a part-time job in a Renault dealership. Later, after the baby arrived, he had requested a full-time position, but was told he would have to wait. So he turned to Arabs like himself who were willing to give him jobs. Car repairs mostly, but also removal of identification numbers. A few tools from the dealership were all he needed. After a while they asked him to go into the field, to help them lift the cars. They appreciated his knowledge of ignition systems and locking devices. He started bringing home more cash and Ghadah stopped complaining. But it was not only the money he liked. It was also the way he felt after each job, especially when they lifted an expensive model, like a BMW. *The kind rich Frenchmen buy for their slutty little wives,* he thought, *les putains, with nothing better to do than drive around and buy things.* Sometimes he found the shoes, dresses and lingerie still in the car. *Le shopping.* It would feel good to whack a Frenchmen or two, the kind who looked down on him and kept him back because he was a Muslim and a foreigner. *Je les emmerde, fuck them.* He would make them pay for putting him in prison. For causing him to lose his wife and child.

Yarkas removed one of the new cell phones Jamal had given him. He flipped it open and shut several times. It was the latest model, with keys for messages. It was time to get moving, he decided. First, he would call someone he knew in Lyon. They had not spoken since Yarkas had gotten out of prison, but the guy would be happy to supply the two cars Jamal required. After the call, Yarkas would stop by the apartment to make sure Hani al-Omari was on board with the new plan. He had reason to doubt his fat friend's commitment after their big argument the evening before. It had started right after al-Omari loaded a new video he had imported from London. "This one is in the new DVD format," he had announced, "the latest technology." Al-Omari always liked to preview films with the group before they sold them to kiosks and street vendors around Saint-Denis. But this time he had another motive, Yarkas recalled. The film was a rousing sermon by *Imam* Abdel Fawwaz designed to recruit young jihadists. Al-Omari had convinced Sheik Musawi to let him show the film at the mosque for that purpose.

Yarkas had crossed his arms and settled into the red sofa next to Benhadj and Essabar. The film opened with an aerial view of the Great Mosque of Mecca. Then the image of the white bearded *imam* appeared on the screen, dark eyebrows accenting his eyes. "Praise be to *Allah*," the *imam* began. "Whoever has been guided by God, he will not be misled. Whoever has been misled, he will never be guided." From the quality of his image it appeared that the *imam* was speaking from a well-lit studio rather than the shadowy mosque.

"What do you think so far?" al-Omari asked after a few minutes, lowering the volume.

"I think he's full of shit," Yarkas replied. "No matter how many Muslim teenagers you send to the Malakand training camp, they will never drive out the Americans. As Mohammed Jamal explained, Afghanistan is the wrong battlefield."

"This only shows that you do not understand God's plan, my friend," al-Omari retorted. "Allah has given us access to American technology precisely to allow us to throw off their oppression." He waved the remote control as if to emphasize his point.

"You think you can defeat planes and missiles with your stupid DVD player?" Yarkas shouted from the sofa. "You're wasting your time with this crazy dream!" His words were drowned out as al-Omari restored the volume. Yarkas stood to grab the remote control, but al-Omari pulled it away.

"But the battle is already raging in Afghanistan!" Essabar added his voice, the fake jewel in his ear flashing angrily in the television light as he rose from the sofa.

"Yes, we have already sent recruits there for training," al-Omari protested. "We promised to join them."

"Shut up both of you." Yarkas felt ridiculously short standing between the muscular Algerian adolescent and the overweight Saudi prince, each a head taller than he. "You've been watching so many videos that your brains have turned to camel dung. The young idiots you have sent to Afghanistan will be killed by the Americans before they can strike a blow."

"Waleed Yarkas is right." Startled by the unexpected voice, all three looked down at the youth with the patchy beard still seated on the red sofa. His deep-set eyes gleamed within their dark circles. "Six million Muslims live in France," Benhadj announced. "Our duty is to defend Islam here. If God had intended us to fight in Afghanistan, He would not have sent Mohammed Jamal to lead us into battle in Paris." Essabar and al-Omari had looked stunned and confused by the unexpected speech, as if they had just witnessed a startling magic trick. Essabar had been the first to react, shrugging his tattooed shoulders and extending his hand to Ali Benhadj.

Still sitting in the *Hôtel de Crillon* lobby, Yarkas laughed quietly as he recalled al-Omari's angry snort and the crashing sound of the remote control he had hurled against the wall. Stifling his laugh, he rose to depart, hoping Mohammed Jamal had remembered to pay for the coffee and croissants.

CHAPTER 9

Third Day of the Investigation

Giles Lambert rushed into the morning meeting with big news. "We've identified the Fiat," he announced to Dupont, panting as though he were a golden retriever dropping a pheasant in front of his master. During the night, they had found a cracked fragment of an automobile transmission buried beneath charred debris in the restroom of the bombed restaurant. Under the floodlights in the *Hôtel-Dieu* garage, they discovered a twelve-digit serial number stamped into the metal. Within an hour, Italian police woke a Fiat official at home and gained access to the company's database. "The car is registered to a resident of Lyon," Lambert continued, still breathing heavily. "We have his name and address."

"Has he filed a theft report?" Dupont asked. Finally, her bloodhound was onto a scent!

"We haven't found one yet."

"Any criminal record?"

"Apparently not." Lambert's nose swung like a metronome as he shook his head. "But I've called the Lyon police to bring him in for questioning. It's unlikely the bombers would have used their own cars, but it's odd the owner hasn't filed a stolen vehicle report."

Dupont thought a moment. "Let's hold off questioning him until we get a warrant to look at his phone records. I'd like to know who he's been talking to before he realizes we know about him."

"Unfortunately, we have Magistrate Joubert," said Yves Bannelier. He stroked his black goatee rapidly.

"*Merde,*" Dupont mumbled. "Why did we have to get Joubert?"

"Dominique wants you to go down personally," Bannelier continued, "and convince him that we may need some flexibility."

"*Merde*," Dupont repeated. "Call me a car."

Hours later, Dupont was back in her office reading a fresh stack of reports. Magistrate Jean-Philippe Joubert had authorized a wiretap for the Fiat owner, but the rest of the investigation seemed to be losing momentum. A painstaking review of the surveillance cameras had not yet revealed the faces she sought. Something always hid them, such as a bus filled with Chinese tourists that had passed the Fiat just as it entered the camera's field. *Globalization is ruining Paris*, Dupont thought wryly. Then there was the half-burned copy of the *Qur'an* bearing a sticker from the library of the *Grande Mosquée de Paris*. When it was pulled from the restaurant rubble, they hoped they had found a link to the bomber, until they discovered that the borrower of the holy book was a longtime employee of the restaurant. His body was found intact, far from the exploded Fiat.

Dupont recalled the words of the analyst Angeline Odette bent over her table at *Hôtel-Dieu* the night before. *It's hopeless.* Maybe she was right. The bomber had blasted himself into a million bloody bits. Even if they pieced him together, there would be no way to identify him, unless his DNA or fingerprints happened to be in some database. *Why don't you take the evening off for a change?* But she could not will herself to go home. What forced her to stay? This case was gripping, of course, but she had been working late nights ever since she had come to DST. *It's the little boy in the park, isn't it?* She had not thought about him for a long time, not since she had told the story to Giles Lambert over lunch during her first year at DST, back in the days when she still accepted lunch invitations from him.

"So what made you decide to join DST?" he had asked.

"The usual reasons people go into public service. Prestige and power, I guess."

"You could have had those back at the law firm."

She hesitated, not sure how to answer him. "Look, I will tell you a story. It happened when I was sixteen." She had gone for a run in the *Bois de Boulogne*, the vast park on the city's western edge. It was early spring and the freshly blooming trees were redolent of a hundred fragrances. Following a path through the woods, she came upon a clearing with picnic tables and a stand selling coffee and ice cream. There, she saw three people: a man, a woman and a little boy. They seemed to be the only people around, except for the vendor working in the food stand. The boy, who looked to be about seven years old, was sitting on top of the table, eating ice cream. The woman sat on a nearby bench, while the man stood a little way off smoking a cigarette. "Approaching on the path, I saw the boy's ice cream fall from the cone onto the table. I caught sight of his face as he looked down at the ice cream and then up at the man. I've never forgotten his expression, because even before the rest of it happened, I could tell something was wrong."

"What do you mean?" Lambert asked.

"The boy should have been angry about the ice cream, but his face expressed fear." Dupont paused to make sure Lambert understood. "Then I saw the man walk over and strike him. He wasn't a big man, but he hit the boy hard. Then he started cursing. He said awful things to the boy, like he was stupid and clumsy, that he should never have been born. The boy just sat on the table frozen while the man cursed and hit him again. The woman looked away with a blank expression. I suppose she was the boy's mother, but she did nothing."

"What did you do?" Lambert asked, brushing aside his long hair as if to gain a better view of the scene.

"That's the trouble. I just stood there. I saw the man raise his hand again, but he must have seen me watching, because he turned, took a drag from his cigarette and then tossed it in my direction on the path. I didn't know what to do, so I started to jog again. I kept thinking I should go back or report it to someone. I mean how could I leave that child in the possession of such stupid, malevolent people with no means to protect himself and no way to escape? But in the end I did nothing."

Lambert sipped his coffee before responding. "So that's why you came to DST?"

"That's right," she replied, wondering if he had really been listening.

It was during that same lunch that Lambert had first admitted to Dupont that he had fallen under the spell of her unusual eyes. Not in so many words, but it was clear enough from his steady gaze as she recounted her story. "Why are you looking at me that way?" she asked, before realizing it might have been better to ignore his attention.

"Your eyes make me feel I'm being judged and forgiven at the same time," Lambert explained, having obviously considered the question for some time.

She had chosen not to pursue his feelings further, but after that lunch she sometimes caught Lambert watching her when she appeared to be unaware. During their workplace conversations, she often detected in him a nervous vulnerability, as though he felt she could read his secret thoughts. In time, Dupont had grown accustomed to Lambert's infatuation, while remaining careful to do nothing to encourage it. The best policy, she believed, was to stick to business.

Dupont turned back to her pile of reports and began reading them a second time, hoping to find some clue she had missed earlier. *Why is the investigation stalling?* She felt no closer to an arrest than she had when the day began.

It was not until late that evening that Angeline Odette returned to the glass beaker labeled "UNIDENTIFIED ELECTRONIC COMPONENTS." During the past three days at *Hôtel-Dieu* she had sorted through thousands of bits and pieces of cameras, telephones, laptop computers, car parts and restaurant equipment. Her back seemed to grow stiffer each hour.

The red-haired analyst dumped the contents of the beaker onto a tray and began picking through the components with a pair of tweezers and a magnifying glass. Something drew her attention to the small chip of plastic and metal she had tossed into the beaker two days earlier. It seemed so different from the other fragments she was struggling to put back together. It was more burnt and warped.

"What is it?" asked her colleague, peering over her shoulder.

"I think it might be a SIM card. You know the little card that goes into a cell phone."

"Too bad it's so beaten up. They may not be able to recover the code."

"I was thinking the same thing," Angeline Odette said. "It's so burnt. It might have been close to the explosion."

They both fell silent.

Half an hour later Dupont and Lambert were rushing on foot to the apartment of Dominique Carpentier, located a few blocks from DST headquarters on *rue Nélaton.* The SIM card was in a plastic envelope inside Dupont's briefcase.

"We found fifty-six cell phones at the scene," she began as soon as they were seated in Carpentier's living room.

"Fifty-six?" Carpentier asked with a tone of surprise.

"They've become very popular with young people," Dupont explained. "Most of the phones have been traced back to victims who have no criminal records or links to radical groups. We should know about the rest of them in the next few hours."

"Which is why you're so interested in this lone chip." Carpentier held up the plastic envelope to the light and peered inside. The head of DST's anti-terrorism unit was dressed in an oriental robe and pajamas, it having been after midnight when his unexpected guests arrived. Dupont glanced around the living room, its bold contemporary furnishings vying for attention with the Louis XVI marble fireplace and the art nouveau moldings around the high ceiling. The eclectic décor reminded Dupont that she had never met Carpentier's wife or heard him speak of her. "Do you really think Big Mac was carrying a cell phone?" Carpentier asked.

"Probably not," Lambert replied. "His handlers would have stripped him of anything that might lead back to them. But we have no other explanation for the chip's condition."

"Yes, it appears quite damaged. How do you propose to reconstruct the code?"

"We think our American friends can help," Dupont answered.

"Is it necessary to bring in the Americans?" Carpentier asked.

"They have better tools for this," Dupont replied. "If they can recover the SIM code for us, we may be able to track down the telephone customer to whom it belonged."

"Of course, they will want to stay involved." Carpentier peered into the plastic envelope as though it might contain a solution to his dilemma. Seated on the edge of an oversize *chaise longue* of lapis-blue suede, Carpentier appeared small and frail, Dupont observed, as though the case had drained him of his customary vigor. "All right," he said finally, "but do this quietly."

As they departed, Dupont glanced down the darkened corridor that led from the living room. No sound had emerged since they had arrived; she wondered if Carpentier's wife was already asleep in one of the silent bedrooms.

A few hours later a DST agent departed from Charles de Gaulle Airport on the morning Air France flight to Washington. As the plane flew westward, Dupont endured another frustrating day in Paris. A few new witnesses were located, but none had seen the drivers or the passengers. The owner of the Fiat turned out to be an innocent victim with no idea who had stolen his car in Lyon. Foreign databases reported no matches for the DNA of Big Mac. Dupont feared that she would have no better luck with the battered SIM card on its way to the CIA.

CHAPTER 10

Two Days before the Paris Attack

Ali Benhadj waited uncomfortably in the elegant lobby while the others buzzed the apartment number written on the card. Moments later they were greeted by a man carrying an *Al Anwar* newspaper. "So this is the young warrior I've heard so much about," the man said as he seized Benhadj by the shoulders and led him toward the elevator.

"I've never been in one this fancy," said Zacarias Essabar, grinning into the elevator mirrors. Hani al-Omari struck him with his elbow, but Essabar seemed transfixed by his own reflection. The pair of Dior sunglasses he had stolen from a nearby boutique that afternoon went well with his earring and tattooed arms.

Their host said nothing more until they entered the apartment on the fifth floor. "My name is Yusuf Ghamdi. Please make yourselves comfortable." He gestured toward a group of white sofas arrayed around a low ebony table.

"How big is this place?" Essabar asked, looking around the room.

"It's nice," al-Omari remarked. "My family has one like this in Marseille, several in fact."

Benhadj looked around with cool disdain. The apartment was located on *Avenue Mozart* in the sixteenth *arrondissement*, one of the richest areas in the city. Why had they brought him here, Benhadj wondered, to this place filled with the vanities of Western culture? A poor setting to prepare for the holy project that Mohammed Jamal had so far described only in vague terms. Yusuf Ghamdi seemed to read his mind. "It serves our purpose to blend in with the enemies of Islam, at least until the moment arrives for your heroic assault."

When Ghamdi left to prepare tea, Benhadj sat on one of the sofas and lit a cigarette. It was the second of the three Marlboros he would allow himself that day. Marlboros came from the decadent West, but his disdain did not apply to cowboys. The ones he knew from childhood movies were solitary and pure, riding on horseback like the first mujahedeen in Arabia at the time of the Prophet. *Heroic assault against the enemies of Islam.* Ghamdi's words reminded him of his long talks with Jamal. Even before their first meeting, Benhadj had sympathized with the rising Muslim counter-attacks against the West. Since his childhood in Algeria, a country dominated by the French for 130 years until the War of Independence, he had been painfully aware of the West's unjustified superiority, its material richness that stood as a permanent rebuke and humiliation to Muslims. He wished fervently to see Islam restored to its former glory, but until now he had seen no role for himself. Could it be that God was calling on him through this messenger Jamal?

"When do you depart for Lyon?" Ghamdi asked al-Omari and Essabar as he served tea.

"Tomorrow morning," al-Omari replied. "We will return with the cars the following day."

"What cars?" asked Benhadj.

"I will explain all this to you soon," Ghamdi replied, placing his hand on the youth's arm. After the tea, Ghamdi rose to his feet. "I suppose you two will need to return to Saint-Denis now, to prepare for your journey. Ali Benhadj will remain here tonight."

"We have much to discuss, my young warrior," Ghamdi said after al-Omari and Essabar had departed. When he smiled, one side of his mouth dropped slightly as the other side rose, giving his grin the odd appearance of an "s" lying on its side, as though nature had ill equipped him to express his benevolent sentiments. *God sometimes chooses strange emissaries*, Benhadj observed. He felt a mixture of respect and sympathy for this deformed teacher who would prepare him for the task he was coming to believe God wished him to perform.

Benhadj suspected, but was not yet certain, that the task would result in his departure from this world. He contemplated the approach of his death, not with terror, but with sadness, as though he were losing his footing on the edge of a precipice and in the moment of falling into the abyss he is seized, not by helpless panic, but by feelings of loss and regret, for he is already looking back upon the earthly life he has left behind. Benhadj struggled to overcome the sadness by reminding himself that death would bring, not personal annihilation, but rather blissful union with *Allah* and Eternity. The tangible world, he knew, was temporary and meaningless compared to what awaited him in Heaven. Only by submitting to the will of God, whatever He required, could he hope to lift himself above the masses of ordinary people, lost in their pursuit of earthly comforts. Still, a part of him hoped that God would not require his death, at least not yet. Death came to everyone, he knew, but going to one's death before it was required was an act of suicide, something forbidden by the *Qur'an*. If God required him to sacrifice his temporary life on earth to achieve His holy purpose, then he would be ready to submit, but he still felt it was permissible to hope that God would not yet require it.

His thoughts were interrupted by a gentle squeeze upon his shoulder. "Come with me," Yusuf Ghamdi whispered, offering another lopsided smile as he gestured toward a large television across the room. Beside it stood stacks of video cassettes and discs.

—   —   —

Mohammed Jamal looked down onto the wide river that sliced Paris into two jagged halves. Beneath the bridge, the last of the day's tourist boats, *les bateaux mouches*, moved up the river toward their nighttime moorings. The night's first freight barges passed under the bridge in the opposite direction. As the boats stirred the dark waters, flashes of color leaped off the surface like shards of broken glass, reflecting the myriad lights of the great city. Jamal looked up from the water and saw the old *imam* approaching slowly across the *Pont d'Austerlitz*. His untrimmed beard flashed white as he passed under the first lamppost. He wore the same loose *djellaba* he had worn in the park the day before. The same fez-like *tarbouch* protected his bald head against the evening chill. But now Jamal noticed that the cap lurched to the left with each step. He realized for the first time that Sheikh Musawi al Amin suffered from a limp, perhaps an injury from his exploits in Lebanon.

Jamal felt confident Musawi was bringing the answer he desired. The old man's absurd vanity would not allow him to back out now. For he considered himself to be among the founding fathers of modern jihad, never tiring of recounting his role in the bombing of the US Marine Barracks in Beirut in 1983. The key to the operation's success, Musawi always insisted, had been his careful preparation of the suicide driver. During their meetings in the *Jardin des Plantes*, Jamal had listened patiently to his stories and advice, assuring him the entire *shura* would appreciate his support. "*Salaam alaykum*," Jamal murmured when the old sheik arrived. "Your young friends have been very helpful."

"Yes, I know," Musawi replied. He stood close to Jamal, looking out over the water. "Al-Omari informed me."

"News travels fast. How did he inform you?"

"Do not worry, he used no telephone. He came to see me this afternoon after they delivered the boy." Two drunks approached and paused near them. One tossed a cigarette butt from the bridge and watched its glow float down to the river. "I discussed with al-Omari the location for the wedding," Musawi resumed after the drunks moved on. "We agreed it should take place in a synagogue." Jamal remained silent, studying the violently dancing colors of the Seine. "*La Grande Synagogue de la Victoire*," Musawi continued, grasping Jamal's arm for emphasis. "We want to paint the walls red with their blood."

"Perhaps a synagogue is not the best target," Jamal said. "At least not for now."

"What target could be better?" The shadow across Musawi's face darkened as he drew back. "It is difficult for our brothers to fight the Jews in Palestine where they are always on guard. We should attack them here, where they feel safe."

"If the attack kills only Jews, no one will care," Jamal whispered. "Just another quarrel between the Arabs and Israelis, the French will say. We have selected an American target."

"An American target?" Musawi asked, leaning closer, his untrimmed beard almost touching the younger man's face.

"Yes, just as you selected in Beirut. Weakening the Americans will weaken the Jews. It is the United States that stands in the way of recovering our lands and our wealth."

"But it did not work in Lebanon," Musawi objected. "Despite our successful blow against the Marine Barracks, the Jews still occupy Palestine. We must strike the Jews directly to end our humiliation, even if we are not yet able to drive them from our land."

"It has been decided. It will be an American target."

"I see." Musawi said nothing more for a moment, looking down at the flowing river. "So when will this event take place?"

"The day will depend upon the boy, but the hour will be around noon."

"Yes, yes." The timing seemed to reassure Musawi. "The place will be filled with people at lunchtime, perhaps including children." He paused to consider the prospect. "It is regrettable, of course, that children should be harmed. They are not responsible, especially those who are not even Jewish. They should not be slaughtered unnecessarily, it is written in the *Qur'an*. But for the operation to be effective, the television cameras must show their parents crying, why did our little ones have to die? Then they will blame the Jews for their occupation of Muslim lands." Jamal said nothing, but Musawi continued. "When the bloodshed becomes sufficiently revolting, the enemy becomes sick at heart and can no longer tolerate the battle. This is the correct path to victory."

"*Inshallah*," Jamal replied. *If God wills it so.* As the last syllable left his lips, Jamal sensed the bridge had become quieter, momentarily emptied of cars and pedestrians. "Then may we count on your support?"

"Yes," Musawi agreed. "I will tell the others."

Jamal strained to read the old *imam's* face in the shadows. A passing car briefly illuminated his white beard and the deep wrinkles that surrounded his wild eyes. Satisfied, Jamal removed a large envelope from his jacket. "Your ticket to Beirut," he explained, extending the envelope. "Also, something for your expenses." A welcome supplement, he thought, to whatever Musawi skimmed from *zakat* donations at the mosque.

"Yes, of course." Musawi smiled, as though these were details he had temporarily forgotten. "We agreed it would be best for me to leave Paris before the battle begins. The police will surely try to capture the leaders."

The leaders, Jamal thought as he watched Sheik Musawi hobble back across the *Pont d'Austerlitz*, moving slowly because of the limp. According to the old man, the attack on the Marine Barracks had inspired all the jihadist attacks that followed. His imitators had merely added improvements such as coordinating attacks in multiple cities or using boats and airplanes in place of truck bombs. *Look at him now*, Jamal thought. Shortly after his Beirut triumph, Sheik Musawi had been forced by a rival militia to flee to asylum in Paris. *The twisted old camel driver believes a plane ticket back to Lebanon will regain him a place among the shura.* Jamal was happy to let him enjoy his delusions.

Something about Sheik Musawi reminded Jamal of his own father. Perhaps it was the insufferable habit of offering guidance when it was least welcome. Such as the way his father had always pressed Jamal to finish the university and get a cushy government job like his older brother Hassan. Jamal had other plans for himself, plans too big for his father to understand, plans far greater than anything his saintly brother would ever achieve. *Allah* be praised that his father was no longer around to hold up Hassan as a shining example. Jamal's only regret was that Hassan had not followed his father into the basement that day.

CHAPTER 11

Fourth Day of the Investigation

Doyle O'Gara took a seat in Douglas Grebb's conference room just as the face of Christine Dupont appeared on the video screen. It was the first time Doyle had seen the leader of the French investigation. Dupont's dark hair was cut short on the sides and parted into an arc that swept boyishly across her forehead, giving her a distinctly French look that Doyle found professional and chic at the same time.

"Before we get down to business, Christine," Grebb began, "let me introduce Howard Silver from Sentinel Systems." From his seat next to Grebb, Silver straightened and smiled into the camera. "Sentinel is one of our best technology consultants, so we asked them to help us with the SIM card you sent over earlier today."

"An outside contractor?" Dupont asked. Her eyes widened on the video screen. "I thought the CIA had limitless resources."

"I'm afraid not, Christine. Even we can't keep up with all the new technology."

Doyle's attention was caught by Leslie Jumana who rushed into the room nodding apologies and took a seat at Grebb's other side. Looking down the table, Doyle's eyes met Leslie's. She arched her dark eyebrows in ironic disapproval, as if she had read his mind and detected some lascivious thought. Before his lips had time to betray a smile, Doyle turned to receive a sheet of technical data from Suresh Kumar beside him.

"Let's begin by asking Howard to tell you what they've learned so far."

"I'll start with the condition of the SIM card," Silver began. "As you know, Ms. Dupont, it is severely damaged. It has been exposed to intense heat and explosive force. The entire card is warped and one of the edges is burned."

"Have you been able to reconstruct any of the code?" Dupont asked.

"Some, but not much. We have just enough to believe it was a prepaid card issued by Swisscom."

"Prepaid," Dupont repeated. "Can you determine how the purchaser paid for it?"

"Not yet," Grebb interjected, "but I'm betting he paid by cash."

"That's what I was afraid of," Dupont said. Doyle understood her frustration. Anyone could buy prepaid cards at newspaper stands, tobacco shops or supermarkets. If the buyer paid cash, there was no record of his name.

"So are you saying you've reached a dead end?" Giles Lambert asked. His long hair and large nose filled the video screen next to Dupont, obscuring Doyle's view of the DST participants seated behind him.

"Not at all," Howard Silver replied. "We're still working on the code. If we can recover enough digits, the phone company in France should be able to identify every call made to or from that SIM card."

"That would be very helpful," Dupont said, smiling for the first time.

"You're assuming it belonged to Big Mac," Grebb observed.

"No, Doug. I'm just hoping. We don't have a lot of other leads."

After the call ended, Grebb began issuing orders to the Langley team. The ball was theirs and he expected them to run it all the way to the end zone. They needed to deliver as much of the code as possible to Paris by the end of the night. But whatever they gave the French, Grebb wanted to get back at least as much, especially phone records. This was an American investigation, too. The CIA had no intention of riding in the backseat while DST drove.

Doyle already knew what role he would be playing. He had been invited to the conference call thanks to a recent promotion. In addition to his continuing role in improving and testing surveillance software, Doyle was now managing Sentinel's translation team. "But, Suresh, I'm too busy to get involved with translations," Doyle had objected when his boss first asked him to take on the additional job two months earlier. It was true;

developing and field testing the new software had been keeping him in the office nights and weekends.

"We feel it's time for you to take on some new challenges, Doyle."

"But I'm no good at languages," Doyle persisted. It was one reason he had studied computer science instead of liberal arts.

"You don't have to be good at languages," Suresh countered. That was the job of the translators. Doyle's role would be to coordinate the translation work more effectively with Sentinel's other activities. A versatile manager could coordinate anything, Suresh assured him.

Doyle could see why coordination was critical, even if he *had* flunked high school Spanish. Developing software to search foreign language messages and translate them into English required dozens of software engineers and translators working together. Even more complicated was the role of translators in supporting CIA investigations. With the volume of intercepts increasing, the CIA relied on new automated systems, but too often the machines made mistakes. For important messages, human experts had to go back to the original intercepts to verify or correct the automated translations. *Yes, lots of coordination will be required*, Doyle thought.

"I've been managing the translators up to now," Suresh explained. "But there is too much going on. Howie thinks you are the perfect one to take this off my back. Let's drop by his office so he can congratulate you on your new assignment."

"Whatever you do," Howard Silver said as they shook hands, "do not sacrifice the accuracy of the translations."

Doyle's mind returned to Grebb's conference room at the sound of Suresh snapping shut his briefcase next to him. "Take a break, Doyle," Suresh said as he rose from the table. "We won't require translation support until they finish with the SIM card; that could take hours." Doyle agreed. He expected that as soon as Sentinel extracted enough code, the CIA would identify intercepted messages requiring urgent translation, but he already had the Sentinel team standing by with the right skills and languages. He might as well take a break while he had the chance.

Doyle remained at the table pretending to study the technical data while the others hustled from Grebb's conference room. What really occupied his mind in that moment was the delicate scent of Leslie Jumana that still floated in the air, the same fragrance Doyle had watched her apply in her bedroom that morning. His thoughts drifted back to the splendid afternoon they had spent together the day before. Leslie had insisted they attend the Egyptian exposition, an event somewhat outside Doyle's normal range of cultural pursuits, but when he picked her up at her apartment he was delighted to see that Leslie had arrayed herself in ways that appealed to his more basic interests. Dressed in blue jeans and cowboy boots, she had pulled back her auburn hair into a braided ponytail, accentuating her high cheeks with their sprinkling of impish freckles, the slight imperfections that Doyle found so irresistible in her fresh-cream complexion. As she descended the stairs of her apartment building, her pert breasts seemed to bounce beneath her plaid blouse in rhythm with the ponytail.

Leslie savored the spicy secrecy of their romance as much as he did. If anyone saw them together in the National Gallery, she had planned, they would pretend they had simply run into one another at the exposition. He would just have to keep his hands to himself and concentrate on the Egyptians. It had not been easy. Afterward, as they walked together along the Mall, he had the constant urge to toss Leslie behind the nearest hedge and make love to her on the federal lawn. He was rewarded for his restraint and sense of public decency when they arrived back at her apartment.

They had been seeing each other for over a month, Doyle calculated, yet they had never gone out to the same place twice. Leslie seemed to know an endless variety of trendy haunts around Washington, including hole-in-the-wall galleries, theaters and concert halls where Doyle secretly delighted in allowing her to fill in the cultural gaps of his Midwestern background. And then there was Leslie's charming little apartment near Langley. He took another moment to enjoy the delicious memory of their prior evening. The wonderful things she had done to please him; the sensation of the delicate gold chain that had hung from her neck; the way she had taken her pleasure from above him. For a moment, the images and sensations surged through his mind and his body as though they were still entwined, straining together toward the heights of their passion. Doyle was confident that none of the others had noticed their brief exchange of glances during the meeting they had just finished in Grebb's conference room. *In the heart of the CIA!* Doyle smiled at their audacity. They had been working together here constantly, yet none of their colleagues seemed to have detected that he and Leslie Jumana were in love.

But then he asked himself the question that had been troubling him for several days: How much longer could their surprising romance survive?

CHAPTER 12

One Day before the Paris Attack

Rashid Badawi began to prepare the first duffel bag in the rented garage. This section of former East Berlin was ideal for his work; no one paid attention to the abandoned factories and warehouses, but unemployed workers from the old arms industry could still be found in the local bars. Badawi unzipped the duffel bag and lined it with plastic bubble wrap. The bag was waterproof, but he liked an extra layer of protection against moisture and shock. He placed the first layer of chocolate into the bottom of the bag. Eight bricks, each half a kilogram.

Chocolate was Badawi's code name for Semtex B. He liked it for his work because it was relatively safe to handle. Palestinian bomb makers preferred TATP, what they called "the Mother of Satan," but for Badawi it was too volatile; it had killed several bomb makers by accident. Semtex B was more difficult to manufacture, but it resisted premature detonation from heat or impact. *Government quality*. He smiled as he finished packing the third layer of bricks into the bag. Into one of the bricks, Badawi inserted an electric blasting cap 10 centimeters long, leaving its two electric wires protruding. The blasting cap contained PETN, penta-erythritol tetra-nitrate, an even more powerful explosive. He taped the ends of the wires so they could not contact any electrical source by accident. It would be for Mohammed Jamal to connect the wires to the detonators in Paris.

It was at the university in Damascus that Badawi had first met Jamal. You had to be careful whom you talked to back then, especially about politics and religion. Badawi had sensed that Jamal was someone he could trust. Not a friend, exactly, but someone who shared his goals. After the first bond of trust, they had a network, a network of two. Then one of them found another person to trust, so there were three. The networks grew that way, one trusted person at a time. Each network was connected to others somehow, but no one saw all the connections. It was safer that way. Not like the loudmouthed students who protested in the streets, the ones who were arrested first when Hafez al-Assad struck back. The ones they interrogated in the middle of the night in concrete basements where no one except the interrogators could hear the screams.

Badawi zipped the first bag shut and started packing the second. By the time they had joined the Muslim Brotherhood, Jamal and Badawi were certain that a few explosions in the right places would bring down the hated Assad regime. The bombs they placed in cafés and markets sounded to them like the voice of God Himself, thundering against the apostates. They had only suffered one accident, Badawi recalled, though it had been a horrible one. It would never have happened if Jamal's father had not gone down those stairs and poked his nose into boxes and sacks that were none of his business. But Jamal had overcome the loss of the old man and pressed on with the campaign, even more determined.

Badawi turned to the second blasting cap and the taping of the wires. Victory had not come to them in Syria, at least not yet, so Jamal had extended the battle to Europe. Provoking the West would help topple Assad, that was Jamal's idea. He was one of the leaders now. Badawi felt no envy, but he sometimes wondered if Jamal still shared the goals that had first bound them together in Damascus. He was content to follow Jamal into Europe, so long as the new path led them to victory. But sometimes it seemed that *Allah* was withholding victory to test their faith. Perhaps it was His will that they go on fighting forever. He zipped the second duffel bag shut. *Wedding cake*, he smiled. That was the code name the pick-up man would use. Badawi had been surprised when Jamal said he was working with neophytes in Paris: urban jihadists with no experience, led by an old *imam* from Beirut. But these were matters for Jamal to decide.

He looked at his watch. The pick-up man would not reach Berlin for another hour. Preparing his dinner, Badawi thought about the other man, the one who would detonate the bomb. He would never meet the man, but he had worked carefully to ensure the success of the man's sacred task. He imagined the man's soul rushing directly to heaven, propelled by the holy explosion.

Waleed Yarkas had started his drive early that morning. On his way out of Paris, he had dropped Hani al-Omari and Zacarias Essabar at the station to catch the TGV. Yarkas drove his twelve-year-old Mercedes 300E. A bit of black smoke spewed from its tailpipe during acceleration, but it would get him to Berlin and back. He had purchased it second-hand, even though he could have lifted a new one for free; he was smart enough not to drive around in a stolen car. Ghadah had been proud when he brought the Mercedes home. Her happiness had made Yarkas feel rich back then. Now, he felt sick every time he thought of her. He had been arrested for car theft when the baby was only a few months old. It was almost funny, his getting caught stealing a Mercedes for a customer when he had been so careful to buy his own. The court-appointed lawyer said he had no defense to the charge, but he could plead for leniency on the basis of his young wife and new baby. Yarkas had expected a short sentence, since it was his first time getting caught. But then the judge ordered six months in prison, saying he should have thought about his wife and baby before he decided to steal cars. *Fils de salope, son of a whore.*

Yarkas glanced at his watch and calculated that his friends were already in Lyon, probably enjoying lunch. *Le train à grande vitesse* took less than three hours to reach the ancient Gallo-Roman city at the threshold of the Rhone Valley. Hani al-Omari would insist they go to one of those little *bouchon* restaurants where he could wrap himself around a plate of *andouillette* sausages. He was a strict Muslim until it came to his own stomach.

Ghadah cooked well enough, he remembered, at least she had before he went to prison. Being separated from her for so long had been torture, but seeing the change in her feelings after he got out had been even worse. Perhaps he should have given her more time to adjust to his return, but he had wanted to make up for all the lost months on the first night. Maybe his new scar frightened her—she did not say—but she became cooler, more formal. She spent more time in her parents' apartment; at least, that was where she said she went. He had his suspicions. It would have been easy enough for her to meet someone else while he was locked away.

Yarkas saw signs for the German border about three that afternoon and felt pleased with his rapid progress. *So easy to travel now that the controls are gone.* But his regrets about Ghadah kept returning. Had he overreacted by imposing the rules on her? He was only following the advice of his Islamist friends, the ones who protected him from the bigger men in prison. She had resisted at first, until he appealed to her parents. After that, she always threw on the *hijab* before she left the apartment, so he felt safer, at least until he followed her one day and caught her stuffing the veil into a shopping bag on her way to visit a friend. The friend had been female that time, but who knew about the other times?

It was nine in the evening when Yarkas reached the outskirts of Berlin. After leaving the *Stadtring*, he drove to *Alexanderplatz* on the east side of the former Wall. There, he called the number Jamal had written on the business card. Following directions from a male voice, he drove further east along *Karl-Marx Allee* until he reached a dimly lit industrial street. The brick buildings on either side looked dark and abandoned. *Where are the famous nightclubs?* he wondered. Stepping outside the car, he detected no sign of life except a low growl of traffic passing somewhere far away. Through a rusted fence, he raised his gaze to the forlorn buildings, suddenly menacing in their immensity, like vast factories of horror in a former concentration camp. *No one is here*, he thought as he peered down the lifeless street. *Not even a blond streetwalker.* He got back into the car and closed his eyes.

The rapping on the window next to his ear awakened him. After hearing the words "wedding cake" through the glass, Yarkas opened the door and slid over to allow the man to take the wheel. The man drove through the dismal quarter without speaking. Yarkas started to ask him what he knew about the Paris operation, but he stopped himself, not wanting to seem too talkative about such matters. After a few minutes of silence, Yarkas lit a cigarette. It was his second pack of Gitanes and the cigarette tasted sour, so he rolled down the window and threw it outside. He saw the first drops of rain fall on the windshield.

The man turned into an unlit driveway, parked the car next to a wire fence and then departed into the darkness. Yarkas stepped outside and lit another cigarette. Looking up, he let the rain fall on his face while he exhaled smoke and urinated through the fence. He heard a metal door swing shut somewhere and saw the man emerge from the darkness carrying two duffel bags. Yarkas unlocked the trunk and reached for one of the bags.

"Not yet," the man said. He returned a minute later with several sheets of foam rubber. Together they lined the bottom of the trunk before placing the two bags inside and wedging sheets of foam rubber around the sides. The man covered the bags with the last of the sheets and pressed the trunk lid shut. "Drive carefully," he said before disappearing into the blackness.

The rain was coming down harder now. Starting the Mercedes, Yarkas realized he had not asked the man's name or anything about him. What did he do between operations? It took him some time to find his way back in the rain, but once on the autobahn he accelerated and merged into the fast lane. *Drive carefully.* He smiled as he recalled the importance of his cargo. He wondered if Ghadah would ever guess that her husband was behind the event that millions would soon be watching on television.

The thought of Ghadah turned his elation into regret. How many times had he hit her? It had not been that many, surely not enough to justify her refusal to return. Besides, she deserved it, treating him so coldly, sneaking around unveiled behind his back. The rain grew heavier, forming thick sheets on the windshield. He had been surprised when her parents had not sent her back the next morning. *How will she find another husband with a newborn baby?* He increased the wiper speed and felt the nausea of his regret turn to anger. He knew girls in Paris besides Ghadah, girls who did not mind being hit a few times. *Girls like Amara.* The memory made him shiver. He steadied the car and recalled the afternoon they had spent with her in al-Omari's apartment. They had first seen her on the street arguing with her older brother over the length of her skirt. Even from a block away, Yarkas could see it was the kind of skirt that made men turn their eyes. *So short you imagined touching her cunt when she leaned over.* But still, it had been tricky luring her into the apartment. She only agreed to go up for a few minutes after Essabar made up the story about his new music system and al-Omari assured her that other girls were present, but even then she hesitated at the apartment door, so all three of them had to shove her inside. She struggled pretty violently on the red sofa, too, until Essabar crammed the towel into her mouth and al-Omari punched her a few times on the shoulder. After they had finished, they made her promise not to tell anyone before they let her leave, although maybe the promise was not even necessary. No one would have believed her story about being forced into it, not the way she dressed. Yarkas was pretty sure she had not talked, since no one had said anything to them, but if he ever saw Amara in the neighborhood again, he intended to tell her that it had been for her own good, to teach her to follow the rules. A fifteen-year-old girl who wore skirts like hers was asking for trouble.

Yarkas yawned when he saw signs for the Belgium border. It was nearly six in the morning. The rain had stopped sometime during the night, but he could not recall when. His eyes had drifted shut several times, but he had no problem re-opening them. He never had trouble staying awake. He slapped his face again, but a few moments later felt his eyes closing. He would let them remain closed a moment longer, just long enough to refresh himself. Something caused his eyes to jerk back open and he saw his hands, the scarred hands of an auto mechanic, wrench the steering wheel to the right and then to the left, fighting to bring the swerving car back into the lane. The vibration of the tires on the shoulder must have awakened him. His heart pounded as he steadied the car and felt his terror give way to relief. The image of a shattered wreck seen years before flashed through his mind.

Breathing deeply, he saw another sign fly past: 370 kilometers to Paris. Maybe he should slow down or even stop in the next rest area. He would still reach Paris sometime in the morning, he estimated, even if he took a quick nap. Sunday morning, just as he had promised Mohammed Jamal. He smiled in anticipation of his return, realizing that everything that lay ahead depended upon him. Thanks to Waleed Yarkas they would soon unleash an angry roar that would echo across France. Maybe across the entire world. All thanks to Waleed Yarkas. Maybe Ghadah would finally realize how grievously she had undervalued her husband.

CHAPTER 13

Fifth Day of the Investigation

"What do you mean by significant segments?" Dupont asked.

"The segments we're sending you may be enough for Swisscom," Grebb replied over the phone. "We're still working, but unfortunately much of the code may not be recoverable."

Within hours after Dupont received the mixed news from her American colleague, Swisscom determined that the burned SIM card found in the restaurant had probably been among those shipped a month earlier to a travel shop called *Bon Voyage Accessories* at Charles de Gaulle Airport. When Dupont and Lambert reached the shop, the manager said he had no record of when the specific SIM card had been sold, but the *Bon Voyage* inventory normally turned over within three weeks, so the sale had probably occurred a week or two before the bombing.

"Excuse me." They turned to a salesgirl standing behind the counter. "Are you asking about prepaid SIM cards?" she inquired. They moved closer to the girl. "I recall one customer purchased several last week. That was kind of unusual."

"Do you remember how many he purchased?" Dupont asked.

"Three, I think. Yes, three and he paid cash. He seemed to have a lot of it." She paused to recall more. "He had a mustache, not too big, and he wore a black KISS T-shirt." She saw their puzzled looks. "The American rock band," she explained. "He seemed a little old to be wearing it, but he was not bad looking."

Armed with evidence that the Big Mac SIM card may have been purchased with two others, Dupont requested Magistrate Joubert to order

France Telecom to turn over records for all calls involving SIM cards shipped to *Bon Voyage* during the prior three weeks. They were especially keen to check names of callers against lists of known extremists. Magistrate Joubert granted only a portion of the request; for the time being, DST could review only records related directly to the one SIM card found inside the restaurant.

"Why are we cursed with this Neanderthal judge?" Dupont shouted when they got back to *rue Nélaton*. "Doesn't he realize we have mass murderers on the loose?"

"We may have asked for too much, Christine," Yves Bannelier responded. "After all, the store sells hundreds of SIM cards each week."

"Including three sold to the bombers!" Dupont protested.

"We can't prove that yet," observed Bannelier, stroking his goatee slowly. "Even if we could, the vast majority went to innocent people. Joubert hasn't forgotten the Mata Hari case."

"Let's get back to work, gentlemen," Dupont snapped. Earlier in her career, she had persuaded the magistrate to allow surveillance of several websites visited by illegal arms dealers. One of the sites, called Mata Hari, turned out to be a Middle East escort service that was also patronized by European diplomats. When the overbroad surveillance came to the attention of the Minister of Foreign Affairs, Dupont and Joubert nearly lost their jobs.

Shortly after the new search order reached France Telecom, call records appeared on the DST computer screens in Paris and, an instant later, on the CIA screens at Langley. Angeline Odette, the red-headed DST analyst Dupont had transferred to the telephone team, was first to notice that the Big Mac SIM card had been used to call two numbers for which France Telecom had no customer names. Odette confirmed with Swisscom that both numbers corresponded to SIM cards recently shipped to *Bon Voyage Accessories*.

"*C'est fantastique!*" exclaimed Dupont, throwing her arms around the young woman. As the others drew closer, Dupont reviewed the evidence aloud: A guy wearing a KISS T-shirt had purchased three prepaid SIM cards at the same time, for cash. A card from the same store wound up in the rubble of the restaurant after having been used to communicate to two other SIM cards, also purchased from the same store.

"And look at the date and time of the last call," Angeline Odette exclaimed.

"Sunday, September 1, at 1:08:32 p.m.," Dupont read, "the date of the bombing and ..."

No one spoke until Lambert uttered what they were all thinking. "Five seconds before the explosion." Surveillance cameras near the restaurant had recorded the first car bomb detonating at 1:08:37 p.m. "Big Mac was inside the restaurant when he made the call."

"Yes, and the call went to the *Pomme Frites* SIM card," said Odette, pointing to her computer screen. "That's what I call the second anonymous SIM card."

"Big Mac calling for *Pomme Frites*." Dupont smiled. "What do you call the third card?"

"*Fromage.* What Americans put on their hamburgers."

"Big Mac with cheese and fries," Lambert said, nodding. "Easy to remember." They all erupted into laughter. After five days, they finally had a breakthrough.

Dupont looked at her watch. It was nearly eight in the evening. "Magistrate Joubert may already be home. Call and ask for an emergency meeting. I think we have grounds to obtain the telephone records for the other two SIM cards, and maybe a lot more than that." She noticed that Lambert's admiring gaze rested on her a moment too long.

"This is the worst case you've ever had," Dupont's mother remarked a few hours later. "Don't you think you should get more rest?"

"That's why I came home, Mother." The meeting with Magistrate Joubert had finished late, so Dupont had directed the taxi back to her apartment. When she arrived, her mother was reading on her customary sofa, her political magazines stacked on the coffee table in neat piles.

"They say you're planning to arrest all the Arabs in Paris."

"They're exaggerating, Mother." She watched the older woman, dressed in her turquoise *robe de chambre*, rise from the sofa and draw near to embrace her. She seemed to move more slowly and stiffly than normal. Or, was Dupont just too tired to see her correctly?

"If you want my opinion, Christine, this has been coming for a long time. If we had not colonized the Arabs and treated them so dreadfully, they would not behave this way." Dupont found it difficult to listen to her mother's words. They seemed faint and garbled, as though they were coming through water. Something needed to be done about the living arrangement, she reminded herself, as soon as the investigation was over. Maybe she could send her mother on a long cruise. With a little luck, she might even meet someone. "I know this recent event was terrible for the victims," the older woman continued, "but it was also an alarm clock for society. We need to pay attention to what they are trying to tell us."

"I don't feel like discussing it just now, Mother. If you don't mind, I'm going to bed."

— — —

While Dupont fell asleep in Paris, Doyle O'Gara looked up from his desk to see one of the translators rush into his office waiving a transcript energetically, as though she were trying to flag down a taxi. Jihan Ammar had just finished the latest batch of Echelon interceptions from France. The transcript she thrust into Doyle's hands was of a conversation recorded from a phone located in Lyon. *Lyon,* Doyle thought as he began reading, *the city where the Fiat was stolen.* "When did this call take place?" he asked a few moments later. He noticed Jihan Ammar was wearing new glasses, their large plastic frames decorated with black and white stripes that reminded Doyle of a zebra

"Several hours ago," she replied as she brushed back her dark hair, still disheveled from her run to his office. "Early evening in France." Doyle began reading the transcript again, this time more carefully.

Hello. Hello. Is that you? I can't [inaudible].
Yes, it's me. Can you?
Okay. It's okay. I'm on the street now.
I can hear you. So, what time does the boat arrive?
Surely this Sunday, God willing, about five maybe a little later.
Okay, no problem, Sunday morning. That is a good hour; they change shifts at six; our friends in customs will be anxious to get home to their wives.
[laughter]
You must be there to take on the cargo before.

Yes, before, as we discussed. We will take care of the little bomb[s]
[laughter] [inaudible words] big explosion[s] in France.
By Sunday night, God willing. Frenchmen will be exploding.
[laughter]
I have work to do. You know, the vans, all the rest.
Okay, call me later.
[They hang up.]

Doyle looked up from the transcript. "When it says 'laughter,' what exactly did you hear on the recording, Jihan?"

"They laughed, both of them. It was pretty loud each time." Jihan had been an exchange student from Jordan when Sentinel had hired her, just a few months before Doyle had arrived. Her English was excellent and she was smart enough not to ask questions beyond her security clearance.

"You're sure they talk about an explosion? You've gone back to the Arabic intercept?" Doyle had seen plenty of errors in machine-generated translations, especially with code words, local dialects and slang.

"I think so," Jihan replied, "though it is hard for me to tell if it is one explosion or several. The recording is very scratchy. Can you get a better copy?"

"I doubt it," Doyle said, "but we need to be sure what this one says."

"The man whose phone is under surveillance—his name is Abdallah Ramadan—he speaks in the Maghreb dialect, probably from Algeria or Morocco. He uses a word that can be translated as bomb, although it could also be something that explodes or has a big impact. The other person I understand better: he uses Levantine Arabic spoken in Jordan, where I grew up, as well as in Lebanon and Syria. He definitely talks of an explosion; I am sure of that."

"We must be exact."

"I understand, but the recording is scratchy. I cannot hear all the words."

Doyle looked at his watch. "I expect the client will want to see this tonight. I need to track down Suresh Kumar right away. Keep working and call me if you make any corrections." Doyle slipped the Ramadan transcript into his briefcase. Fortunately, Suresh was meeting with Leslie Jumana and others at the CIA that evening to review Echelon field tests.

Running to his car, Doyle was struck by how exciting the translation job had turned out to be. *Just as exciting as Ozzie led me to believe*, he thought, recalling his friend Khalid Osman, the translator he had met months before he took charge of the department. Not for the first time, he wished Ozzie had remained at Sentinel, at least long enough to help him adjust to his new duties. But his abrupt departure had not really surprised Doyle. He had always felt that Ozzie was destined for something greater than translations.

During his drive to Langley, Doyle thought back to their first fortuitous encounter. Sentinel's office building contained a spacious cafeteria facing an atrium garden, the company evidently wishing to discourage employees from leaving the building for a mere bite to eat or breath of fresh air. Doyle had just seated himself for lunch when Ozzie wandered up to his table appearing a bit lost. Doyle nodded toward the empty place across from him.

"What kind of work do you do for Sentinel?" Ozzie asked without preliminaries. His eyes remained fixed on Doyle, observant yet friendly. From his lean build, Doyle guessed he was in his early thirties, although something about his face seemed older. It was not until later that Doyle noticed the rimless glasses hovering before his eyes.

"I'm not permitted to say."

They both laughed to cover the awkwardness. Doyle's evasive response was not an uncommon one at Sentinel. He had no need to ask Ozzie's job, as he had already guessed it from his accent. Twenty or thirty translators from the Middle East occupied a maze of cubicles on Sentinel's first floor, their ears clamped between headphones and their eyes staring intently into computer screens. Ozzie explained that he had studied public administration in Lebanon and was planning to enter law enforcement. That was why he was eager to learn how Sentinel helped the CIA with terrorist surveillance. Doyle was cautious in his replies, not speaking about particular projects, but sharing a few techniques that had already been reported in the media. Perhaps detecting Doyle's hesitancy, Ozzie asked only a few questions during that first lunch, but spoke freely about his own work. Much of it sounded like traditional translation of Arabic into English. But some of it was more high-tech, such as developing Arabic language search engines and translation software.

Although Doyle was not to become involved in translations until months later, he was already intrigued by the technical hurdles. His new friend Khalid Osman was remarkably knowledgeable and helpful. His explanations were concise and articulate, as though Ozzie had prepared little lectures for Doyle's enlightenment. Indeed, with his neatly sculpted features and unobtrusive glasses, Ozzie seemed almost professorial at times. They must have talked for another hour that day before they returned to work. As they parted, Ozzie suggested they get together again some evening in one of the local sports bars. He professed a passion for baseball.

Pulling his car into the Langley parking lot with the Ramadan transcript in his briefcase, Doyle tried to remember if he had ever given Ozzie his e-mail address. It was possible, but he could not recall.

CHAPTER 14

Sixth Day of the Investigation

When Christine Dupont arrived at DST headquarters that morning, she wore a charcoal pinstripe suit, elegant but not too provocative. Lambert's renewed glances, infrequent though they were, had started to worry her. Entering the main war room, she sensed that the investigation was gaining momentum. Hanging from the walls were hand-drawn charts showing relationships among the telephone numbers, locations and times. One chart had been edited violently with colorful grease pencils. Before Dupont could decipher the chart, Angeline Odette rushed into the room carrying a stack of France Telecom records. She had identified a call from the *Pomme Frites* SIM card to a number in Lyon, just two days before the attack.

"Lyon!" Dupont exclaimed. "That's where one of the cars . . ."

"Both of the cars," Giles Lambert corrected. "We traced the Renault Clio this morning. It was also registered to a Lyon address and was stolen on the same day as the Fiat."

"I see you've been busy during my little nap," Dupont said with a smile. "Go on."

"The number called by *Pomme Frites* belongs to a certain Abdullah Ramadan," Odette said. "It's a cell phone, too."

"What do we know about Mr. Ramadan?"

"Not much," Lambert confessed. "No criminal record, no radical connections."

"Let's get a surveillance order for the guy," Dupont said. "If he talked to *Pomme Frites*, we need to know who he is talking to this morning and what they are saying."

"The magistrate may not go along," Yves Bannelier observed, "unless we show evidence that Ramadan is involved in a crime."

"But the guy was called by someone linked to the bombing," Dupont exclaimed.

"It's not a crime to receive a phone call," Bannelier replied. "The magistrate will point out it could have been a wrong number."

"Can I add something?" Odette asked, flipping impatiently through her stack of phone records. "It looks like Abdullah Ramadan also received a call from the Big Mac SIM card. It was one day before the attack."

"Two wrong numbers?" Dupont asked Bannelier in an ironic tone.

A secretary appeared at the door. "You have an urgent call from the Central Intelligence Agency, Madame Dupont. It's Mr. Grebb."

Dupont looked at her watch, puzzled; it was the middle of the night in Langley. "You can transfer it here on the secure line. Yves, while we take the call, please find out how soon Magistrate Joubert can see us."

"I have with me Leslie Jumana of my team," Douglas Grebb began after exchanging greetings with Dupont, "as well as Doyle O'Gara from Sentinel Systems. I think you met them both during our last video conference."

"You're keeping them up late, Doug. I hope it's been worthwhile."

"That's why we're calling you, Christine. We reviewed the latest records you got from France Telecom. We see they included only first-level contacts of the three SIM cards."

"That's all we've been able to get so far."

"None of those contacts was in our files," Grebb continued, "so we put all of them under surveillance. We found that one of them is involved in some very odd activities."

"Surveillance?" Dupont asked.

"Yes," Grebb replied, "monitoring their calls and movements."

"You are speaking of people in France?"

"Yes," Grebb said. "We are particularly interested in a Mr. Abdallah Ramadan in Lyon. As you've no doubt discovered, he was contacted by Big Mac and one of the other SIM cards, and he has a criminal record."

"I do not want to hear any more," Dupont interrupted. She glared at Giles Lambert. Angeline Odette rose abruptly and rushed out of the war room.

"I think you do," Grebb continued. "Especially his phone conversation earlier tonight."

"No, I must ask you to stop," Dupont snapped. "I do not want a French judge to dismiss our prosecution on the grounds of illegal wiretaps, especially those of the CIA."

"We are entitled to conduct such surveillance under US law."

"That is irrelevant under French law, Mr. Grebb."

"We are trying to be helpful, Christine."

"I am sure you are, Mr. Grebb, but I think it is best to end this particular conversation."

An uncomfortable silence followed before Dupont put down the receiver. She turned quickly to Lambert. "Why does the CIA think Ramadan has a criminal history?"

"He came up clean on our records," Lambert replied with a frown. "Maybe they have the wrong guy."

"*Merde! Putain!*" shouted Odette as she reentered the room with Bannelier. She was carrying a computer printout. "We misspelled his name in the search request last night. It is 'Abd-a-llah' with an 'a', not 'Abd-u-llah' with a 'u'. It appears that Mr. Abd-a-a-a-llah Ramadan"—she stretched out the "a" for emphasis—"has a long history of arrests for car theft and smuggling."

"*Mon Dieu*," Dupont said. "No wonder the CIA has been listening to him all night! Did anything else come to light while I was chatting with them?"

"We've analyzed more of the phone records, "Bannelier replied. "The *Pomme Frites* and *Fromage* SIM cards were each used to call a mobile phone registered to a certain Hani al-Omari with a billing address on *rue du Landy*."

Rue du Landy, Dupont thought, *in Saint-Denis*. Now they had a physical address. Things were starting to fall into place.

"*Pomme Frites* also called a number in Berlin," Bannelier added, "and the *Fromage* card was used to call England."

"Tell me about the Berlin call," Dupont asked quietly.

"It is very suspicious. *Pomme Frites* places the call Saturday night, August 31, about 9:00 p.m. The call lasts less than a minute."

"The night before the bombing. Who did he call?"

"The receiving number is not registered with Deutsche Telecom," Bannelier said. "It's another anonymous SIM card and it was used only once in their system."

"So someone in Berlin bought a SIM card just to receive the call from *Pomme Frites*."

"Right, but there's something more interesting," Bannelier continued. "*Pomme Frites* accessed the Deutsche Telecom system from a location near *Alexanderplatz*."

"What was *Pomme Frites* doing in Berlin, for God's sake?" Dupont wondered aloud.

"He doesn't stay there long. He is near Liège in Belgium around seven the next morning when he receives a call from *Fromage*."

"So *Pomme Frites* is heading toward Paris. Where was *Fromage* calling him from?"

"That's the most interesting part. We think the call came from *Avenue Mozart* somewhere near *rue de la Source*. We can't determine the exact address."

Dupont was already on her feet heading to the door. "Get records of everyone who occupies an apartment on that block of *Avenue Mozart*. While we're waiting, let's see Magistrate Joubert about a roving wiretap for the guy in Lyon."

"A-b-d-a-l-l-a-h Ramadan." Angeline Odette spelled the name out loud as they ran down four flights of stairs.

"Don't forget the new guy, Hani al-Omari," Dupont added. "We'll need an order to search his apartment on *rue du Landy* while we question him."

"I've already prepared the request," Odette replied, patting her briefcase. Her youthful enthusiasm and flaming red hair were energizing the entire team, Dupont thought as the group crowded into a taxi.

"Now you can tell me about that call *Fromage* made to England," Dupont said to Bannelier as she pulled playfully on his goatee.

— — —

"The ungrateful fools!" Doyle exclaimed angrily. He was back in his car after the brief call with Paris. *After all our hard work, they couldn't find a way around their stupid rules to hear what we discovered about this guy*

Ramadan. Can't they be a little more creative? Maybe Doyle was just irritable after working half the night, but he found Dupont's frigid caution quite discouraging after the warm reception his team had received from the CIA. Was it due to cultural differences? *Yes*, he thought, *Americans are more open than the French.* Look at the CIA, for example; in place of Cold War compartmentalization, the Agency now embraced Silicon Valley collaboration, reaching out to the technology companies. *Reaching out with a warm embrace,* Doyle thought, remembering the invitation Leslie had whispered to him after the aggravating call. He would reach her apartment in a few minutes. While looking forward to the pleasures ahead, Doyle's mind slipped back to the first days of their unlikely affair, still amazed about how it had all unfolded.

It had begun during the so-called camping trip, he recalled, when the Sentinel team installed itself at Langley to test the improved Carnivore software. Doyle had been happy that the CIA team included the young woman with the intriguing eyes he had spotted during his first meeting. He soon learned that Leslie's new unit analyzed terrorist organizations, including their hierarchies and decision-making processes. Grebb seemed to consult her frequently.

One evening in late June, with the Paris attack still months away, Doyle found himself alone with Leslie for the first time after others had left the room. They continued working silently on opposite sides of the table until she closed her laptop and stood to leave. Whether intentional or not, the movement displayed her lovely proportions to full advantage.

"How long will you be here?" she asked as she moved past Doyle, her tweed skirt arresting his attention mid-thigh. "Your group, I mean."

"Several more weeks," he said as he looked up. Seeing her smiling, he had the terrifying impression that she was peering down at his plump belly. He had lost five pounds, thanks to his early morning runs, but knew he still had more to lose.

"Good, that gives us plenty of time." She remained standing next to him, as though waiting, but before he could compose a follow-up line, she added: "After all, we still have lots of software to test."

It was not until she resumed her progress toward the door that Doyle asked if she knew any good restaurants near Langley. She turned back, holding her laptop to her chest. Doyle explained that he didn't know the area very well. She swayed gently from side to side, evidently considering his question. "What kind of food do you like?" He replied that he didn't really care and just wanted to get out of the building. Maybe they could get something nearby, in case she needed to get back to work. "Meet me in the lobby in fifteen minutes," she instructed him. "In front of the truth motto."

The CIA lobby, a wonderful place to begin a love affair, Doyle thought as he stopped his car before Leslie's apartment building. Despite the late hour he expected she would offer him something healthy to eat. She blamed his bizarre bachelor diet for his excess weight. But working so close to her the entire day had left Doyle hungry only for her. Ravenous, in fact. The thought of her full lips yielding under his kisses turned the hunger into a throbbing urge.

"He would like to see you immediately," Dupont's secretary informed her. "I told him you were on the way back from your meeting with Magistrate Joubert."

Dominique Carpentier was standing when Dupont entered his office. "*Bonjour*, Christine. Any progress?"

"Yes, we have several fresh leads. I was intending to brief you as soon as I returned."

"Unfortunately, that will have to wait. I'm more interested in *arrests* than leads. It's been six days. How many people do you have working on this?"

"Nearly five hundred. Plus our friends abroad."

"Are you sure that's enough?" Carpentier asked with a frown. "The Socialists are grumbling we are inept, we could have prevented the attack, we should have tracked down the culprits by now, blah, blah, blah. We need an arrest or two to shut them up." Carpentier appeared more robust than he had in his living room three nights earlier, but the daylight revealed a nervous impatience Dupont had not seen in him before.

"Then you'll have to help me with Magistrate Joubert," she countered. "He insists on playing by the book. That's not going to work in a case like this."

"Joubert is no more of a fan of the restrictions than you are," Carpentier said. "But what choice does he have under these damned privacy laws?"

Does his impatience have something to do with his retirement? Dupont recalled the dark corridor leading to the silent bedrooms, wondering what plans Carpentier and his wife might have for the future. *If he even has a wife.* She remembered his oriental robe and pajamas, the strangely eclectic furnishings.

"Joubert may be trying to make a point to the Socialists," Carpentier went on. "Unfortunately, we get all the blame." He rubbed his knuckles and glanced out the window. "What do you need from him, exactly?"

"So far, he has limited us to phone records that directly involve the three SIM cards. We need to see the calls of indirect contacts, out to the third or fourth level."

"That may involve thousands of people," Carpentier objected.

"In addition to phone records," Dupont pressed, "we need wire taps for everyone connected directly or indirectly to the SIM cards."

"You are asking for a lot, Christine. The press will go crazy."

"All three SIM cards have been silent since the day of the attack, Dominique. The bombers have obviously gone into hiding. We need to monitor indirect contacts if we hope to pick up their trails again."

"Very well. I'll see what I can do about Joubert. In exchange, I want you to have some arrests to announce before tomorrow's protests."

"Protests?"

"Haven't you heard?" Carpentier asked. "The French Council of the Muslim Faith plans to march around *Place de la République* at noon on Saturday."

"That's outrageous! We haven't arrested a single Arab, at least not yet."

"Don't jump to conclusions, Christine. The march is to protest the attack on the *Champs-Élysées*. They want to make it clear to everyone that the killers do not represent the views of Muslims in France. A rather heartwarming gesture, I thought."

— — —

Two armored police vehicles approached the apartment building on *rue du Landy* linked to the mobile phone account of Hani al-Omari. Immigration records indicated that al-Omari was of Saudi Arabian origin, having emigrated five years earlier with his family. His father was evidently wealthy, having purchased three apartments in Marseille, one of which was occupied by Hani al-Omari and his young wife. It was not clear why the younger al-Omari also maintained an apartment in Saint-Denis.

From the street, the apartment on the third floor appeared dark. Half a dozen armed officers in protective clothing climbed the stairs and knocked on the apartment door. No answer. A second time, more loudly. A curious neighbor came into the hallway, staring at the strangely attired men. They were not home, she told them. She believed there were three who lived there, maybe four, but she hadn't seen any of them for a week. An officer knocked again and then, after there was no response, he liberated the door from its hinges with a swift kick. All the officers entered with weapons drawn and moved quickly through the rooms. Strong odors greeted them in the kitchen where they found unwashed dishes in the sink and an overflowing garbage pail. Satisfied that the apartment was unoccupied, they began a visual search, taking care to touch nothing.

The two bedrooms contained mattresses without beds, desks loaded with computers and recording equipment, and several cardboard boxes containing clothing, magazines and video materials. A set of exercise weights lay next to one mattress. Returning to the main room, they noted a red sofa before a large television and more boxes of video tapes and discs.

"Fils de salope!" remarked one officer. *Son of a bitch.* "Have you ever seen anything like that?" He pointed to a poster taped on the wall.

"Putain," his colleague replied. He stepped closer to the wall and took a photograph.

CHAPTER 15

Sixth day of the Investigation

It was noon in Washington when the National Security Advisor, Stephen Holbrook, received an urgent request to attend a meeting at the Russian Embassy. No reason was given, but Holbrook knew from experience not to decline such invitations.

Besides the Russian Ambassador, two other officials were seated in the office when Holbrook arrived. After coffee, the Ambassador passed out an agenda that listed several long-simmering issues concerning North Korea. Holbrook glanced at the agenda and then turned it over as though looking for something more. "Pardon me, Mr. Ambassador," he said, "but if I had known this would be the subject, I would have brought along our Korea experts." As if his words were a cue, the others rose and left the room.

"What I have to say is sensitive," the Ambassador began after the door closed. "If any of this were to become public, I would be forced to deny it. Today's meeting is solely to discuss North Korea."

"I understand," Holbrook replied.

"About two weeks ago my country became the victim of a theft of radioactive material," the Ambassador continued. "The theft occurred at a research center outside Rostov. It was an armed robbery. We believe the robbers entered the facility during the day, perhaps with help from an accomplice inside. During the night, they killed several security people, seven I believe, and then escaped in three trucks."

"What did they steal?" Holbrook asked.

"They left with a thermal generator containing over 20 kilograms of Strontium-90, along with six containers of Cesium-137 totaling about 37 kilograms." The Russian paused to allow Holbrook to absorb the significance. "The loss was not discovered until the shift change the next morning. We found all three trucks abandoned within a 25 kilometer radius, so we assume they transferred the material to other vehicles."

"Do you have any idea who they were?"

"As you know, there are certain groups that wish to separate the region of Chechnya from the Russian Republic through violent means. I believe you have similar criminal groups in the United States that object to the role of your federal government." Holbrook did not react to the comparison, so the Ambassador continued. "We suspected the robbers were Chechen separatists due to the brutal nature of the theft, so we conducted raids at several locations in Grozny. Yesterday, we learned the material had been sold."

"Sold? To whom?"

"To a man carrying a false Egyptian passport. We do not know whom he represents."

"May I ask how you know about the sale?"

"From the sellers," the Ambassador explained. "They told us."

"I don't understand."

"After the raids, several Chechens were invited to Grozny police headquarters. We need not discuss methods and sources, but one of them eventually described the transaction in some detail."

Holbrook raised his eyes and pretended to study one of the Ambassador's abstract paintings. "Do you have any more information about the purchaser?" he asked after a moment.

"Not much. It seems the man traveled under the false name Hosni al-Sheriff. The Chechens liked him well enough to take his money, but so far they claim to know nothing about the group he represents. Through other sources, we believe the man who called himself al-Sheriff recently completed a series of bank transactions in Abu Dhabi, whereupon he departed on a flight via Istanbul to Sochi."

"One of your ports on the Black Sea," Holbrook commented.

"I am impressed by your knowledge of Russian geography," the Ambassador replied. "It is also where the Chechens delivered the radioactive material to the purchaser."

"Where is it now?"

The Ambassador frowned. "Yes, therein lies the problem. Our sources tell us the material left the Port of Sochi a few days ago, on a vessel called the *Izmir Queen*." He glanced down at a piece of paper. "It is a Turkish vessel. We have not been able to locate her, but perhaps she is hiding in a port somewhere in the Black Sea or the Mediterranean."

"Perhaps we can help you find the vessel."

"That is our wish. We would like to get the stuff back, quietly." They both studied the abstract painting for a moment. It looked to Holbrook as though it had been painted by an untalented child during a temper tantrum. "One more point," the Ambassador resumed. "We believe the purchaser returned to Istanbul and took an Air France flight to Paris on August 27 using a different passport." He paused to allow Holbrook to consider the date and itinerary. "We don't know what name he assumed, but perhaps your CIA colleagues have picked up his trail."

"Have you told anyone else?" Holbrook asked.

"We shared this information with our French friends, since the man flew to Paris, but only at the highest levels and in the strictest confidence, of course."

"Of course. Let me see what I can find out."

— — —

Magistrate Jean-Philippe Joubert issued an expanded order that evening allowing DST to obtain telephone records for three levels of contacts with Big Mac, *Fromage* and *Pomme Frites*, as well as to conduct electronic surveillance of the first two levels. He gave no reason for the sudden expansion, but it did not surprise Dominique Carpentier. He knew the *Élysée Palace* had earlier that day called Joubert's superior, the president of the Court of Assize, to express concern that, without broader electronic surveillance, the government would have no choice but to interrogate each known contact, most of whom had Arabic names. Considering the prospect of busloads of police visiting Muslim homes, mosques and markets, the court president agreed that a bit more electronic eavesdropping was less threatening to French civil liberties than a possible civil war.

As the new records flowed in, DST identified over 500,000 calls among the three levels of contacts during the two weeks surrounding the attack.

DST computers analyzed the calls to identify suspicious patterns. Amidst the piles of printouts, Angeline Odette and five other analysts argued late into the night over the implications. How many people were involved in the plot? How wide had it spread? Where would it next rear its monstrous head?

— — —

Two constables drove to the address in Blackpool, England.

"Do they really believe the fellow living there is connected to that bombing in Paris?" Albert Baldwin asked.

"They sounded doubtful," responded his partner William Lennon. "They just want us to pay him a visit and see if anything looks odd."

Lennon knew that the Secret Intelligence Service, better known as MI-6, had received a telephone call from a CIA woman named Leslie Jumana a few hours earlier. She told them that a SIM card linked to the Paris investigation, code-named *Fromage*, had been used to call a number in England. Ms. Jumana wanted to know why those preparing the Paris bombing made that call. Were they seeking instructions? Could they be organizing more attacks? MI-6 traced the *Fromage* call to a number in Blackpool registered to one Mustapha Yazid Hamza. He had emigrated six years earlier from Pakistan and had been granted a British visa for permanent residency. However, MI-6 had no criminal file regarding Mr. Hamza or any combination of his three names.

"Why didn't they send up the specialists from Vauxhall Cross?" Baldwin asked.

"They want us to do an advance reconnoiter before they commit any resources," Lennon explained. "They've never heard of this Mr. Cheese that the CIA woman spoke about. But they said she was very insistent. Called them back twice on the encrypted line."

"Mr. Cheese?" Baldwin asked.

"*Fromage*," Lennon clarified, "the suspect in Paris who called Mr. Hamza's number."

The address belonged to a small house near the beach, the kind that tourists rented during the summer. Lennon rang the doorbell, while his partner walked to the back. No response greeted the bell, so Lennon tried the door. It was locked and the curtains were drawn. Baldwin returned to report the same conditions at the back of the house. "Do you suppose we could get a warrant to search the place?" Baldwin asked.

"Simply because the bloke is a Paki and received a call from Paris? I doubt it." Lennon opened the letter box and saw it contained several days of mail. *Interesting that Mr. Hamza left around the same time as the Paris bombing.* Reaching up, Lennon patted along the window frame while Baldwin, the shorter of the pair, stooped down to look under the doormat. When they found nothing, Lennon began checking beneath the flower pots.

It was Lennon who eventually found it under a cracked planter at the far end of the porch. It was old and corroded, as though it had been hidden there and forgotten years before. Lennon inserted the key into the door lock, pushing and jiggling it to overcome the rust. He was amazed when the key turned the cylinder. *God bless you, Mr. Hamza, you haven't changed the lock.* Lennon looked toward the beach. The sun was setting and several young couples were strolling toward the water. *Maybe you went to watch the sunset, too,* Lennon thought. He hesitated before turning the knob. *But you wouldn't stay there for several days.*

The door opened directly into the living room. Lennon's nose detected a sharp chemical smell. Stepping inside, he headed down a short corridor that led to the kitchen at the rear. Arrayed on a large table in the center of the kitchen were glass bottles, plastic sacks and cardboard containers. "My, my, look what we have here." Lennon said.

"Looks like a real fire hazard," Baldwin said behind him.

"More like a bomb factory," Lennon exclaimed as he read the labels.

Stacked on another table were books, magazines and catalogs. "Holy mother of God," Baldwin whispered as he leafed through one of the books. Lennon drew back one of the curtains. Dusk light flowed into the kitchen, illuminating the tables and their contents. The two constables returned to the front of the house, closed the door and replaced the key under the old planter. Then they walked around to the back and looked through the rear window.

"The experts from Vauxhall Cross should have no trouble getting a search warrant now," Baldwin observed.

"It's shocking, what some people will leave in full public view," Lennon agreed.

CHAPTER 16

One Day before the Paris Attack

"At last, some company," Yusuf Ghamdi exclaimed as he opened the door.

Entering the apartment, Mohammed Jamal saw Ali Benhadj seated on one of the plush sofas. The young man had been in the *Avenue Mozart* apartment for over twenty-four hours; it was time for Jamal to see how he was progressing. Benhadj was dressed in a white *dishdasha* with a green belt circling his waist. A long, curved saber had been thrust under the belt. Tied around his head was a band of cloth bearing a slogan in black Arabic letters. A leather bound *Qur'an* lay open before him on the low table. Video discs were scattered on the carpet near the television. "I'll prepare tea," Ghamdi said. "After that we can begin the filming."

"Excellent," Jamal said. "Let me help you." He pressed his hand gently on Benhadj's shoulder, signaling him to remain seated, and followed Ghamdi into the kitchen.

"I'm not sure, yet," Ghamdi whispered.

"Will he be ready by tomorrow?"

"Don't be impatient, my friend." Ghamdi's lips twisting into his odd smile. Jamal nodded. Ghamdi was among his earliest comrades from the Syrian uprising and had several times demonstrated his talent for such preparations.

Jamal returned to inspect the dining room. Covering one wall was a colorful poster depicting the Al Aqsa Mosque in Jerusalem. An armchair stood before the poster. Two strong lamps illuminated the scene. A video camera waited on the dining table. Jamal's inspection was interrupted by the ringing of his cell phone. His face broke into a smile as he listened.

"Don't start filming until I get back," he told Ghamdi as he headed for the door.

Below, two cars were parked before the building. Zacarias Essabar sat in a Fiat Punto minivan, perhaps ten years old. Its color may have originally been black, but age or abuse had turned it to a powdery gray, as though it had long been over-used as a delivery van. *It will be perfect*, Jamal thought. Hani al-Omari occupied a yellow Renault Clio, a five-door hatchback model. It was newer, perhaps only five years old, but considerably smaller. Al-Omari's corpulent, bearded body filled the entire space between the driver's seat and the steering wheel.

Jamal paced around the tiny Clio. He had expected a larger car, one more in line with the scale of the enterprise. *Trusting the fat fool's judgment was a mistake.* But it would have to do, he decided. At least it was unlikely to be noticed by the police if reported stolen. Millions of Clios swarmed the French roads.

Jamal directed the two men down the ramp into the underground garage and then into the parking spots assigned to the apartment. As al-Omari squeezed out of the Renault, Jamal noticed something odd: instead of his customary Saudi headgear, he now wore a green French beret. Even odder, he had trimmed his bushy black beard, reducing it to two neat strips along his jaws that converged into an "O" encircling his mouth. *He looks like a chubby Che Guevara*, Jamal thought sarcastically.

When Jamal returned to the apartment with al-Omari and Essabar, he spotted Benhadj in the dining room, seated on the large armchair listening to instructions from Ghamdi.

"Hey, you look Japanese," said Essabar, tugging the headband. "Like a kamikaze pilot."

"Or an Arabian warrior," Jamal corrected.

"Whatever." Essabar seemed more interested in showing Benhadj the new Sony Discman he had stolen in Lyon. Benhadj listened a moment without smiling and then abruptly handed it back.

"Are you ready to begin, my young mujahedeen?" Ghamdi switched on the filming lamps. "You can begin speaking whenever you like."

Benhadj positioned the sword across his lap and sat upright in the armchair as though it were a throne. He looked a bit undersize for the regal setting, Jamal observed with regret.

Benhadj began in a clear voice without hesitation, having evidently practiced the speech: "In the name of *Allah*, the merciful . . ."

"Wait, the camera is not running yet," Ghamdi said as he fiddled with the device. "Okay, now you can begin."

"In the name of *Allah*, the merciful, the compassionate. May God's peace and blessings be upon the Prophet Mohammed and his household. My name is Abu Salem of the Islamic Army of Jihad in France."

Abu Salem, a nice touch. Jamal felt reassured.

"I speak on behalf of the Muslims of the world, especially those who have suffered at the hands the global crusader alliance led by America, Britain and Israel."

"Can I say something?" al-Omari interrupted. The words seemed to jump through the bristly "O" of his beard.

"What is it?" Ghamdi asked, pausing the camera.

"I don't think Ali should talk about Britain." He shook his index finger to emphasize his point. "Our plan is to attack America, right?"

"The British are *fils de salopes*, too," Essabar interjected.

"True," Jamal agreed, "but perhaps Hani al-Omari is correct. Let us not mention the British in the speech of Abu Salem."

Essabar shrugged and returned to his music.

"The evil influence of America has grown intolerable," Benhadj resumed his speech. "The collapse of the Soviet Union has made the United States even more haughty and arrogant than it was in the past. America has come to see itself as the master of the world."

A sharp knock came from the apartment door. Jamal motioned for the others to dim the lights and remain silent. He shut the dining room door as he left.

"Our neighbor," Jamal explained when he returned a minute later, carrying several pairs of shoes. "She objected to our leaving them in the corridor."

Ghamdi slapped himself on the head.

"Yes," Jamal agreed. "We must be more careful."

Ghamdi restored the lights and resumed filming. Benhadj had adjusted the saber so it now stood upright in his right hand.

"America seeks to plunder Muslim oil and supports governments that impose man-made laws upon Muslims. If we resist, America says we are terrorists. What a lie! They are the terrorists, occupying Muslim lands and desecrating holy sanctuaries!" Benhadj thrust the sword toward the poster behind his head. "Even the third holiest site of Islam, is today occupied by the Zionist allies of America."

"You should add something about yourself," Jamal suggested.

Benhadj nodded and resumed his speech. Describing his childhood in Algeria, he told how his life had acquired meaning only after he began following the Straight Path of Islam. He explained how he had come to France with dreams of becoming an engineer or architect, expressing his bitterness that the university had rejected him because he was a Muslim and a foreigner.

The intercom buzzed at the apartment door. Ghamdi looked at his watch. "It must be the delivery," he said to Jamal. "Abu Salem selected tonight's meal."

Jamal looked up at the ceiling and shook his head. "I will get it," he muttered. "You finish the film."

It is not a bad speech, Jamal thought as he carried the pizzas and soft drinks into the kitchen, *although I've heard better ones.* Still, it might be adequate to inspire other recruits, provided the boy completed his task. Sitting down to smoke a cigarette, Jamal tried to recall the many things Ali Benhadj had revealed about himself, looking for signs that might tell him whether the youth was up to the challenge. He began with the story of how Ali had arrived in Paris, alone and without much money or any clear plans. He must have sensed his vulnerability, Jamal thought, causing him to wonder what God intended for him. His father had given him the address of a friend in Paris, a man with whom the father had worked years earlier in the Algerian gas industry, but the friend seemed strangely unprepared to receive Ali. He eventually offered to let the youth stay in the apartment, but on condition that he share the expense.

Jamal removed his glasses and placed them on the kitchen table. His eyes felt dry and tired, but he had no desire to sleep. He recalled how Ali had described the man's two little girls running into the front room laughing. They had reminded Ali of his sisters in Algiers. He seemed especially drawn to the younger one who had studied him shyly from the security of her father's lap. *His affection for children roots him in this world,* Jamal observed. *Will he be able to overcome the attachment when the moment arrives?* Ali had seemed reluctant to tell Jamal about the other person he had met that day. The presence of the host's young wife in the small apartment apparently disturbed him. *What was it about her that made him so uncomfortable?* His host worked nights as a waiter, so Ali had found himself alone each evening with the wife and two little girls. He tried to maintain his prayers and to study the *Qur'an*, but he had found it difficult to concentrate with the television blaring out children's cartoons. It was even worse after the girls were put to bed, for then he found himself alone with the young woman. It seemed that she dressed correctly when she went outside, always donning a long dress and *hijab*, but inside the apartment she wore shorts and T-shirts, apparently oblivious to their effects upon Ali. A man must keep his thoughts pure to discern God's will, Ali had explained to Jamal.

Jamal stroked his mustache as he recalled their first meeting in the Saint-Denis mosque. The self-righteous youth yielded almost too easily to his guidance, his adolescent virility seeming almost feminine in its receptivity. For it was not only his quest for moral purity that rendered him suitable for martyrdom, Jamal realized, but also his lack of plans for the future. The young man dreamed of making the Hajj pilgrimage to Mecca, but submitted to his father's insistence that he first complete his education. He arrived in Paris with a brochure from *École Polytechnique* but with no assurance of admission. Not surprisingly, when he first visited the campus he was told that to qualify for entry, he would need at least two years of preparatory courses and top scores in the entrance examination. After all, *École Polytechnique* was no ordinary engineering school, but one of France's prestigious *Grandes Écoles*. After his anger subsided, he later told Jamal, Ali decided the rejection was a sign from God that he should return to his religious studies. *Nudged back onto the spiritual road, but is he prepared to travel as far as we require?*

Jamal had grown fond of the boy, but his death was essential to give meaning to the operation. They could achieve the explosion without sacrificing him, of course, simply by detonating the bomb with a remote control. But such a cowardly attack would be meaningless. It was the martyr's willingness to die that confirmed the truth of the message behind the attack. The Christians had proved this long ago; it was thanks to their martyrs that Christianity had attracted so many followers. Not just the

Chief Martyr, tortured and nailed upon the wooden cross, but all the others who had followed him: burned at stakes, eaten by lions, pierced with arrows, roasted over hot coals. Every church and museum in Europe was filled with lurid portrayals of their martyrdoms. Jamal wondered if pictures of the modern-day Islamic martyrs would someday hang in museums, heroic portraits of those who had sacrificed themselves in planes and automobiles.

But will Ali Benhadj be among them? He was playing the role well with his *nom de guerre* before the video camera, but would he persevere through the final act? Jamal suddenly recalled another story Ali had related, a story that might contain the answer he sought. When Ali was still a schoolboy in Algiers, he learned that the world contained five billion people. His teacher explained that in a lifetime a person could not even count to one billion. The unimaginable size of the earth's population left the boy with an uncomfortable sensation of personal insignificance. With so many people in the world, how could he distinguish himself? He feared he would grow up to become an anonymous nobody lost among a multitude of other people. He would be forgotten the moment he died, as though he had never existed. *Yes, that is an encouraging sign.* Jamal finished his cigarette and smothered it among the others in the ashtray. It was 10:30 p.m. on the microwave oven. *The midget courier should have picked up the wedding cake in Berlin by now, if he hasn't crashed the car somewhere.*

"Our brother mujahedeen recently struck America at its Achilles Heel and destroyed its greatest buildings." Ali Benhadj was reaching the most important part of his speech by the time Jamal returned to the dining room. "May God's peace, mercy and blessings be upon our brothers. America has been filled with terror, from north to south and from east to west, praise and blessings to God. What America has suffered is but a small taste of what Muslims have endured for centuries." Benhadj hesitated, as if trying to recall the proper order of ideas, the sequence they had selected for the best effect.

Al-Omari, still wearing the green beret, signaled Ghamdi to pause the filming. "He should explain how America's usurious global economy exploits Muslims."

"I think he has already covered that, Hani," Ghamdi replied. "Let us continue."

Jamal wondered how many times the overweight Che Guevara had interrupted the filming while he had been thinking in the kitchen.

"Should I announce the attack now?" Benhadj asked.

"Yes, Abu Salem, just as we agreed. The film will not be shown until afterward."

"Instead of heeding this great warning, America has persisted in its repression of Muslims, so we are forced to take further reprisals today." Benhadj paused and reconsidered. "Should I say *today*?"

"Yes, that is right," Ghamdi replied. "The film will be released the day of the attack."

"It will be on every television the same evening," al-Omari added. "They will replay it around the world for weeks."

Maybe for a day or two, Jamal thought. Most media would omit the speech entirely.

"Today, the world will witness another glorious attack against America. It shall be the first of many attacks around the globe unless America satisfies our just conditions." Benhadj sat up higher in the armchair throne and raised his saber as he recited a list of six demands. As he approached the conclusion, Ghamdi zoomed the camera closer to his face. Looking over Ghamdi's shoulder into the video display, Jamal saw that the youth's gleaming eyes, set deep in his gaunt face, now appeared menacing. The intensity of his dark glare, accentuated by the spiky patches of his adolescent beard, rendered his face almost terrifying.

"I, Abu Salem of the Islamic Army of Jihad, will lead today's attack. I go joyfully—" His voice broke mid-sentence as he paused to lift a plastic bottle of water to his lips. In the silence that followed, the rap lyrics of a hip-hop artist could be heard emanating faintly from Essabar's stolen Discman, until a sharp look from Jamal caused him to pause it.

"I, Abu Salam, go joyfully to my death today, because it will serve to humiliate America." The youth's voice had regained its full strength, but it was strangely hoarse now, like a voice of an older man. "Faced with an army of martyrs, the cowardly oppressors must at last admit they cannot withstand the bravery of Muslim youth." He drew a breath for the final prayer. "All praise be to *Allah*. He is our protector and we are his humble servants. May we be allowed to assist in His glorious victory."

Hani al-Omari began clapping. "That was a stirring speech, my brother. Soon the entire world will be listening to your words."

The young man rose from the armchair, still holding the Arabian saber, and emerged from the harsh glow of the filming lights to approach Jamal.

"Your father will be proud of you," Jamal said quietly, placing his hands firmly on the youth's shoulders. "Your uncle will be proud, as well. I will be proudest of all."

CHAPTER 17

Sixth Day of the Investigation

Alarmed by the call from the National Security Advisor, coming on top of the latest French intercepts and the English house search, Douglas Grebb added more resources to the CIA investigation.

Ronnie Lapoint, one of Grebb's sallow-complexioned lieutenants, now led the intelligence gathering team. Known for his extraordinary analytic ability, Lapoint had helped track down Ramzi Youssef, the terrorist responsible for detonating a giant car bomb in the underground garage of the World Trade Center in 1993, the first attempt to topple the twin towers. When they were attacked the second time in 2001, Lapoint was heard mumbling for days, "We should have seen it coming." Ramzi Youssef's uncle, Khalid Sheik Mohammed, had organized the second attack.

Stan Stebbins, another of Grebb's light-deprived deputies, led the operational team. As more intelligence flowed in, the perpetually hunched-over Stebbins would recommend what actions the CIA should take in the field. He had joined the Counterterrorism Center only recently, having come from the covert operations side of the Agency where he had helped track down those who planned the simultaneous bombings of the embassies in Kenya and Tanzania.

Grebb had assigned the most difficult job to himself: convincing the National Security Agency to provide more Echelon resources. His opening request was for Echelon to analyze all messages intercepted in Europe and the Middle East during the prior three weeks. He proposed they search for a dozen key phrases in French, Arabic and Turkish.

"Are you shitting me, Doug?" asked his NSA contact.

"Fuck you. This is important."

"Can't do, Doug. You have no idea how much computer time that would take."

"We're looking for radioactive material sold in southern Russia and shipped to France," Grebb pleaded. "The culprits could be in any of a dozen countries along that route."

"What makes you think I can tap into communications in all those countries?" asked the NSA man. Grebb knew the NSA never divulged such information, even to the CIA, so he merely shrugged. After a moment, his NSA friend relented. "I can maybe filter messages for the last week," he offered, "if you limit the target phrases."

Even after accepting such limitations, Grebb had to promise an adequate number of analysts and translators to work through the night. The NSA refused to waste supercomputer time to find messages the CIA would not take time to review. In addition to Lapoint and Stebbins, Grebb assigned twenty CIA analysts led by Leslie Jumana. He was keen to deploy Fluent, Sentinel's new system for automated translations, as well as Sentinel's latest enhancements to Echelon, so he asked Howard Silver to assign a dozen more analysts and translators headed by Doyle O'Gara.

— — —

War rooms were organized on the fifth floor of the Original Headquarters Building. When Doyle found his place in the Lockerbie room, he noticed it was located between Kandahar and Mogadishu, and realized that rooms in the Counterterrorism Center were named after cities where terrorists had murdered American citizens. Other rooms bore names such as Aden, Beirut, Cairo and Dar es Salaam; they appeared to continue through the entire alphabet.

Doyle opened his computer and began to plan for the night ahead. In his continuing role as software developer, he would be responsible for resolving any glitches they detected in the latest versions of Echelon and Fluent. Field tests had not yet been completed in Arabic and Turkish, so Doyle anticipated at least a few significant problems. But it was in his newer role as manager of the translation team that Doyle expected greater challenges. He knew that serious disputes were likely to arise between the CIA analysts and the Sentinel translators during the coming hours. It might begin with a simple question, such the spelling of an intercepted address. The CIA might have found a different spelling in a message months before. Couldn't the two addresses be one in the same? Then there would be pressure from CIA analysts to approve strained translations that supported their preferred theories. Please go back to the Arabic original, the CIA might demand, and consider this background from our database. Doesn't that change your interpretation?

An hour later, Doyle had completed his planning and felt that his team was as prepared as possible for the challenges ahead. He expected several hours would pass before the NSA delivered the first batch of intercepts. He looked around the Lockerbie room, wondering how he would spend the time until then, when he noticed that Leslie Jumana had taken a seat at the other end of the table. Doyle had mixed emotions. He still felt the bliss of fresh love, but his feelings had grown complicated since the prior evening. Was it just the strain of maintaining a secret liaison under the eyes of their colleagues? He had suggested coming out in the open, but Leslie was not ready for the office publicity. He waited for her to look up, but she seemed absorbed in her work. She brushed aside a strand of her auburn hair, reminding Doyle of the evening when their friendship had unexpectedly turned physical.

It happened in mid-July, perhaps a month after they had first met. She invited him to her apartment for a glass of wine on their way to their fourth restaurant, the one they would never reach. He waited until they were seated on the sofa before asking the casual question he had been preparing for days. "So, I was just wondering, are you seeing anyone?" He nodded toward a framed photograph displayed on an end table: Leslie with her arm around a man, slender and older, both of them brightly dressed for the ski slopes.

Leslie swirled the wine in her glass as if to study its color. "Not now," she replied, lifting her alluring eyebrows. "Who knows? This could be your big opportunity." It was not the first time she had made a seductive remark, but he was still wondering if she was in earnest. He took a small sip of wine, just enough to overcome his timidity, then leaned forward to test her intentions, that is until he felt her fingers press gently back on his shoulder. "First, I want to know how you got into the spy support business," she said. "I really don't know much about you, Doyle."

Was she playing coy or was she still uncertain which way she was leaning? It was too early to say, he decided, so he sat back and began describing his early career with the Ann Arbor office. "Did you ever worry about privacy?" she asked, raising her eyebrows like two fuzzy question marks. Doyle had to admit that privacy issues had never concerned Sentinel Systems very much. Occasionally, their lawyers would call about a complaint or an inquiry, but his team never felt they were invading people's privacy. Visiting a website was like walking into a shopping mall. A shopper could not complain if a sales clerk noticed how many jackets he tried on, what size of shoes he purchased or which credit card he used. If a person did not want others to keep track of such matters, they reasoned, that person had no business shopping on the Internet.

"Very interesting," Leslie remarked, as if she were considering the implications. She leaned forward to set her glass on the table. When she sat back she had moved closer to him. "So you have no qualms about letting the government use the same technology?" She brought her fingers to his chest and drummed them gently, as though to drive home her question.

"Do you?" Doyle asked, watching her fingers and wondering if his waistline was more noticeable sitting on the sofa. He had lost more weight thanks to his continued jogging and Leslie's admonitions against desserts, but he suddenly doubted he had lost enough.

"Not really," Leslie replied. "I don't think the CIA abuses the technology, but I'm curious how the private sector feels." He leaned toward her lips, which had remained slightly parted after her last word, but he felt again the gentle resistance of her fingertips. "Not so fast," she warned, smiling. "This is a big decision for me."

"I don't have any qualms, either," Doyle resumed, his eyes remaining on her lips. "I figure the privacy issues should be decided by Congress and the Supreme Court. People like Howard Silver worry mostly about what technology the CIA wants to buy and how much they are willing to pay for it."

"Tell me something naughty about that stage of your career," Leslie asked. She hoisted her bare feet onto the sofa and nestled closer to him, as though she were making herself comfortable to listen to a long story. Doyle glanced down at the skirt stretched across her thighs and wondered if she was wearing anything beneath it.

"Naughty?" he asked. "There was a lot of partying during the evenings, if that's what you mean." He recalled the frequent trips to pitch software to Sentinel clients, the weeks away from home to help install and test. Sentinel had a liberal expense policy; they were expected to wine and dine the clients. "We called them team-building sessions," Doyle explained. "They broke down barriers and often led to good ideas for the projects."

"I bet they led to other things, too," Leslie whispered into his ear. Her close breath caused him to shiver, but her comment left him pensive. *Yes, they certainly had*, he thought. People moved from one romance to another as easily as from one party to the next. It had not hurt that business was booming and the company was paying generous bonuses. Money, alcohol and sex seemed to lubricate everything. New cars appeared each week in the parking lot. Someone was always organizing wild excursions to exotic locations like Las Vegas, Hawaii or the Bahamas. Maybe it was the vacuity of it all that finally prompted Doyle to flee the Ann Arbor office, he told Leslie. If his career were ever to have meaning, he needed to find it in Washington, in this place and this time.

Leslie leaned away to study his face. He reached forward and moved aside her fine reddish-brown hair, as though he merely wanted to see her charming freckles better. It was a tentative gesture from which he could easily retreat, if necessary. She remained motionless, except for the slight enlargement of her eyes searching his, so he leaned closer, watching her reaction, until his lips came to rest upon hers. It was a surprisingly successful kiss. When it was over, she sat back against the sofa and smiled. "I think I've learned enough about you for now, Mr. O'Gara." She yawned and then moved her shoulders luxuriously against the sofa. "So, do you want to spend the night?"

Doyle jolted upright in the Lockerbie war room when he heard the NSA couriers entering to deliver the first batch of transcripts. It was well after midnight. The transcripts contained hundreds of phone calls, e-mails and website postings matching their search criteria that had been intercepted by Echelon and translated into English by Fluent. The review team sprang into action, first verifying the translations and then beginning the slow process of wringing actionable intelligence from the messages.

As work progressed, the Lockerbie walls became covered with hand-drawn diagrams of possible links between obscure phrases and potential terrorist plots. Tables grew heavy under computer printouts analyzing relationships among people, places and things mentioned in messages. Maps became dotted with colorful pins marking locations of senders and receivers. NSA couriers scurried through the hallways, delivering still more transcripts to the sleepless review teams. As Doyle anticipated, the application of Echelon and Fluent to new languages exposed software glitches. Doyle spent half the night calling in Sentinel specialists to correct the bugs. Also as expected, efforts to squeeze meaning from the messages generated debates over translations. Doyle spent the other half of the night trying to resolve the issues to the satisfaction of the CIA analysts and the Sentinel translators. He sometimes found it maddening that a word or phrase could take on several equally-plausible meanings due to the suppleness of language, the molding pressure of context and the twisting force of competing theories. Between the software emergencies and translation battles, Doyle found time to review transcripts already read by others, hoping to unearth some valuable nugget that might somehow have been overlooked.

Yet, as the long night came to an end and unfamiliar sunlight stabbed into the stale interior of the Lockerbie room, the review teams had still found nothing relevant to the investigation. Feeling frustrated, Doyle cast his sore eyes down the table and saw that Leslie Jumana was half asleep at her computer. Another analyst was snoring beside her, his head resting on a pizza box. Gazing at the piles of seemingly banal transcripts before him, Doyle's mind began to wander. It eventually came to rest upon the mysterious Internet messages that he continued to receive outside work.

Even as his romance with Leslie had bloomed, Doyle had continued his online chats with 22excited, often stopping at the MouseTrap café on his way home. The latest e-mail had directed Doyle to yet another chat room. His anonymous friend awaited him there. *you've been gone a couple of days. i missed u.*

Sorry, busy at work, Doyle had typed in reply.

so i've noticed. nu problems in the translating department?

New problems? Doyle had hesitated, trying to recall how much he had said in prior messages. There had been so many. *How do you know about that?* he finally replied. It must be someone at Sentinel, he thought. Who else would have such information?

i know more than u imagine.

Who are you?

i can't tell u yet.

Give me a hint, he pressed. *Are you a man or a woman?*

which do u want me 2 b? came back the answer. Could it be Leslie? It certainly sounded like her. The first message had come around the time they had first met. He looked suspiciously around the MouseTrap café trying to recall when he had first given her his e-mail address. Of course, she could have gotten it before then from several people at Sentinel.

I'd like to meet you in person, he typed.

i'd love 2 get 2gether 2, doyle, but first i need 2 know more about u. i'm still curious about your work. tell me more about the fluent upgrade.

Fluent? He thought about logging off, fearing he had already revealed more than he should. Surely, he had said nothing about the upgrade, had he? *You must know I can't talk about that,* he typed after a moment.

that's not fair, doyle. there's so much i want 2 reveal 2 u. While he was trying to decide how to respond, another line appeared. *wouldn't u like 2 talk 2 the other side?*

He thought again about ending the exchange, but then typed, *Other side?*

u know, the 1s we watch 4 the client. wouldn't it be simpler just 2 talk 2 them? Suddenly Doyle felt certain who it was. The question was so preposterous, he could detect Suresh Kumar's sharp ironic humor and even hear his high-pitched Pakistani voice.

Come on, Suresh, knock it off, he had typed.

u caught me! was the reply. *but it's safer 2 joke out here than in the office.*

But then Doyle no longer felt so sure. He had abruptly logged off.

"You have to report it," had been Leslie's immediate reaction. He had not told her about his Internet chats until a few nights before the Paris bombing. Even then, he had not disclosed the full content of his exchanges; that would have been a bit awkward, like talking to her about another girlfriend. At first he had been inclined to follow Leslie's advice. Still, the strange contacts had been outside work and nothing important had been exchanged. Besides, everyone was so busy with the field testing, there was no time to submit a lot of forms about insignificant messages. It might have been a little embarrassing, too, considering some of the suggestive lines he had written.

Doyle's thoughts were yanked back to the present when another stack of Echelon intercepts was delivered to the Lockerbie room. Gazing at the new documents with a mixture of boredom and dread, Doyle smelled a delightful aroma. Some unknown angel had thought to send fresh coffee along with the oppressive transcripts. Sipping the rich brew and feeling his spirits revive, Doyle returned to the messages from 22excited. It would be even more awkward to report them now, he decided, in the midst of the investigation. It would be enough for him to stop going to the MouseTrap. Break off the affair, so to speak. But he found something irresistible about the mysterious exchanges; their anonymity made them all the more intriguing. It would be okay to visit his Internet friend once or twice more, Doyle concluded, just long enough to verify whether it was really a flirtatious female or just Suresh. He could always file a report if he detected anything more suspicious than he had so far.

CHAPTER 18

Morning of the Paris Attack

Yusuf Ghamdi woke Ali Benhadj after he had slept only a few hours. "Stand up, my young warrior," Ghamdi instructed. "Today is the great day. It is time for you to bathe." Benhadj rubbed his eyes and seemed unable to recall where he was. As he struggled from the bed, Ghamdi detected the scent of floral perfume he had sprinkled on the sheets.

In the bathroom, Ghamdi helped the youth remove the warrior's robe and enter the shower. It was not until the water splashed on his face that Benhadj seemed to register Ghamdi's words. "You said *today*?" he called through the shower curtain.

"Yes, indeed," Ghamdi replied, his words accented with musical tones. "Waleed Yarkas is bringing from Berlin everything you will need for today's glorious event. Right on schedule."

Actually, Yarkas was behind schedule and Ghamdi was worried, although he took care not to alarm his young charge. If Yarkas did not arrive in time, he feared Benhadj might lose his current resolve. He recalled the disturbing telephone call that Mohammed Jamal had placed a few hours earlier. Several tense moments had passed before Yarkas finally answered.

"Where are you?" Jamal asked without introduction. "*Huddah!*" he exclaimed after another moment. *Shit head!* Jamal held the telephone an instant longer. "Alright, alright, I understand. I'm sorry I lost my temper. Get back on the road and call me again when you reach the apartment. Let's not waste any more time."

"*Huddah!*" Jamal repeated as he hung up. "The idiot stopped to eat near Liège and fell asleep in the restaurant parking lot. That's somewhere in the middle of Belgium. He won't get here before eleven."

"Perhaps sooner, *inshallah*," Ghamdi said soothingly. "Praise be to *Allah*, it is Sunday morning so traffic into Paris should be light."

Ghamdi decided to awaken Benhadj despite the uncertainty over when Yarkas would arrive. He had overcome such problems before. What Jamal praised as his skill with martyrs consisted mostly of patience and persistence. "When you finish bathing," Ghamdi called through the shower curtain, "please shave the hair from your body." He passed a razor to Benhadj. "Do not forget to shave under your arms and around your private parts." Through the plastic curtain, Ghamdi could see the young man bend and stretch as he shaved. "Come out and I will help you finish," he called over the splashing. Ghamdi set to work with another razor, first shaving the youth's back and the rear of his neck, then stooping to remove the remaining hair from his legs. When the shaving was complete, he sprayed perfume—the same fragrance he had applied to the sheets—upon the young man's chest, shoulders and back. Ghamdi left the bathroom to allow him to dress.

"We will keep your things for you during the operation," he called as he swept Benhadj's few possessions from the bedside table into a paper bag: a wristwatch, a wallet and the half-empty carton of Marlboros he had purchased duty-free on the flight from Algiers. At the rate of three cigarettes a day, the remaining packs would have lasted him another month. Benhadj emerged from the bathroom dressed in blue jeans, a gray T-shirt and a light blue jacket. "You have nothing in your pockets, do you?" Ghamdi patted him to make certain. Then he motioned for Benhadj to kneel on the rug beside the bed.

"In the name of *Allah*, the merciful, the compassionate . . ." To keep the youth's mind on the divine task ahead, Ghamdi began with the first of the Five Pillars of Islam, the *shahada*, the Islamic declaration of faith: ". . . I witness there is no god but *Allah* and Mohammed is His messenger." From their hours together Ghamdi knew that these holy words formed the bedrock of Ali Benhadj's beliefs. Even before the boy had learned to speak, he had heard the name of God sung out by *muezzins* from atop the minarets five times each day, echoing in melodic waves over the rooftops: *Allah*, like the Mediterranean surf he heard reverberating from the Bay of Algiers up the hillsides; *Allah*, like the desert wind he felt blowing through the alleyways into his bedroom window, causing his curtains to dance like phantoms while he fell asleep; *Allah,* like an unseen force of nature, ethereal yet tangible.

———

Jamal kissed the young man on both cheeks when he emerged from the bedroom with Ghamdi. Freshly showered and shorn of his adolescent beard, Benhadj appeared more relaxed and cheerful than the night before. "Where in God's name did you get that outfit?" Jamal exclaimed when he saw Hani al-Omari emerge from a different bedroom. He was dressed as a Palestinian fedayeen, complete with a headscarf, khaki tunic and an empty ammunition belt hanging across his broad chest. "Do you want to stand out like a freak on the *Champs-Élysées*?"

Al-Omari made no move to return to the bedroom. "Curses on your mustache, Mohammed Jamal. This is our business, too."

The two men glared at each other, until Ghamdi broke the tension. "Let's have breakfast," he said brightly. "This will be our last meal together before the heroic operation. We should celebrate."

Zacarias Essabar came out yawning, dressed only in his underwear, and followed al-Omari into the kitchen where they attacked the plates of bread and fruit that awaited them. Benhadj ate nothing, as was his custom in the morning, but drank several cups of coffee. The caffeine seemed to raise his spirits further. He began laughing when Essabar told the story of how he had nearly been caught shoplifting in *Galeries Lafayette*, running down three flights of stairs with security guards in hot pursuit. Unable to stop laughing at the end of the story, Benhadj hugged his friend until tears came to his eyes.

"It is time to look at the target," Ghamdi announced. He led Benhadj, still giggling, back to the dining room where photographs had been spread on the table. Jamal watched them from the doorway. This would be the first time the youth would learn the details of the operation.

Brushing aside his tears, Benhadj studied the images of the restaurant taken from various angles and distances. He seemed to grow serious when he saw the name and logo. "A worthy target."

"We have chosen to attack when the site will be crowded and busy," al-Omari declared, raising a toothpick to emphasize the point. "A warrior should strike while the enemy is confused." He returned the toothpick to his bearded mouth to finish cleaning the remnants of his breakfast.

The cell phone in Jamal's pocket rang. He glanced at the time. Could Waleed Yarkas have reached Paris already? "What?" he exclaimed into the phone. "You should be on the flight to Beirut." It was Sheikh Musawi al Amin. Walking quickly back to the kitchen, Jamal whispered violently: "We have no time to discuss that again. The airports will be blocked this afternoon!" Jamal hung up. *Meddlesome old fool*, he thought angrily. *Still arguing about the choice of the target; still lecturing me on how to prepare the driver.* He returned to the dining room.

Ghamdi was now showing Benhadj an enlarged photo of the two-story restaurant. Crowds of people could be seen passing on the sidewalk, their images reflected off the glass façade. Through their reflections more people were visible inside the restaurant. "There are many children," Benhadj remarked.

"It is permissible to kill the children of the infidels because they kill ours," Jamal said, perhaps too sharply. He was still thinking of Musawi's call.

"An eye for an eye," al-Omari added as he returned to the dining room. Jamal saw that al-Omari had left to change into slacks and a striped shirt. With his bizarre beard and protruding stomach he still looked conspicuous, but Jamal said nothing. "Only when our enemies lose their children in the same way we lose ours," al-Omari continued, "only then will they lose the taste for aggression against—"

"I think Abu Salem understands all this," Jamal interrupted. He noticed Benhadj was staring silently at the big photo, his expression now strangely vacant.

"Let's have a look at the route," Ghamdi chimed in. Spread on the table before him was a large map of Paris with a red line marked from the *Avenue Mozart* apartment to the restaurant on the *Avenue des Champs-Élysées*.

Ghamdi had driven the route several times that week to ensure there were no closures or construction.

"It should take us half an hour," al-Omari declared, tracing the red line with his toothpick.

Jamal's phone rang again. It was almost eleven. *God help us if this is not the dwarf delivery boy.* Raising the phone to his ear, Jamal felt his face relax into a smile. "*Allah* be praised! Our brother has returned safely from Berlin and he is already entering the garage below!" He picked up his aluminum briefcase and motioned for al-Omari and Essabar to follow, but then turned back to Benhadj.

"Have some more coffee after Yusuf Ghamdi finishes with you." He tickled the young man playfully on the ribs. "You need to stay awake."

— — —

". . . Lord, when the confrontation begins, let Abu Salem strike like a champion who has no wish to come back to this world." Ghamdi recalled that for Ali Benhadj the act of prayer, like the other Pillars of Islam, was founded upon the bedrock of his childhood experience. The daily recitation of prayers, *salat,* imbued young Ali with a sense that the entire physical world was a reflection of God and was subject to His will. The rising of the sun, the appearance of rain from the sky, the growth of corn from the dead earth: all were signs of God's miraculous power and His awesome presence beyond the visible world. "We ask you Lord to accept Abu Salem among the prophets, martyrs and pious men. We ask you to bless his joyful family and provide them the greatest of rewards." Benhadj had once confided to Ghamdi that he found the act of prayer so intense that he sometimes heard God's voice offering him guidance. Now, after so many hours of prayer together, Ghamdi hoped the young man could also see God's hand beckoning him toward his place in Heaven.

— — —

In the garage, Jamal spotted the diminutive figure of Waleed Yarkas urinating in the shadows next to the Mercedes. Yarkas turned and smiled, the loathsome crescent rising on his cheek, then stepped forward to throw his arms heartily around Jamal's chest. Jamal tolerated the short man's clasp a moment before steering him toward the Mercedes. Together they opened the trunk and removed the foam rubber sheets, exposing the two duffel bags lying side-by-side like twin corpses. Jamal unzipped the bags and straightened the wires that led from the blasting caps that Rashid Badawi had inserted in Berlin. Jamal next removed from his briefcase two detonators. Each could be activated locally by means of a switch attached to a long cable or remotely by means of a radio antenna.

"Sometimes the switch fails," Jamal explained to Yarkas. "So we have the antenna, just in case." Jamal inserted fresh batteries into the detonators and tested both to ensure they were functioning. After locking them to prevent accidental activation, he connected the detonators to the blasting cap wires. Finally, he zipped the duffel bags shut, leaving the long cable and radio antenna protruding from each bag.

Jamal and Yarkas carefully slid the first bag into the rear of the Fiat Punto minivan and passed the switch with its long cable to Essabar in the front seat. Essabar secured the switch with tape next to the seat, within easy reach of the driver. Al-Omari dragged over boxes of nuts, bolts and fasteners he had purchased near Lyon and began arranging their contents around the duffel bag. The sight of the loose metal made Jamal feel uneasy; it would enhance the killing power, he knew, but he considered it messy. He liked working with bombs, neat bricks of explosives connected by wires, but the loose metal always disturbed him.

They repeated the preparations with the Renault Clio. Since the tiny car had hardly any trunk, they squeezed the second duffel bag into the rear bench and slid back the front seat until the bag was snug. "You can skip the metal," Jamal said. "In case the car is stopped."

"What about the switch?" al-Omari asked.

"Leave it inside the bag." *Unless you plan to stay in the car to push it*, Jamal almost added, but decided he had already antagonized the bearded buffoon enough. Al-Omari slammed the door shut. Jamal winced but continued to hold his tongue. The dull sound echoed briefly through the half-empty garage and then died. The preparations were nearly complete; there remained just one more important step. "Give me the phones used in the operation," Jamal ordered. He would dispose of them afterwards, he explained, so they could not be traced back to the group.

When they reached the apartment, Jamal located Ghamdi and Benhadj in the large bedroom, still praying. "We're ready downstairs," he announced. The two men rose from the carpet. Ghamdi nodded and disappeared down the hall. Jamal grasped the young man's shoulders. "Remember, Abu Salem, the Prophet promises that death for the martyr is no more painful than the bite of a gnat."

"I understand, *imam*."

"Every man must die one way or another." He shook the youth's shoulders gently. "You have been chosen by *Allah* to die as a martyr. It is the most honorable way, Abu Salem, in submission to God's will." Jamal removed from his pocket the cell phone he had retrieved from al-Omari. "Here, take this, just in case you need to speak to me during the operation."

Benhadj examined the phone a moment and then slid it into the pocket of his jeans. "I want you to have these," he said, removing the half-carton of Marlboros from the paper sack. Jamal took the gift and spread his arms to enfold the young man. "Could we . . . ," Benhadj began in a whisper. Jamal barely heard the words, but he felt the youth surge forward into his arms, causing him to return a clasp more intense and prolonged than he had intended, the squeeze strengthening into a mutual embrace that felt to Jamal like the warm hug of a father and son bidding each other farewell or, he admitted to himself, like the desperate clutch of two lovers parting forever. After a long moment, Benhadj straightened upright to recover his stature, as Jamal allowed his arms to fall aside. Stepping back, Jamal was relieved to see that the young man's countenance still appeared alert and resolute.

CHAPTER 19

Seventh day of the Investigation

It was a few minutes past noon, when Christine Dupont fell asleep at her desk in Paris while studying the latest telephone tree diagrams. She awoke when her face hit a slice of broccoli quiche that her secretary had brought her for lunch. *I've got to get out of here*, she thought, as she wiped off the moist egg.

Ten minutes later she was jogging along the *Quai Branly*, having changed into running shoes and sweats, heading toward the *Champs de Mars*, the great rectangular park from which the Eiffel Tower soars 320 meters into the Paris skyline. How long had it been since she had last gone jogging? It had always been her passion, but that was before the bombing a week earlier. The constant work and lack of sleep were draining her energy and dulling her concentration, she realized. She could not afford to lose focus now, not when they were getting so close. An hour of fresh air would revive her.

She was still jogging when she reached the park and felt the soft earth replace the pavement under her feet. She lengthened her stride on the tree-lined path, heading away from the tower. The myriad facts and connections of the case still filled her mind, but the sensation of motion lifted her above the oppressive detail. They were making progress, she told herself. Another piece of the puzzle was about to fall into place.

Suddenly, a small child ran shrieking across the path ahead of her. In the split-second before the scream turned to laughter, Dupont looked down and saw the headless corpse of the other child, the one in the restaurant rubble, as though it were writhing on the ground before her.

Looking past the hideous image, she struggled to recompose herself, straining to see the faces of the killers, trying to visualize their next move. Had they slithered away to hide in a distant hole or were they still curled up in France preparing to strike anew? *Either way, I don't have much time.* If she didn't secure an arrest soon, Dominique Carpentier might not be able to protect her from skeptics in the government. He might not even be able to protect himself much longer. *Well, I'll just have to take the risk.* She needed an hour to revive herself. The damned investigation could wait one more hour.

She was already half-way through her run, on the other side of the *Champs de Mars*, coming back down the path toward the Eiffel Tower. Maybe she would even take time for a decent meal instead of that lousy quiche and coffee at her desk. No, that would have to wait. The air flowing into her lungs and the rhythmic pounding of her feet on the earth sharpened the feeling that she was getting close to another breakthrough. Then she saw the people on the path ahead—three of them—running crazily toward her. She identified the faces at the same instant she heard the voice.

"You've got to see this!" Giles Lambert gasped. Behind him was Angeline Odette, running with her computer under her arm, followed closely by one of the translators. They were all panting, but Lambert looked the worst, his hair bouncing frantically around his oversize nose as he came to a halt. He pushed a transcript into Dupont's hand.

"One of them is the Lyon car thief, Abdallah Ramadan," Odette said breathlessly, her flushed face perspiring in the mid-day sun. "We haven't yet identified the other speaker." Dupont brushed back her hair and began to read as the others collapsed onto a bench beside the path.

Hello, Abdallah.

Yes, I can hear you.

Listen, I spoke to our friends. They expect a storm in the morning [unintelligible].

Later? [Obscenity, obscenity] They will delay the wedding.

No, a little later, the Izmir Queen should arrive by six maybe.

Okay, okay, but I do not believe this about the storm. Are you sure they are not eating the wedding cakes?

[Laughter]

There will be plenty of chocolate left for the party. We will light lots of candles.

France will be on fire.

[More laughter]

You will delay the other boat, the little one for the special cargo?

Yeah, yeah. It will be arranged.

I will call you when they are near, on the other telephone I gave you.

No, no, [obscenity], we will be there if they are.

[Unintelligible] I will call you perhaps three this morning. Be sure you are awake.

No, I welcome the wedding cakes. Give thanks to our friends in the East.

Okay, I call you later. Get some sleep before.

[Obscenity] We will be ready.

[They disconnect]

Lambert started to speak, but Dupont motioned for him to remain silent as she turned to the translator. "What do you make of that?" she asked, pointing to the phrase "wedding cakes" marked twice in yellow. "Maybe they are just getting ready for a wedding."

"The context suggests a different meaning," the translator said. "An Arab family would not delay a wedding due to an early morning storm."

"It appears this wedding will result in France burning," Dupont observed.

"Yes," the translator agreed. "Ramadan says to give thanks to their friends in the East. Wedding cakes come from local bakeries, not from friends in the East."

Dupont studied the transcript again. "It doesn't say specifically to thank them for the wedding cakes."

The translator removed the original Arabic intercept from a folder. "That is true, but he gives thanks right after he mentions the cakes. He has nothing else to thank them for."

"What could they be bringing to France?" Dupont wondered aloud.

"More of what they used on *Champs-Élysées*," Lambert suggested.

"Perhaps worse," Dupont muttered. "Where did Ramadan received this call?"

"He was on route A-7, about ten kilometers south of Lyon," Odette answered.

"Where is he now?" Dupont asked.

"He is sixty kilometers further south."

"On his way to Marseille," Dupont observed. "I think it's time to arrest Mr. Ramadan. Also, find out everything we can about the boat he mentioned, the *Izmir Queen*, particularly whether it is scheduled to dock in Marseille or some other port."

"The next flight leaves Orly at 4:05." Odette was checking airline schedules on her laptop computer. "It will be tight," she shouted. Dupont was already jogging back down the path in the direction of the office.

The *Direction de la Surveillance du Territoire* maintained seven regional Directorates, including one in Lyon and another in Marseille. In the taxi to the airport, Lambert phoned Marseille to hear the latest on their efforts to apprehend Ramadan. "What?" he shouted. "We knew where he was half an hour ago!" Marseille had lost contact with Ramadan's phone. Perhaps he had switched it off, suspecting he was under surveillance, or maybe the battery had run out. They had contacted the *gendrmerie national*, France's countrywide police force, to stop his car on the A-7, but no cars were registered in Ramadan's name.

As the taxi neared the airport, Dupont was on her phone giving orders. "You heard me right. Get every available detective down to the port. I want them talking to every dockworker, drug dealer and prostitute. If a big smuggling operation is coming down, someone there will know about it."

Aboard the plane, Lambert seemed to sense Dupont's anxiety. "Don't worry, you were right to hold off arresting him. Ramadan was leading us to another operation and to other members of the group."

Lambert's words did nothing to reassure Dupont as she gazed out the window. Carpentier would be livid to learn that she had let the first potential arrest slip through her fingers. The Minister would be demanding her head before nightfall. But there was nothing more she could do until they landed. *Marseille*, she thought, *perhaps the oldest city in France.* Founded by the Greeks of Asia Minor in 600 BC as a trading post, known in antiquity as Marsalla, today the country's second largest city and by far its most violent. A vibrant mix—some would say clash—of two cultures, the best and worst of Provence and the Maghreb. Why did it not surprise her that the terrorist plot had led them to Marseille?

She felt Lambert's eyes upon her, but when she turned, his gaze was on his laptop. She looked past him to Angeline Odette asleep across the aisle. It would be a lot simpler if her bloodhound took an interest in his vivacious young teammate, she thought, provided they were discreet about it. She felt fatigue overcoming her. Lambert's shoulder looked inviting, but she decided to tilt herself toward the window before she closed her eyes and dozed off.

CHAPTER 20

Morning of the Paris Attack

They emerged from the *Avenue Mozart* lobby into the mid-day sunshine with Ali Benhadj between them. Ghamdi opened the driver's door of the Fiat minivan and pointed to the switch taped between the two seats. "Do not touch that, under any circumstances," he instructed. "Not until you are inside the target. Do you understand?"

"Just keep your mind on the driving," Jamal said with an encouraging smile.

"Am I to drive?" Benhadj asked. "I've done so in Algiers a few times, never in France."

A few times! Jamal stepped back from the car and slammed his fist onto the roof. *Allah the merciful, the magnificent, how have we overlooked something so important?* He grabbed Ghamdi's arm and pulled him onto the sidewalk, away from the others. "Why have we been cursed with this gang of imbeciles? None of them thought to mention the kid cannot drive!"

"Calm down," urged Ghamdi, offering his grotesque smile. "I can teach him on the way."

"Teach him on the way! Are you insane?"

"He will only need to drive alone the last few blocks," Ghamdi reassured him.

Jamal closed his eyes and tilted his face skyward. How had he allowed this to happen? He breathed deeply and felt the caress of the sunshine transform his dark mood. *It could be worse.* It could have been raining that day, yet the glorious summer weather ensured large crowds on the avenue and light for the reporters to film the aftermath. Surely, this was proof that God smiled on their enterprise.

He reopened his eyes, nodded to Ghamdi, and began issuing final instructions to the others. Al-Omari would lead the way in the Renault Clio. Benhadj would follow in the Fiat Punto with Ghamdi and Essabar. Yarkas would drive the Mercedes back to the Saint-Denis apartment to await the others. Later, he would transport the gang to a new hideout in the South of France. All this had been said in the apartment several times, but it reassured Jamal to repeat the instructions.

Once the others were inside the cars, Jamal opened the rear door of the Fiat, unzipped the duffel bag and turned the key of the detonator. The bomb was now activated. It could be triggered by the switch taped to the seat next to Benhadj or by the radio transmitter in Jamal's briefcase. Jamal shut the rear door carefully and moved on to the Renault. Al-Omari had already squeezed himself into the small car, forcing his seat back against the duffel bag. "Remember to wait ten minutes before you depart," Jamal reminded him once the second bomb was activated. "Then follow the route exactly and make sure Ali follows you."

Jamal saluted Benhadj a final time and then walked quickly toward the Metro station *Jasmin*, carrying the briefcase with the two radio transmitters.

— — —

Hani al-Omari studied his watch. *Ten minutes takes forever when you have nothing to do but wait and think.* He saw Jamal disappear at the corner and suddenly sensed his vulnerability. *One press of that thing in his briefcase.* A terrifying image flashed through his mind. *But the bully still needs me to get the cars to the restaurant*, he reassured himself. He looked at his watch again. A few more minutes still remained. He thought about the other dangers of the drive ahead. *What if the police stop my car?* Should he jump out and run or just stay and hope they ignored the bag?

He watched the second hand count off the last two minutes and then started the engine. After glancing back to ensure no cars were passing, he shifted into gear and tapped the accelerator pedal. The car lurched backward and struck the Fiat Punto behind him. Startled, he looked up into the rearview mirror and saw the horror-stricken face of Yusuf Ghamdi.

"*Huddah!*" screamed Ghamdi. He continued to stare ahead, waiting for the explosion. When the annihilation did not arrive, Ghamdi glanced around at the others. Benhadj clenched the steering wheel tightly, but his face was expressionless, as though he had not felt the collision. In the backseat, Essabar's face trembled, causing his earring to sparkle violently in the sunlight. His heart still pounding, Ghamdi turned toward the front and saw that al-Omari had changed gears and was driving the Renault slowly forward.

At least the asshole didn't have more space to ram us harder, Ghamdi thought. Recovering his breath, he directed Benhadj to follow al-Omari's car.

"Fasten your seatbelt," Essabar muttered from the backseat.

Ghamdi watched Benhadj pull the Fiat away from the curb and follow al-Omari into the traffic. As he had hoped, the youth seemed to know how to drive well enough. He would just need to keep an eye on him. Essabar patted his friend's shoulders rhythmically from the rear seat as though he were playing a conga drum. *It was a good idea to bring him along,* Ghamdi thought. Still watching closely, Ghamdi saw perspiration appear on the young man's brow as he followed closely behind al-Omari's car. Was he too warm in the nondescript jacket they had purchased for him? It looked oversized on his ascetic frame.

"Do you want some music?" Essabar asked, extending his hand over Benhadj's shoulder to offer the Discman. Ghamdi pushed the hand back, gently shaking his head.

Benhadj turned successfully onto *rue de la Pompe*. Wiping the cool sweat from his forehead, he lifted his eyes toward the Haussmann-era buildings that lined the street. They looked strangely familiar. Yes, he remembered, they were in the book of paintings his mother had kept from her student trip to Paris. The shimmering dance of sunlight and shadow that animated the buildings before him, he had seen as a child on the colorful pages his mother had shown him. But he must resist such distractions, he reminded himself. *The brightest colors of this world are mere shades of gray compared to the glories of Paradise.* He must keep his mind on his objective. But his thoughts drifted again. How many cups of coffee had he drunk that morning?

It took another few minutes before he turned onto *Avenue Victor Hugo* and saw the immense monument looming ahead. Being new to the city, he was not aware that the *Arc de Triomphe* stood in the center of a great circular road from which twelve avenues radiated outward through the city like beams from a giant star, hence its principal name, *Place de l'Étoile*. The radiating avenues led to many of the city's other landmarks and cultural treasures: To the east, the great art museum *Le Palais du Louvre*; to the south the emblematic *Tour Eiffel*; to the west the modern skyscrapers of *La Défense*; and to the northeast the bohemian neighborhoods of *Montmartre* ascending to the crowning basilica, *Sacré-Coeur*.

Approaching the great circular hub in the rusted gray Fiat minivan loaded with Semtex explosives, Ali Benhadj felt a pressing need to urinate. He had ignored the growing urge for the past hour, everyone being in a hurry to get on with the operation, but now he felt he must relieve himself soon. He turned to Ghamdi and started to speak. "Charles de Gaulle," cut in Ghamdi, pointing ahead. "We're getting close." The circle's equally famous second name, *La Place Charles de Gaulle*, was familiar to Benhadj. He knew de Gaulle as the French leader who had abandoned colonial rule of Algeria as a result of the glorious War of Independence. He decided he could control the urge a few more minutes.

—   —   —

The slow-moving traffic came to a halt. Ghamdi noticed Benhadj twist sharply in his seat. *Nerves*, he thought. He wished he had brought along the Marlboros so he could offer him a smoke. "Tell me more about how your uncle fought in the war." Ghamdi had heard the entire story the night before, but recounting his uncle's exploits would keep Benhadj focused.

When the light turned green, the traffic resumed its slow crawl toward the *Arc de Triomphe*. Hundreds of cars entered the circle each minute from the twelve avenues, merging into a great swirl of traffic as they crossed and dodged one another in search of different avenues to escape. Benhadj followed the yellow Clio closely into the churning mass of cars until al-Omari suddenly braked to avoid a car darting across his path. Essabar screamed a warning from behind, but the youth's foot had already found the brake pedal and stopped the Fiat a few centimeters behind al-Omari's Clio. A car behind them erupted into furious honking. "*Arrifique!*" shouted Ghamdi out the window. *Fuck you!* France was a nation of big tempers in tiny cars. Sweat moistened Ghamdi's shirt. What if the asshole had struck them in the rear? Another risk that no one had thought about during the careful planning. The infernal honking stopped as traffic started moving again.

Ahead of them, Ghamdi saw al-Omari's car escape the circle, barely missing a motorcycle that tried to pass on its right, and come to a halt along the curb of the *Avenue des Champs-Élysées*. "Pull over behind him," Ghamdi ordered Benhadj. "Remember, Abu Salem, you are about to enter the battle. A true martyr does not turn his face from the enemy until he achieves victory or dies." Ghamdi opened the door and stepped onto the sidewalk, motioning for Essabar to follow. Outside, the sound of the traffic was deafening. Ghamdi leaned back into the car. "Remember, you must stay close behind Hani al-Omari," he shouted. "He will stop at the target. Then, you must complete the attack immediately, just as you have planned."

Inside the car, Benhadj nodded. Ghamdi pointed to the switch taped between the seats. "The moment you push that, your duty will be complete and you will arrive in the Gardens of Paradise, into the embrace of God. Do not hesitate, Abu Salem."

—　—　—

Benhadj started to speak again, but Ghamdi slammed the door and motioned for him to lock the car. Ahead, Benhadj saw the Renault Clio pull away from the curb and ease into traffic. He depressed the gas pedal, pleased that the motion relieved his urge to urinate, and tried to follow al-

Omari, until another car forced its way in between them. Falling behind, Benhadj saw the Clio clear an intersection just as the traffic light turned red.

Forced to wait at the light, Benhadj tightened his groin muscles rhythmically until the painful urge receded inside his body. Across the avenue, he saw a police car approach in the opposite direction. "Oh Lord, block their vision from in front of them, so that they may not see." The police car passed, but the traffic light remained red and the overwhelming pressure returned. "Lord, give me the strength to do Thy bidding." Benhadj shook the steering wheel violently as the extra cups of coffee raged in his bladder. As if in answer to his prayer, the light turned green. He stamped on the gas pedal and the car lurched into the intersection, the motion bringing him another moment of relief.

— — —

As soon as al-Omari saw the Fiat moving again, he pulled the Clio away from the curb. Two long blocks remained to their destination. He looked out at the lunchtime crowds on the sidewalk. The *Champs-Élysées* was lined with restaurants and luxury shops, interspersed with banks, movie theaters and futuristic automobile showrooms. The broad avenue attracted tens of thousands of people each day from around the world. Al-Omari smiled to think that the "fields of heaven" would soon be converted into hell on earth. Tonight everyone in the world would be talking about them. *Even the bloody mujahedeen in Afghanistan*, al-Omari thought, snickering. *They won't know our names, but they will sure know what we've done.*

He looked into the rearview mirror to confirm Benhadj was still following, but saw instead a tourist bus entering the avenue from a side street. *"Tel Hastizi!"* shouted al-Omari as the bus blocked Benhadj from his view. *"Mous zibbee!"*

— — —

Behind the halted bus, tears came to the eyes of Ali Benhadj. He looked frantically outside, but the sidewalk was packed with people. There was nowhere he could relieve himself. He glared at the bus ahead and screamed, "Allah, the Merciful!" Miraculously, the bus started to merge into the next lane, unblocking the lane ahead of him. He accelerated until he spotted the yellow Clio ahead. His oversize friend stood next to the tiny car, pointing with a grin toward the restaurant as though he were beckoning Benhadj to a banquet. *You must complete the attack immediately.* Grimacing in agony, Benhadj slowed the Fiat and turned the steering wheel sharply to the right, bringing the front tires against the curb. *Do not hesitate.* He depressed the accelerator and the minivan began to crawl up the curb, but too slowly, threatening to fall back into the street. His legs began to tremble uncontrollably until he pressed one hand into his groin and stamped harder on the gas pedal. The Fiat lurched up the curb and across the sidewalk, wedging heavily through the crowd before it halted a meter before the glass facade. Tears still flowing from his eyes, Benhadj released a frantic cry. He attempted to tighten his groin muscles one more time, but now he was beyond all ability or desire to hold back the spasms.

He looked back for al-Omari, but his view was blocked by people crowding around the minivan. Someone knocked sharply on the window next to him. Another yelled through the windshield. Through their angry visages, he saw the faces of his father and uncle. They were smiling at the television, listening to the oath of jihad he had sworn before the video camera the night before. He felt the car shake as someone tried to pull open the locked door. He closed his eyes and depressed the accelerator again. *You will arrive in the Gardens of Paradise.*

The car crashed through the glass façade of the restaurant. When the airbag exploded, it drove his head back, causing his foot to make one final thrust against the accelerator. The car struggled deeper into the restaurant, crushing aside the plastic and metal furniture, until his foot slipped from the gas pedal and the car halted again, its motor still running.

His stunned face collapsing into the slowly deflating airbag, Benhadj remembered the switch attached to the cable. *Every man must die, one way or another.* His fingers located the tape between the seats, but he could not find the cable or the switch. Had the crash dislodged them? He thought of the cell phone in his pocket. He could still call Mohammed Jamal and abort the operation. Then his fingers found the cable. The sound of a woman's shriek caused his head to jerk up and he heard a fist pounding on the windshield. He could still unlock the door and flee. He felt along the cable until his fingers found the switch. His other hand felt the cell phone through the urine-soaked fabric of his jeans pocket. But the smell would be too humiliating. *Death for the martyr is no more painful than the bite of a gnat.* He heard more people shouting and crying, something hard beating on the roof, all at once. Through the windshield he saw another angry face. Was it the face of his father? He closed his eyes and saw himself once more on the edge of the precipice, struggling to retain his footing, but already falling into the abyss. *Into the embrace of God.*

— — —

Across the *Champs-Élysées*, Mohammed Jamal watched from an outdoor café. He had arrived at the Metro station Franklin Roosevelt with enough time to walk two blocks and locate a sidewalk table with a clear view of the target across the avenue. By the time the Fiat Punto arrived, he had been served a *café au lait* with a small square of chocolate. Moments later, he heard the roar of the engine and the scream of the tires as the gray minivan lurched across the sidewalk, separating the passing pedestrians into two waves. Still watching from his café table, he saw the Fiat lunge forward a second time to penetrate the restaurant. Hearing the shattering sound of the glass façade collapsing, he watched the pedestrians surge into the street as drivers leaped from halted cars.

Jamal waited patiently. He was in no hurry. After all, he was about to alter the course of history. His goal was nothing short of a complete change of leadership in the Middle East, sweeping aside both the Islamist militants who shackled the people with their medieval religion and the despotic regimes that squandered their oil wealth. He watched crowds pouring out of shops and cafés, merging with the crowds in the street that pressed toward the restaurant to view the destruction and assist the injured. No one seemed to have noticed the overweight, bearded man who had rushed away in the opposite direction. No one stopped to look at the yellow Renault Clio he had left illegally parked on the avenue. Jamal's mind returned to his plan. The eagerness of the religious extremists to take credit for jihadist attacks in Europe would bring the West's initial wrath down upon their heads. Most of them would be imprisoned or killed during the first waves of repression. *But the destruction of the Islamists will be only the beginning if my bet pays off.* With a little luck, the Western repression would also enflame Muslim resentment and ignite protests violent enough to topple several pro-Western regimes.

Still waiting for Ali Benhadj to complete his task, Jamal felt certain of success. Now that the car was inside the restaurant, nothing on earth could stop him. His thoughts were interrupted by the sharp sound of shouting across the avenue. Standing from his café table, he saw that the crowd had pressed its way into the restaurant, concealing the Fiat Punto from his sight. *Why is he taking so long?* Perhaps the crash had left him unconscious. Perhaps they had broken into the car and seized him. Perhaps he had simply lost faith.

Jamal snapped open his aluminum briefcase and placed his hand on one of the radio transmitters. He silently counted off five more seconds. Pushing the button, he thought he heard his cell phone ring once, just before the sound of the explosion, but perhaps it was only his imagination. He could not be sure.

CHAPTER 21

Seventh Day of the Investigation

"Look at this!" Leslie Jumana shouted. She was startled as her voice shattered the silence of the Lockerbie war room like a gunshot. Until that moment, the new day had brought the same fruitless drudgery as the night before. Hour after hour, the team had reviewed an endless stream of probable matches churned out by Echelon, but none seemed relevant to their investigation. As the end of the afternoon approached, Leslie had started to feel that the Echelon exercise was an enormous waste of time, not to mention computer resources. Then, just as she was tempted to go home for a few hours of sleep, she discovered a golden needle hidden in the giant haystack of transcripts.

It was a single, three-minute telephone conversation. One of the callers was located near Aleppo, Syria, not far from the border with Turkey. As she shared the transcript with Doyle, a dozen of their colleagues circled to read over their shoulders. Keyboards began clacking as they crosschecked the telephone numbers and locations in the vast CIA database. Even before the research was complete, Leslie ran down the hallway to report the discovery to Douglas Grebb. Doyle ran behind her.

"My God!" shouted Grebb after reading the transcript. "Who are these guys?"

"We think they are Syrian extremists, Mr. Grebb," Doyle replied breathlessly.

"We haven't yet identified the callers," Leslie corrected him, "but both phones are associated with known radicals from Syria. The audio lab is running voice recognition programs right now."

"It looks ominous," Stan Stebbins said quietly.

"We think so," Leslie said, her eyes on Doyle. "They use the word radioactive twice and they mention the *Izmir Queen* by name." She pointed to two lines highlighted in yellow.

"The Lyon car thief, Ramadan, expected the boat to arrive on Sunday morning," Ronnie Lapoint recalled. "That's about six hours from now."

"I'm going upstairs to alert Burt Brown," Grebb said. "Ronnie, you get back downstairs to see why they haven't located that damned boat yet. Everyone else, get back to work. I want every detail double checked and updated for Burt."

Watching Grebb give orders, Leslie realized this was the first time he had appeared happy in ages. She knew the past few years had been rough on him. After the waning of the Cold War temporarily beached his CIA career, his excessive drinking nearly cost him his wife and children. While his recent rebirth as a terrorist fighter refloated his spirits, the constant stress of the unfamiliar new threat seemed to overwhelm him at times, causing him to lash out unexpectedly at his associates. It was good to see him enjoying this moment of progress. The unaccustomed sparkle of his eyes seemed even to lighten the purplish blotches beneath them.

News of the Syria intercept flashed through the Counterterrorism Center, galvanizing the exhausted review teams. Doyle went next door to Mogadishu to see if anything more had been discovered there. He found Suresh Kumar working with the translator Jihan Ammar. To stay cool, Suresh had changed into khaki shorts and a T-shirt that lent him the rugged air of a Pakistani soccer player. The table before him was buried in piles of transcripts.

"These are from the past couple of hours," Suresh explained. "We're confirming translations, but they appear to contain nothing significant."

Doyle snapped his fingers. "I have an idea. Jihan, let's have another look at the Ramadan intercepts, but going back a couple of weeks." Seconds later a list of intercept numbers and dates appeared on Jihan's screen. "I don't recognize that one," Doyle said. "Do you, Suresh?"

Suresh stood and looked over his shoulder. "I can't say for sure, but I double checked most of Ramadan's calls prior to the French wiretap. Hold on." Suresh raised his cell phone to identify an incoming call. Doyle wondered if the phone had ever left his hand since he'd greeted Doyle in the Sentinel lobby six months earlier. "Stan Stebbins wants me to get over to Fort Meade right away," Suresh announced. The NSA had discovered another problem applying Fluent to Arabic voice intercepts. "Can you keep a lid on things here?" Suresh asked as he dashed out the doorway.

"Sure," Doyle called after him. "I just need to verify this intercept with Jihan." The call was fairly long, a transcript of six pages in English. At first it seemed irrelevant, but toward the end Ramadan and the other caller started talking about events in Paris. Doyle asked Jihan to find the original intercept. She placed a pair of headphones over her dark hair and moments later signaled she had found the Arabic recording.

"Try to find this part." Doyle pointed to the transcript. "Aren't they talking about the bombing?"

She advanced the recording to the passage he had indicated. "Yes, yes, it sounds like they are. They call it the big party on *Champs-Élysées*."

"Does it sound like they were part of it?"

"Perhaps, Mr. O'Gara," she replied hesitantly, "but this conversation occurred the day after the attack. Everyone in France was talking about it, weren't they?"

"Keep listening," he urged. "The translation makes it sound like they're worried about something." He saw Jihan's eyes looked red within the zebra frames of her glasses. She, too, had worked with little sleep since Grebb had ordered the massive Echelon search.

"Yes," she said. "They are worried the police will push them down." Doyle shook his head, puzzled. "Is that not the right phrase? *Push down*, like when they arrest a lot of people."

"You mean *crackdown*, don't you?"

"Yes, crackdown," Jihan sighed. "That is the expression. This guy—I think it is Mr. Ramadan—says he hopes the police don't crack them down before the cargo comes in."

"Then they are part of it, part of the operation?"

"I don't know Mr. O'Gara. They may just fear a police reaction against Muslims. You know, a general pushdown."

"Crackdown?" Doyle suggested.

"Yes, that is what I meant."

Doyle thought a moment. "You said they mentioned a cargo. Keep listening."

Jihan replaced the headphones. "A lot of this part is inaudible," she said after a minute. "Too much background noise."

"But you're sure they use the word cargo, aren't you?"

She motioned for him to be quiet while she listened. Doyle recalled Howard Silver's words, *don't sacrifice accuracy*, as he watched the weary young woman. Unfortunately, Silver had not offered him any additional resources. Waiting for Jihan, his thoughts drifted to another Sentinel translator, his friend Khalid Osman, who had also warned him of the risks of mistranslation. Doyle had accepted Ozzie's invitation to get together at an Arlington sports bar shortly after they had been deployed to the CIA campus to test the new software. In addition to watching the Detroit Tigers beat the Baltimore Orioles, Doyle questioned Ozzie about how Arabic script could be converted to digital forms for computer analysis. As before, Ozzie shared his technical knowledge generously. Of course, Doyle did not realize then that two months later he would be supervising translations and would be desperate for translators as skillful as Ozzie.

"Yes," Jihan replied finally. "They use an Arabic word equivalent to cargo, or at least something carried by a ship. The other guy—not Ramadan—asks if the entire cargo is for Frenchmen. Then Ramadan says he doesn't think they deserve all of it."

"You mean like he's feeling sorry for them?" Doyle heard skepticism in his own voice.

"I don't know. They both start laughing. Then the interception ends, as though one of them hung up." Jihan removed the headphones. "Can I take a break now, Mr. O'Gara? I am tired and I would like to eat something."

"Okay, but please verify the translation one more time before you leave."

"The entire transcript?"

"No, just the parts we discussed. Then you can relax a few hours, but please come back. We still have lots of work to do."

Doyle left the Mogadishu room in search of Howard Silver to brief him on the new discovery. Before he reached the elevator, he had second thoughts about letting Jihan leave. He started to turn back, but then hesitated. There was no point in depriving her of a break just to double check irrelevant portions of the transcript. He had to draw the line somewhere, with Grebb being in such a hurry to update his boss.

He pressed the elevator button. As he waited, Doyle's thoughts returned to his translator friend Ozzie. After their first evening of beer drinking, they had met on a regular basis, each encounter being more fun and informative than the prior ones. It was during a lunch in early May, Doyle recalled, that he found himself talking to Ozzie about Middle East politics. A bus bombing had occurred in Jerusalem and the Israelis had closed the border. Ozzie became agitated, saying that Palestinian extremists were destroying the livelihoods of ordinary Arabs.

"They're crazy animals!" he said over his second beer, almost shouting.

Doyle reached across the table and put his hand on his friend's arm. "Their tactics are indefensible, Ozzie, but if you were in their position..." Doyle hesitated, finding himself on a path he had not intended. Then he pressed ahead. "I mean, how else are they going to convince the Israelis to end the occupation?"

His friend said nothing more, but Doyle had the impression that Ozzie was studying him over his next sip of beer, in the same way that a butterfly collector might examine a rare specimen he had just caught. Something else struck him as odd during that lunch, Doyle recalled. It was then that he first noticed Ozzie was growing a mustache. He said nothing at the time, assuming Ozzie had simply forgotten to shave, but it was just a few days later that Ozzie left Sentinel without saying good-bye. He must have been changing his look in preparation for a new job or something, Doyle now realized.

The elevator finally arrived. *What luck*, Doyle thought as the door opened. Howard Silver was inside. Doyle saw that he had changed suits and gotten a fresh haircut. He wondered when Silver had found the time that hectic afternoon.

Grebb was delighted when Ronnie Lapoint called him to the CIA surveillance room. "I knew you'd find her eventually," he said, slapping Lapoint's back in appreciation. Displayed above them on large television screens were images of the *Izmir Queen*, each with a date, time and geographic location.

"That's the earliest one," said Lapoint raising his finger. "It was taken in the Black Sea a few miles off the coast of Georgia."

"On Monday, the second of September," added a CIA technician. "She apparently sailed from Sochi earlier that day."

"That matches the information the Russians gave us," Lapoint confirmed.

The technician flipped past several photos. "Here is the *Izmir Queen* entering the Port of Trabzon on the north coast of Turkey, later the same day."

"She doesn't leave Trabzon for two days," Lapoint said. "She remains in port until Wednesday, then continues westward across the Black Sea." Lapoint sounded troubled by the two-day stay. He looked quizzically at Grebb as though hoping he might supply the explanation.

More images appeared overhead. "Here she is again as she leaves the Black Sea through the Bosporus," the technician said. "She must have passed Istanbul without stopping and then headed across the Sea of Marmara and through the Dardanelles. Here's the next picture, after she entered the Aegean Sea heading south toward the Mediterranean."

"Do we know where the *Izmir Queen* is now?" Grebb asked.

"Not exactly, but here are the latest shots; she already passed Italy and is moving north along the west coast of Sardinia."

"When can we expect the next images?" Grebb asked the technician.

"Not for another three hours. If I could move a couple of satellites, I could increase the image frequency." Grebb picked up the phone. Normally it required days to alter satellite paths, since any change could potentially compromise national security. In this case, the National Security Advisor was already briefed, so Grebb expected quick approval. While he waited, he called an Air Force base near Las Vegas about another possibility.

Lapoint passed a sheet of paper to Grebb as he hung up the phone. "We just learned the *Izmir Queen* was impounded by Greek authorities two years ago."

"On what charges?"

"Smuggling illegal arms."

"Why am I not surprised?" Grebb said, shaking his head.

Howard Silver entered the room, smiling radiantly. "Doug, I just visited the Echelon review teams. It looks like our Doyle O'Gara has found something exciting."

"Mr. Grebb." It was the voice of a woman standing in the doorway behind Silver. "Mr. Brown would like to see you all upstairs in the control room. He said immediately."

"Let's get going, Howard," said Grebb as he rose. "Tell O'Gara to meet us up there, in case we have any questions for him."

— — —

In the Mediterranean Sea, 140 nautical miles south of France, the USS Roosevelt launched an RQ-1 pilotless drone, known popularly as "Predator." In the Nevada desert, an Air Force lieutenant typed in the coordinates that Douglas Grebb had provided to him by telephone a few minutes earlier. As the lieutenant pulled gently on a joystick, Predator turned northward and began flying toward the French coast, equipped with an infrared surveillance camera and two Hellfire infrared-guided missiles.

CHAPTER 22

Seventh Day of the Investigation

Doyle exited the elevator on the sixth floor of the Original Headquarters Building. No one was there to meet him. He buttoned his jacket and started down a hallway as though he knew where he was going. *So this is it, the nerve center of US intelligence.* He was not as much surprised by the power-exuding décor—plush carpeting and dark wood paneling—as by the absence of order and security. Young men and women darted across the corridor from one office to another pursuing urgent tasks. No one paused to check his credentials or ask where he was going.

Trying to appear purposeful, Doyle continued up the corridor until he reached a large room filled with dark-suited men and a few colorfully-dressed women engaged in intense discussions. *The famous control room,* he thought as he squeezed inside. *Not quite like the movies.* Around the perimeter stood consoles bearing computers, communication gear and random cups of half-finished coffee. Display screens were mounted overhead. With so many people talking at once, the room reminded Doyle oddly of a holiday office party. He spotted Howard Silver near the middle of the room, seated with his CIA clients around a large table of polished mahogany shaped like a huge donut. As Doyle neared the table, Silver raised his gaze and nodded toward the wall lined with chairs. Something in his sharp glance reminded Doyle that he had not shaved since the prior day.

Taking one of the wall seats reserved for support staff, Doyle looked around the room to see if he recognized any of America's top spies. Doyle had never seen the man next to Douglas Grebb, but guessed immediately it must be Burt Brown, the Deputy Director for Counterterrorism. Brown wore a gray patch over the socket of his left eye, reportedly lost during his covert service in Lebanon in the mid-1980s. Doyle had heard rumors, never officially acknowledged, that after the bombing of the US Marine Barracks it was Brown who led the CIA actions to settle accounts with Hezbollah and their Iranian sponsors. Although the patch concealed his missing eye, the extent of Brown's injury was apparent from the scar tissue still visible on his left cheek. *The legendary Burt Brown.* Doyle chuckled to himself. After only six months in Washington, he was meeting with the top brass of the CIA. Just like Doyle's father always said: good looks, hard work and a little luck will take you a long way. But who would have ever thought Doyle would rise this fast?

He saw Brown lean toward Grebb, apparently trying to hear his words over the many conversations echoing through the room. The inclined posture brought the two men so close that Grebb's whispering lips appeared to be nibbling Brown's ear. Seated on the other side of Brown were Lapoint and Stebbins, each staring into the center of the donut, doubtless collecting their thoughts for the debate ahead. They looked to Doyle like two cave-dwelling creatures, hunched over from living in tight spaces, pallid from lack of sunlight. Another two dozen people stood around the room, separated into noisy clusters. One cluster near the opposite wall contained Leslie Jumana. Despite the all-night work, she looked rejuvenated, her auburn hair bouncing as she emphasized some point to her colleagues. An erotic fragrance floated into Doyle's imagination, the memory of a scent that had aroused him violently two nights earlier, the faint remnants of Leslie's perfume warmed by her fresh sweat. He hoped they would not have to remain at work after the meeting.

Doyle awoke from his reverie as people began noisily taking seats around the table and along the walls. Burt Brown had apparently signaled it was time to start. As the seats filled, a few people scurried toward the door, evidently pursuing tasks that had been assigned within the buzzing clusters.

"So it looks like we have a little problem shaping up," Brown began. The room fell silent. "Is that fair to say, Doug?"

"Yes, sir, a problem and an opportunity. The team has been working around the clock on the Paris bombing and we've detected plans for another attack in France." Grebb paused to let the others absorb the significance. "We've concluded that Abdallah Ramadan, the Big Mac contact in Lyon, is about to meet the *Izmir Queen* to receive the radioactive material stolen from our Russian friends. It appears Mr. Ramadan and his group are preparing another attack to take place in Marseille in the next few hours."

Brown scanned the faces around the table with his one eye. "You'd better take everyone through the evidence, Doug."

Grebb nodded. "First, we've confirmed most of the Russian story about the theft of the radioactive material and its shipment aboard the *Izmir Queen*."

"The Russians have been unusually forthcoming," Brown agreed. "What makes you think the stuff is headed for Marseille?"

"We're tracking the boat, sir." Grebb nodded to Lapoint and a map of the Mediterranean appeared on the overhead monitors. A series of dots on the map indicated locations where the *Izmir Queen* had been recently photographed by satellites. The dots formed a line pointing directly toward Marseille.

The map disappeared from the screens and was replaced by the latest image of the *Izmir Queen*, obscured by thick rain and ocean waves. "A storm is moving into the area," Lapoint explained. "We expect Predator will reach her soon so we'll get real-time shots." The excitement of the pursuit seemed to have lent a rosy hue to Lapoint's wan countenance.

"How do you connect Mr. Ramadan with the boat?" Brown asked.

"We've been analyzing his calls since the French first identified him as a contact of the Big Mac SIM card," Grebb replied. "The new tools from Sentinel Systems are helping us speed up the process." Grebb turned to Howard Silver when he mentioned Sentinel. Silver smiled, casting nods around the table. Even under the artificial light, he appeared tanned and fit, as though he had just walked in from a golf course. "The intercepts contain an abundance of code words," Grebb continued. "But it is clear that Mr. Ramadan was involved in planning the attack on the *Champs-Élysées*, that he is expecting radioactive material on the *Izmir Queen* and that the stuff is to be used for a dirty bomb in France. Do I have that right, Howard?"

"You are correct, Mr. Grebb," Silver replied. "We were able to recover and translate his recent cell phone calls thanks to our enhancements of the Echelon and Fluent software. As you point out, he uses code words, but the message could hardly be clearer." Silver glanced toward Doyle seated against the wall.

Hardly be clearer. Doyle wondered if he should pass Silver a note. Ramadan had talked about the *Champs-Élysées,* that was certain, but it was not so clear he was part of the planning. *But what difference do such questions make?* Even if Silver had embellished the translation slightly, it was clear from other evidence that Ramadan was linked to the Paris plotters and the boat was carrying nuclear material. Doyle's attention returned to the meeting. No one looked to him for clarification. The dozen people seated around the donut-shaped table appeared immobile, their expressionless eyes still fixed on Howard Silver, like a dozen mannequins cast from the same mold.

Doyle heard Grebb's voice again. ". . . so there are numerous facts linking Ramadan to the terrorist network. First, Ramadan received calls before the attack, not only from the SIM card later found in the Paris restaurant, but also from another SIM card purchased at the same time at Charles de Gaulle Airport."

"Purchased by a Middle-East guy with a rock-band T-shirt, correct?"

"That's right," Grebb replied to Brown. "Second, both the cars used in the bombing were stolen from Lyon where Ramadan operates."

"Any evidence he was involved in the thefts?"

"Not directly, but he has been arrested for car theft in the past."

Doyle was still thinking about the Ramadan translation. *A dirty bomb in France.* Maybe Ramadan had not used that exact phrase, but he had referred to explosions and to the *Izmir Queen.* That certainly ruled out the benign interpretations that Jihan Ammar said were possible. Doyle had mentioned the ambiguities to Silver downstairs, he was sure, although it might have been better if Jihan had stayed to parse through the Arabic with him.

"Big Mac's phone was also used before the Paris attack to call a number registered to a guy named Hani al-Omari." Stan Stebbins was now talking. "We don't know much about al-Omari—no criminal record—but his apartment contained this poster." Stebbins had apparently dressed up for the occasion, Doyle noted. Gone was his customary black knit sweater. From somewhere he had retrieved an ill-fitting sports coat and colorful tie.

"Good Lord," one of the mannequins said as Stebbins passed a photo of the poster. It showed an atomic mushroom cloud erupting over a map of the United States.

"The martyr flying toward Heaven looks like you, Stan," said Brown wryly, as if to break the tension, but he did not smile. "Have the French tracked down Mr. al-Omari?"

"Not yet," Stebbins replied. "He and his roommates apparently abandoned the apartment two days before the bombing. We suspect they are going to meet Ramadan in Marseille."

"Any proof of that?"

"No; they've vanished for the moment," Stebbins admitted, adjusting his unaccustomed necktie. "We lost contact with Ramadan, too."

"But this is only part of the evidence," Grebb resumed. "You recall the Big Mac card was purchased with two others. One of them was used to call a rental house in England that was later discovered to contain bomb making materials." The kitchen of the Blackpool house appeared on one of the monitors. "That's a cookbook for dirty bombs on the counter." Grebb said as the image zoomed larger.

"The house was called a few hours before the Paris attack," Stebbins added. "It appears to have been abandoned suddenly the same day."

"So you think the caller dispatched them for the next job?" Brown asked.

"Looks like it," Grebb replied. "Our British friends have not yet found the occupants."

A new figure entered the room and took a seat next to Burt Brown. "Nice you could join us, Russell," Brown said. "We're just getting to the interesting part." Doyle guessed the new man was Russell Fairbanks, the CIA's general counsel. The lawyer wore a green bow tie and a pair of broad suspenders beneath a tan linen suit, giving him an appearance midway between a Southern politician and a college professor.

"Perhaps of greater significance," Grebb resumed after Brown had conducted a brief whispered conference with Russell Fairbanks, "Ramadan's own words confirm the reason he is meeting the *Izmir Queen*. Can you elaborate, Howard?"

"As you've seen from our translations, Ramadan makes unmistakable references to his rendezvous with the *Izmir Queen* and a dirty bomb attack in France." Silver nodded around the table. "It's easy to see through his transparent code words in this context."

Silver did not glance at him this time, but Doyle wondered if he should speak up to clarify. Some intercepts did refer to a cargo of radioactive material, that was true, but had Ramadan actually used the term dirty bomb? Doyle had read so many transcripts he was having trouble keeping them straight. He opened his briefcase to check, but saw he had brought only the latest transcript he had discussed with Silver before the meeting. He looked over to Leslie and the group of analysts on the other side of the room. *They must have double checked all of them, even triple checked.*

"Doug, do you mind if I ask a few questions?" A new voice was speaking.

Grebb raised his hands from the table and parted his arms slightly, as though welcoming the fresh line of inquiry from Russell Fairbanks.

"What makes us so certain they are bringing the stuff in for a dirty bomb?" the lawyer asked. His thumbs slipped under the broad suspenders as he tilted back. "Maybe they're just planning to do some medical research." A brief laugh came from someone on the opposite side of the circular table. Brown did not join the laughter, his good eye remaining fixed on Grebb.

"I admit, I was skeptical myself, despite all the evidence," Grebb said. "That is, until earlier this evening, when we received additional proof that clinched the deal for me." Grebb pointed toward one of the screens where a two-page document had appeared. "This is a translation of an Arabic telephone conversation intercepted by Echelon." A rhythmic bounce animated his lanky frame as he strode closer to the text. "It takes place five days ago, the same day the *Izmir Queen* lay in the Port of Trabzon in Turkey."

"Interesting," Fairbanks conceded as he read. "Who is speaking?"

"We believe they are both with Muslim Brotherhood of Syria."

"Muslim Brotherhood?" The question came from a man seated next to Ronnie Lapoint. "I thought Hafez al-Assad eliminated those guys from Syria during the Hama massacre."

"You're mostly right," Grebb acknowledged, "but the hard core escaped to other countries. They filter back into Syria now and again to see if the time is ripe for another uprising. In this case, one of the speakers is

Maher Arar, a top operative, calling from Paris. The other may be Babar Bakri, a weapons expert, who received the call near Aleppo. You can see they clearly refer to the *Izmir Queen* and to a nuclear cargo." He read aloud several lines highlighted in the text:

Now we will need twenty kilos of Semtex.

That will be enough?

Yes, plenty to blow the radioactive material into dust. A thousand meters into the air. The wedding party will leave the city uninhabitable for a hundred years.

"A hundred years," Brown repeated.

"We believe Bakri's people were in Turkey to meet the boat and prepare the dirty bomb," Grebb continued. "That explains why she spent two days in Trabzon."

"What do these guys have against the French?" Fairbanks asked.

"We're not sure, but now the same boat is nearing Marseille, and Ramadan is on his way to meet it with plans to launch another attack. Bakri's code word *wedding* is the same one used by Ramadan."

Fairbanks turned his attention back to the words on the screen. "You are confident about the translations?"

"The translations have been verified several times, thanks to Sentinel," Grebb confirmed, "and they jibe perfectly with all the rest of the evidence we've gathered, including what the Russians told us about the cargo. It all fits together."

Fairbanks leaned toward Burt Brown and another whispered conference ensued. "We don't seem to have much choice," Brown said when they finished. "We need to stop them before they attack again." As Brown spoke, new pictures appeared on the screens overhead.

"Predator is right on time." A hint of a smile fluttered across Grebb's lips. The pilotless drone had caught up with the *Izmir Queen* and was now broadcasting pictures of the boat tossing on the Mediterranean Sea. The eerie green images jerked violently from the combined movement of waves rocking the boat and turbulent winds shaking the drone. Some showed the *Izmir Queen* at a distance, surrounded by a large expanse of water, while others showed her close up, nearly filling the screen.

"What the hell is that?" Brown exclaimed. Everyone turned to the monitor to which he pointed. A wide-angle shot showed the *Izmir Queen* occupying one corner. A smaller gray shape inched toward her from the opposite corner, traveling diagonally across the screen.

"It looks like a motorized skiff approaching the *Izmir Queen*," said Lapoint, squinting into the image. "Why would such a small boat be out there on a night like this?" No one replied, but several men nodded as though the answer to Lapoint's question was inescapable.

Grebb was already talking on his cell phone. "Our closest military ship, the destroyer *Roosevelt,* is still sixty nautical miles away," he announced as he disconnected. "We've located a French navy vessel a little closer, off Cannes, but it will take her at least two hours to reach the area."

"By that time, the skiff will have taken off the nuclear cargo and be back to Marseille," Brown said. "That's the biggest port in the Mediterranean. If they set off a dirty bomb there, it will cripple the European economy." The room fell silent. Brown's left hand reached up to adjust his eye patch as he raised his right eye to the overhead screen. Four thousand miles away, Predator's infrared camera circled high above the two boats. In each jerky image, the skiff crawled closer toward the *Izmir Queen.* "Get me the National Security Advisor," Brown said finally, speaking into his phone. Seated against the wall, Doyle expected the Deputy Director to clear the room, but he gave no such order. The support staff was allowed to remain, momentarily forgotten along the edges of the control room.

CHAPTER 23

Seventh Day of the Investigation

Christine Dupont lay awake in her hotel room, still thinking about the strange voice-mail Dominique Carpentier had left on her cell phone during her flight to Marseille. He would handle the contacts with the Americans, he informed her, so she could concentrate on finding Abdallah Ramadan. Maybe he just wanted to impress the politicians with his hands-on leadership, like Napoleon touring the front before a big battle, but this intervention went beyond Dominique's usual effort to play the general. He sounded too insistent about the Americans, all the while trying to sound casual.

Thick clouds had covered the airport when they landed, the first sign of a storm moving northward across the Mediterranean. Rain had begun falling by the time they caught up with Thierry Christophe at the *Vieux-Port*. The head of DST's regional office had deputized twenty local *gendarmes*, but when they checked the list of incoming ships, they found no mention of the *Izmir Queen*. Sailors at the *syndicat maritime CGT* claimed they had never heard of the boat. Local thugs who hung around the old harbor looking for unlocked cars or open warehouses knew of no one named Ramadan, or so they said. Following a reluctant tip from a taciturn bartender, Dupont and Angeline Odette eventually stumbled into a wharf-side brothel. The operator expressed no surprise—she had evidently seen stranger pairs of customers—but she had no answers to their questions.

After a brief, cheerless meal in her hotel room, Dupont had called Paris to check progress. The telephone trees continued to grow and sprout new leads, she learned from Yves Bannelier. Among the third-tier connections of the *Pomme Frites* phone was a call to an Islamist radical from Strasbourg. A team had rushed to the city in northeastern France to interrogate him, but he appeared to have a solid alibi and no connection to the Paris plot.

Still lying on the bed, Dupont propped a pillow behind her head and placed a call to Dominique Carpentier to see if he had learned anything new from the US. Her call was answered by one of Carpentier's assistants who said he was in a meeting and could not be disturbed. Yes, he would call her back as soon as he was free. It might be later that night or first thing in the morning. Something big was happening, Dupont suspected. Did it involve her case or something else? *Most likely politics if it's keeping Dominique at the office so late.* Were they about to reshuffle the cabinet?

She felt exhausted, but left the light on so she would not fall asleep. Thierry Christophe had promised to call if he found Ramadan, no matter how late. Why did the inquiry seem to be sputtering to a halt again? The day had brought a series of tantalizing leads followed by dead ends. Searching her mind for any clues she might have overlooked, she looked at her watch. It was nearly midnight.

When the ringing woke her, the light was still on and she was lying on the bed fully clothed. Her watch showed a few minutes before 4 a.m. "Sorry to wake you, Christine." It was the voice of Dominique Carpentier when she picked up the phone. "I need your assessment of this guy Ramadan."

"We haven't found him, yet," she said, wondering what he was after.

"I know, but based on what you've seen so far . . ?" He left the question unfinished.

"It is hard to say. He and his friends are expecting an important cargo to arrive this morning. In Marseille, we think."

"Do you think it is nuclear in nature?" Carpentier interrupted.

In the darkness Dupont pictured his lean aged face, still hungry for victory, but weary from the endless struggle. "Nuclear?" she repeated. "I suppose that's possible. Several intercepts suggest a big explosion is being planned, although our translators find some of the words ambiguous."

"What do you think?"

His impatience alarmed her. "It was pretty scratchy at times," she said cautiously. "The reception broke up when he passed through the hills north of Marseille."

"We need to decide. The Americans think he's preparing another attack."

"Really? What exactly are they saying?"

"I'm not at liberty to share that."

"I see."

"How clear is the link between Ramadan and the *Izmir Queen?*" Carpentier asked.

"Very clear. Whomever he's talking to tells him what hour the vessel is expected to arrive. Ramadan is to provide another boat, a little one, to receive part of the cargo."

"A little boat," Carpentier repeated. "Thanks, that's helpful."

"Is there anything more you can share with us?" Dupont pressed. "We might be able to help."

"Nothing more for now. Just find Ramadan as soon as you can." Carpentier hung up, but his urgent tone reverberated in Dupont's mind. It seemed to involve something more than the investigation. Maybe it was his impending retirement. *He must feel pressed to achieve something memorable,* Dupont imagined, *before he becomes just another name in the ledger of forgotten public servants.* Dupont rose from the bed and removed her clothes. The air felt warm and humid against her exposed body. Pulling back the covers, she slid beneath a single sheet and turned off the light. She lay thinking about what Carpentier had said and what he had not said. As she stared into the darkness, the curtains suddenly glowed and an instant later she heard thunder. She listened until the noise passed. *What more did the Americans know about the Izmir Queen?* The evidence she had seen might point to a dirty bomb attack, but . . . The lightning came again, followed closely by more thunder. Her fingers traced the firm curve of her breast, absently at first but then more intentionally, an old habit. Her thoughts drifted to her lover at the Ministry of Foreign Affairs. She had not seen her diplomat for over a week. Maybe she should let the too-neat affair come to a friendly end, she thought. Find someone to whom she could really give herself, have a baby even, it was not too late. She could take care of her own child, instead of trying to protect all the children in France. *But is that what drives me?* Was it really about that defenseless little boy being beaten for dropping his ice cream? Maybe it was more about herself, as she sensed it was for Carpentier. Didn't she, too, want to accomplish something big before it was too late?

Her mind loosened its grasp, no longer able to hold onto her questions, as she slipped back into sleep. If she had any dreams, they were shattered when the telephone rang a second time. "We found him," said a voice after she found the receiver.

"Where?" She listened as Thierry Christophe gave her the address of the local police station. Then she remembered she was in Marseille. "We'll be there within an hour." Hanging up, she looked at the bedside clock. It was 6:15, Sunday morning.

— — —

Two hours earlier, the National Security Advisor, Stephen Holbrook, had called the French Ambassador at his home in Washington. "I assume your government has been briefed," he began without the usual pleasantries.

"Yes, we understand the urgency. I've spoken to the President of the Republic despite the late hour." The Ambassador paused, seeming to choose his next words carefully. "We would see no objection if it were to become necessary for the United States to intervene."

"No objection," Holbrook repeated. "Does that mean public support?"

The Ambassador ignored the question and continued. "Of course, we are confident the French navy will intercept the boat at sea or arrest the crew promptly if they reach our coast. We will not allow radioactive material to fall into the hands of criminals on our territory."

"So you believe the situation is under control?" Holbrook asked.

"Yes, I would say so, at least for France. Of course, there is a risk they will transport the cargo to some other country, perhaps even to the US, so we can see the situation presents a threat to your interests as well." He let the implications of his remark settle.

"Then we have your support?" Holbrook asked, impatient with the length of the pause.

"So, we have no objection if you choose to take appropriate action, particularly while the ship remains outside French waters."

Holbrook hung up and immediately dialed the Central Intelligence Agency. He looked at his desk clock while the call connected; it was 10:18 p.m. in Washington.

The screens in the CIA control room showed the small boat alongside the *Izmir Queen*, the images having grown brighter as the storm abated and dawn approached over the Mediterranean. Through Predator's shaking eye, the two boats now appeared to be a single heaving mass upon the rolling sea.

"What's your verdict, Russell?" Holbrook's voice asked from the speakerphone resting on the donut-shaped table. All eyes turned toward Fairbanks.

The lawyer continued to gaze up at the images as though searching for some additional detail that might affect his advice. He straightened his green bow tie and cleared his throat. "Based on the facts presented to me, the Agency has authority to proceed with deadly force under the Presidential Finding." His thumbs had found their way back under the suspenders. "We have strong evidence that the ship is controlled by terrorists and contains radioactive material to be used in an imminent attack. No legal means appears feasible to seize her within the limited time available."

"Are you sure about that last premise?" the National Security Advisor asked from the speakerphone. "Can't we get the Navy out there to stop and board the ship?"

"Unfortunately, no," Burt Brown replied. "The Navy advises that our closest vessel cannot intercept the *Izmir Queen* before the cargo reaches shore."

"The French ambassador seemed confident they could intercept her," Holbrook pressed.

"So they claim," Brown said. "But we calculate that by the time the French get there, the bad guys can detonate the bomb in Marseille harbor or hide it in some smaller port nearby."

"Are we sure of their intentions?"

"Yes, we are. The key is this guy Ramadan. The interceptions confirm he is part of the same group that bombed Paris a week ago and that he expects the radioactive cargo will be used for another attack in France."

Howard Silver was still at the table but he had said nothing since Fairbanks had entered the room. He glanced at Doyle for a fraction of a second, as though to confirm his presence.

"Can we contain the radioactive material?" the voice from the speakerphone asked.

Brown nodded to Grebb. "That should not be a problem, Mr. Holbrook. The water there is less than a thousand meters deep, so even if the boat sinks, we should be able to recover the material quickly."

"What if the explosion causes it to escape the shielding?" Holbrook persisted.

"We've already asked the Navy to coordinate with the French to cordon off the area," Grebb replied. "It will be less costly and dangerous to clean up a radioactive mess twenty miles offshore than in the middle of a French port or city."

A long silence followed.

"Sometimes we have to take risks to protect the country," Holbrook said finally. "The risks in this case seem manageable. If we do not move now, the consequences could be disastrous. Disable the boat."

"Yes sir," Brown answered. "May we assume you speak on behalf of the President?"

"You may."

—   —   —

At Nellis Air Force Base northeast of Las Vegas, the officer controlling Predator reached forward and flicked two switches that in combination armed the drone's Hellfire missiles. With the joystick control, he gently steered Predator northward about two miles toward the coast of France and then turned her back toward the target. On the Langley television monitors the *Izmir Queen* came back into view, its gray-green bulk rolling on the choppy sea. The small skiff was now pressed close against her side, like a whale calf suckling its mother. In the Nevada desert, the officer squeezed a trigger on the joystick and a radio signal flashed nine time zones around the world. In a process known as painting the target, Predator projected a laser beam to guide the Hellfire missile. As the drone passed through turbulent air, its infra-red camera eye tilted briefly upward, causing the target to drop momentarily from the screens at Langley. When the camera eye settled back down, the CIA team saw that the *Izmir Queen* and the companion skiff had been transformed into a mass of flames upon the water.

Cheers erupted in the control room. Some stood and slapped high-fives. Others exchanged hugs. Doyle remained seated against the wall. It had all the excitement and camaraderie of a college football game, he realized.

CHAPTER 24

Eighth Day of the Investigation

They had found Abdallah Ramadan in a hotel room near the *Vieux-Port*. The hotel was of the cheap kind, without any stars. Ramadan was a short man with small eyes that darted nervously from place to place. The darting eyes may have reflected instinctive distrust of his unexpected visitors or perhaps chronic irritation from the cigarettes ever-present in his mouth.

Although it was not yet dawn, he was dressed and smoking when they entered his room.

He did not seem surprised to see them, having encountered police often enough before. What may have come as a surprise was their number; in addition to the four who crowded into the tiny hotel room, three more waited outside in the hallway. Ramadan's eyes darted from one face to another, perhaps trying to recognize them from past visits. He agreed to accompany them to the station. Resistance would only make them more suspicious, he evidently knew. His surprise may have grown when he saw still more police in the street below.

— — —

As her taxi hurried toward the Marseille *gendarmerie*, Dupont saw the overnight storm had passed. She thought she saw smoke on the dawn-lit horizon, but had no time to ask about it before the taxi halted and she found herself racing after Lambert and Odette into the station. When they reached the interrogation room, Dupont saw Ramadan seated alone on the far side of the table. Thierry Christophe sat on the near side with two local detectives. Ramadan's eyes darted toward Dupont and his lips curled into a weak smile.

"Good morning, Mr. Ramadan. My name is Christine Dupont. I'm an investigator from *Direction de la Surveillance du Territoire*." Ramadan glanced at her credentials without betraying any recognition. Dupont took a moment to arrange her papers in order to give Ramadan time to worry about DST's interest in him. She observed his possessions lying on a plastic tray in the middle of the table: car keys, a mobile telephone, a wallet that appeared to contain a lot of money and a package of Gauloises cigarettes. Ramadan shifted his feeble smile to Angeline Odette, evidently finding the fetching red-head more interesting than Dupont's preparation, or at least wishing to give her that impression.

"We'll begin with the stolen cars." Ramadan shrugged. He could not have been surprised that Dupont knew he was a car thief. He had been arrested three times in the past five years, although charges had been dropped each time due to insufficient evidence. He specialized in luxury vehicles, which were plentiful in the Rhone Valley wine country and in great demand in Eastern Europe. What he probably did not know was that his file had attracted renewed attention during the past twenty-four hours. The recently stolen vehicles the police had found in his Lyon garage would be enough to earn him a prison stay of at least a year. "We're particularly interested in a Renault Clio and a Fiat Punto." She saw Ramadan blink. News reports of the Paris bombings had not yet divulged the car models involved, but Ramadan must have guessed the connection by now. Dupont heard him whistle softly to himself, perhaps wondering how to exploit what he had just learned.

"Suppose someone lifted those cars, but that person knew nothing about what happened to them after they were delivered." Ramadan reached for one of his cigarettes as if to allow Dupont time to consider the hypothetical case. "Would you prosecute that person?"

"If that was all the person knew?" Dupont asked. "In that case, I would tell that person we are not interested in prosecuting car theft."

"So such a person could walk out of this room without any further problems?" Ramadan looked to Dupont for confirmation, then to the others. "Okay, I think we have a deal." Cigarette smoke flowed from the sides of his mouth as he attempted another smile. "A week or so ago I received a special order from an acquaintance in Paris. He wanted two cars in good running condition, popular models that were several years old. I usually do not bother with such cheap cars, but the price he offered was interesting."

"Who asked for the cars?"

"Waleed Yarkas." Thierry Christophe stood and left the room. Within minutes they would have police records of every Yarkas in France. "I don't know him very well," Ramadan continued. "He has a business similar to mine in Saint-Denis, just outside Paris. I sometimes help him find buyers for his cars, and once in a while he has a customer for one of mine. No big deal."

"How did he reach you?" Dupont asked.

Ramadan glanced at the plastic tray on the table. "He called me on that phone."

"Didn't he tell you why he needed the cars?" As Ramadan shook his head, Dupont pressed. "You said it was a special order. He must have told you something."

"A lot of people call me about cars. They don't ask where I get them. I don't ask what they do with them."

"How did you deliver the cars?"

"Yarkas sent two other guys. One was named al-Omari, a fat guy."

"Hani al-Omari?" Dupont asked.

"Yeah, I think that was his name." Ramadan's voice betrayed a note of surprise. "The other one, a younger guy, was called Essabar. He had flowers tattooed on his arm—a *pédé*, maybe. They called me when they got to Lyon." He nodded again at the cell phone on the tray.

Dupont looked down at her notes to help herself concentrate. She did not buy his story about not knowing how the cars would be used. Not with so many connections. She decided to change direction. "What do you know about the *Izmir Queen*?"

The question hung in the air for several seconds. Ramadan's eyes darted from face to face, evidently trying to judge how much they knew. His gaze came to rest upon his mobile phone. "I would like to speak to a lawyer."

"Listen, Mr. Ramadan." Dupont raised her voice slightly. "We will tell you when you can talk to a lawyer. This is not an American crime movie.

You are in the middle of an investigation by the anti-terrorism authorities of France."

Ramadan looked back without betraying any emotion, apparently searching for some clue that might guide his next move. "Anti-terrorism? What makes you think the boat has anything to do with terrorism?" Dupont did not reply, so he continued, "Look, I will tell you what I know, as long as our deal includes the boat."

"Let's hear your story first."

He explained that, on the assumption he was involved at all, he might have been asked by certain friends from Turkey to help unload certain cargo from the boat. Naturally, he would have assumed that such Turkish friends had taken care of any customs or immigration matters relating to such cargo. His job, assuming any of this had occurred, might have also included distributing the cargo, since he had access to vehicles and young men to serve as drivers.

"What kind of cargo?"

"Are we agreed, no prosecution?" Ramadan asked.

"Just answer the question," Dupont said sharply. "If you're not involved in terrorism, then you have nothing to worry about."

"We know the boat contains explosives," Lambert interjected. "What are you going to do with them?"

Ramadan straightened. "No one said anything about explosives! I think they said *girls*."

"Girls?" Lambert repeated, looking puzzled. Seated beside him, Odette drew a transcript from her briefcase.

"You know, girls from Turkey," Ramadan continued. "They need such girls to work in France, maybe in hotels or restaurants, I don't know. I assumed their visas were in order."

"That's not true," Dupont interrupted. "You spoke to your friends about chocolate. That was a code name for explosives, wasn't it?" Lambert and Odette leaned together over the transcript, Odette drawing back Lambert's long hair so she could see the page better.

"The girls from Turkey are dark and sweet." Ramadan put his fingers together against his lips and made a kissing sound. "Delicious. It should be easy for them to find nice husbands."

"No, you spoke about explosions in France," Dupont pressed.

"Sure. It's what happens between a man and a woman." Watching her reaction, his lips spread into a condescending smile bordering on a sneer. "Perhaps you never had the experience."

Dupont watched him coolly. She had half expected a story of this kind. "Look, Mr. Ramadan, if what you say is true, it should be easy enough to verify. The boat, the *Izmir Queen*—when is it due to arrive?"

Ramadan released a derisory gasp. "I thought you guys knew everything." An aroma of tobacco and garlic reached Dupont across the table. "They told me the boat would dock early, but your *gendarme* friends met me at the hotel before I could find out. They said there would be about two dozen girls, so I sent them four vans and drivers."

"So you don't know if the vans met the *Izmir Queen*?"

"I've heard nothing." Ramadan raised his empty hands as if to show his innocence.

A phone rang. Ramadan's eyes darted to the tray, but it was not his. An officer entered the room. "Madam Dupont, it is Monsieur Carpentier calling from Paris. He says it is urgent."

———   ———   ———

The first ship to arrive was *Le Floréal*, a French frigate patrolling the country's southern coast. In the dawn light, the captain easily spotted the smoldering wreck, wisps of black smoke still rising into the sky. Pursuant to orders, *Le Floréal* halted at a distance of one kilometer. With the aid of binoculars, the captain saw that a large part of the cabin and upper deck was blown away where the missile had entered, but the hull seemed to be intact. The *Izmir Queen* was still afloat. A small skiff, apparently empty, bobbed in the sea next to it. The captain adjusted the binoculars when he saw several people in life preservers floating near the wreck. Before he could decide if his orders permitted him to approach for a rescue, he saw the *USS Roosevelt* on the horizon.

The American destroyer was specially equipped to detect and contain radioactive materials. The captain watched her approach at flank speed, then shifted his binoculars back to the floating survivors, spotting others he had missed the first time. Members of his crew moved to the prow to get a closer look. Minutes later, the captain of *Le Floréal* received word that the *Roosevelt* had detected levels of radioactivity somewhat higher than normal, but not dangerous. It was safe to begin the rescue.

A skiff from *Le Floréal* was first to reach two life preservers floating a hundred meters from the paralyzed *Izmir Queen*. They pulled aboard two young women, both alive but barely conscious from shock and cold. A motor launch from the American ship passed them, heading toward another group of life preservers closer to the wreck. More rescue boats arrived, some pausing to pull aboard motionless forms that floated near the surface. A boat equipped with radiation detectors reached the *Izmir Queen*. The exposed interior was filled with twisted metal and smoking debris. The rescuers located more survivors and several lifeless bodies inside the wreckage. The survivors were swiftly brought to *Le Floréal*, while a temporary morgue was organized aboard the *Roosevelt* for the corpses. The French ship had been selected for the survivors because its officers included Turkish and Arabic speakers. After the most seriously injured were taken to the infirmary, they began to question those capable of responding. The interrogators were under orders to get to the bottom of the plot as quickly as possible.

Still in shock, the survivors seemed unable at first to comprehend the questions. Two of the young women began to cry, demanding to know why the *Izmir Queen* had exploded. Then one of the crewmembers, a Turkish sailor who spoke passable French, offered to provide answers. They were carrying mostly passengers this trip, he explained. No, there was nothing unusual on board. He seemed puzzled when they asked about nuclear material. He knew nothing about such a cargo. Then one of the women said they were all from Turkey and were seeking work in France. No, they had no visas, but they intended to apply for them as soon as they arrived. A second crewman said this was the first he had heard about the visa status of the girls. If anyone had known of such a problem, it was the captain and unfortunately he was not aboard *Le Floréal*; perhaps he was among the bodies on the other ship. No, he did not know why the small boat had approached as they neared the Port of Marseille, but perhaps the captain had wished to avoid customs for certain items from Turkey.

"What items?" asked one of the questioners. The two crewmen shrugged in unison. Apparently the purpose of the early-morning transaction with the small boat was a mystery to them. One of the women asked again if the French navy knew why the boat exploded.

"About two dozen," the first sailor said after the interrogators ignored the woman's question and asked him about the number of passengers. When they pressed him once more about their visa status, the first sailor offered a new explanation: "Perhaps they were seeking work in Europe that requires no visas."

"Yes," agreed the second sailor with a smile. "They are all very pretty." The young woman who had asked about the explosion began to cry.

—　—　—

Burt Brown dismissed everyone except Douglas Grebb from the control room around midnight. "Get some sleep," Brown ordered. "We won't know anything more until morning." When the door had closed behind the last departing CIA analyst, Brown removed a pair of cigars from his coat pocket and offered one to Grebb. "Tonight I think we're entitled to ignore the rules." He raised the brow over his good right eye as he lit Grebb's cigar.

An hour later, they read the first reports from the *USS Roosevelt* twenty nautical miles south of Marseille. "They got the right boat," Grebb observed. "But they haven't detected much radioactivity, yet."

"It's still early. Give them time."

"Excuse me, sir." A CIA analyst appeared at the door. "Mr. Carpentier is calling on the secure line from Paris."

When Brown hung up a few minutes later, he was no longer smiling. "Dominique is flying down to Marseille. He says he wants to make sure everything is handled correctly. I suspect he just wants to get his share of the credit."

"A dramatic photo at the scene of his latest victory over terrorism," Grebb quipped.

"Yes, but I also sensed he's nervous about something." After a pause Brown added, "You'd better get over there, too. Make sure they spin things correctly, in case anything got fucked up."

"I was thinking the same thing." Grebb's bony fingers combed back his graying hair.

"Let the French run things, of course. It's their show."

Grebb sighed and stood to leave.

"And, Doug. Don't forget to take someone from Sentinel with you."

CHAPTER 25

Eighth Day of the Investigation

"Was it okay for you?" he asked. They had gone directly from the Agency to her apartment. It started off pretty wild, both of them stirred up by the evening's events, but in the end they lost steam. Was it simply exhaustion from working through the prior night? No, he knew it was something else.

"Yes," she replied after a moment. "It was great."

He remained silent in the darkness as he considered her answer. *Great*. For him it had been something less the last couple of times. The contours of her delicious body still stirred him, but the feelings were not the same. "But something was different, wasn't it?" he asked. "I could feel it." But what was the difference he was feeling? He grasped for the right word. *Mechanical*, he decided. It had become mechanical. But no, it was something more than that.

"Like I told you, Doyle, this has been great, but . . . ." She continued speaking in the darkness. He listened for a while, until after she asked if he could drop off the clothes she had left in his apartment, but he was too tired to reply, too exhausted to sort out his feelings. Sometime later the ringing of the telephone woke him. Leslie lifted the receiver and listened silently before handing it to him. It was two in the morning, he saw on his watch. It took him a few seconds to realize who was speaking. "What did he want?" Leslie asked, now sitting up in the bed, her reddish-brown hair the color of cinnamon under the lamplight.

"He wants me to go to Andrews Air Force Base as soon as possible." She said nothing while Doyle dressed, but he knew what she was thinking.

Their clandestine affair had been discovered, just when she had decided to end it.

Doyle was unable to get back to sleep during the flight to Marseille. He kept asking himself why Howard Silver had selected him to go. He had made the trip sound like a boondoggle, a reward for his good work. Sentinel would have no big role to play, Silver expected, but Doyle could always call them in Washington if any surprises arose. With more plotters to round up, the French might even want to buy some of their software. It could be a big opportunity for a rising star like Doyle, he joked before hanging up. But Doyle sensed there was something Silver had not told him.

Across the aisle two rows ahead, he saw Grebb pour his third miniature bourbon. Collapsed in his seat, he resembled a scarecrow, his iron-gray hair protruding at unkempt angles, his wrinkled suit pitifully oversize for his gaunt frame, looking as though it had been slept in for a week. The air grew turbulent, causing the small CIA plane to shudder and plunge. Staring out the window at the shaking wing, barely visible in the pre-dawn darkness over the Atlantic, Doyle was suddenly seized by a sense of vulnerability. Could enough turbulence tear the wing from the plane? But there was no point in wondering about that: thinking about it would not cause it to happen, and if it did happen, no amount of thinking would save him. Better to think about something else.

As the turbulence subsided, Doyle tried to return his mind to Leslie. *Meet me in the lobby,* he remembered her saying at the start of their spontaneous first date. *In front of the truth motto.* He smiled at the irony of Leslie choosing the truth motto, of all places, for their initial rendezvous. For she had never been truthful with him. Not fully anyway, not about what really counted. But perhaps he had no right to judge her. After all, she had never made him any promises. Maybe it was his fault for misreading her intentions. Another violent bump caused him to look up. A stewardess staggered down the aisle checking seatbelts and appeared relieved to see Doyle still there, as though he might have been tossed overboard. She offered him a drink, whenever the turbulence ended, but he asked only for a glass of water. He wanted to keep his mind sharp while he sorted his confused feelings into rational piles.

When the plane finally landed, it was already mid-afternoon in Marseille. Looking at his fellow passengers, Doyle sensed that the meeting with DST was not going to be the victory celebration that Silver had led him to expect. Grebb had been on the phone several times during the flight and was now speaking in hushed tones to Ronnie Lapoint across the aisle. Lapoint's leaning visage looked intent and mirthless.

When they arrived at the DST regional office, no one was in the lobby to greet them. Doyle spotted a copy of the *International Herald Tribune* on the vacant reception desk. "US ATTACKS TURKISH BOAT NEAR MARSEILLE," the headline read. After a twenty-minute wait, a secretary led them to a large office where Dominique Carpentier sat with Christine Dupont. They offered perfunctory handshakes, but their faces appeared stiff with embarrassment, as though they were greeting former colleagues who had just been convicted of publishing child pornography. "The purpose of this meeting, Mr. Grebb," Carpentier began, after an awkward pause during which no coffee was offered, "is to understand why the United States conducted this shocking military operation near French territorial waters."

"I'm surprised by your question, Dominique. You knew the boat was carrying stolen radioactive material destined for use by terrorists."

"That is what your National Security Advisor told us, and we had similar information from the Russians, but we have seen no hard evidence." Carpentier turned to Dupont.

"We've been interviewing the crew and passengers all afternoon," she said, "at least the ones who are able to talk. None of them knows anything about a radioactive cargo or terrorists. Have you found anything on the boat?" Awaiting Grebb's response, Dupont brushed aside her long forelock as though to observe him better. It was the first time Doyle noticed the unusual color of her eyes, a striking feature that the video conferences had failed to convey.

"Not yet," Grebb admitted, "but we're still looking."

"I am instructed by my government to demand an explanation," Carpentier pressed.

"Come off it, Dominique!" Grebb snapped. "You guys supported the intervention."

"We acknowledge the French government sought American cooperation to investigate the recent events in Paris, but we deny any involvement in the attack on the *Izmir Queen*. France will not accept responsibility for faulty intelligence and imprudent action on the part of the United States. Anything short of a stern rebuke would outrage our public, particularly those of the Muslim faith."

"Why don't we drop the political posturing and try to figure out where we go from here?" Grebb said. "We have plenty of evidence linking the boat to the Paris attack. Your investigation corroborates that, I assume."

"The only link we've confirmed is Abdallah Ramadan," Dupont replied. "He admits he supplied the two cars, but says he had no idea what his customers planned to do with them. We've interrogated him for hours and his story hangs together."

"I'm afraid you're being naïve, Madame Dupont," Grebb said. "You are obviously not considering recent intercepts of Ramadan's plans to meet the *Izmir Queen* and receive the stolen radioactive material."

"Slow down," Carpentier interrupted. "The calls we intercepted— legally, I might add— contain several references to the *Izmir Queen*, but we've seen no evidence the boat was carrying anything radioactive, other than the initial report from the Russians."

Doyle was already reaching into his brief case. "Please look at this transcript," Grebb directed. "It's a call we intercepted in Syria yesterday. You will see references to the *Izmir Queen* and her cargo of nuclear material."

"I'm sorry we didn't see this earlier," Dupont said after she finished reading. "It could have helped our investigation."

"You asked not to see them," Grebb reminded her.

"That applied only to recordings made illegally in France," Dupont retorted.

"But if the *Izmir Queen* was carrying radioactive material," Carpentier cut in, his voice betraying impatience, "where is the material now?"

"We're wondering that, too," Grebb replied. "Whatever they did with it, Ramadan's group was planning to use the stuff for another attack in France. That's what justified the intervention."

"No, that is where you lose me," Dupont replied. "How do you link Ramadan with plans for a dirty bomb attack in France?"

"Look at his other calls, Christine. You can see the links in his own words." As Grebb spoke, Doyle passed out more transcripts.

Dupont flipped through her copies, noting the dates. "Some of these calls were intercepted before Magistrate Joubert granted us the wiretap order, weren't they?"

"I suppose we can look at them informally," Carpentier ventured. "We had nothing to do with the intercepts and we won't use them in any French proceeding." The room fell silent as everyone began reading.

"Who translated these?" Dupont asked after a few seconds.

"The translations were handled by Sentinel Systems," Grebb replied, turning to Doyle for confirmation.

"That's right. We contracted with several Arabic translators."

"We intercepted some of the same calls after the wiretap order," Dupont said, "but our translations are different."

"There are always differences among translators," Grebb objected. "But here the references to 'bombs' and 'explosions' are unmistakable. Some of it is in code, of course, but words like 'weddings' and 'cakes' in this context are clearly references to attacks and explosives. We've seen the same codes from other terrorist groups."

"They even talk about France burning and Frenchmen exploding," Doyle read from a transcript. "That seems clear enough."

"We believe they were talking about girls," Dupont replied. "What you've translated as 'cakes' and 'bombs' is Arabic slang for prostitutes. The references to 'weddings' are sexual encounters. All the talk about 'burning' and 'exploding' is . . . how do you call it in English?"

"Orgasms?" Grebb suggested.

"Yes, exactly," Dupont replied. "That is why the boat was full of young women. They were destined for the brothels around Marseille."

"Our translators did say some of this was ambiguous," Doyle admitted. "But with all the evidence that the boat contained nuclear material, it seemed like a reasonable interpretation." He paused abruptly. Ronnie Lapoint studied him from a corner of the room, his bloodless face looking ghostly under the florescent lights.

"A reasonable interpretation," Grebb repeated. "You didn't mention ambiguities in Langley last night." The room fell silent as Grebb appeared to calculate something mentally. "We better go through all the original interceptions again," he resumed. "Do you guys have any good Arabic translators here in Marseille?"

While they awaited the experts, Doyle sat in silence, just beginning to realize the mistake and the consequences, but still resisting the idea that he might be responsible. Looking around the office, his gaze fell on Christine Dupont, whom he found even more alluring in person than he had during the video conference a few days earlier. So much had changed since then, he reflected. Prior to that first discussion of the mutilated SIM card, his duties at Sentinel were growing, rather rapidly it seemed to him at the time, just as some of Sentinel's projects were merging into the CIA's operations. But afterwards, his job transformed in ways that seemed subtle at the time but radical in retrospect, a tiny quantum leap of responsibility. Still, he did not foresee that he would play such a central role, albeit a minor one, in the investigation that swiftly followed. But looking back now, he realized that the video conference with Dupont had pulled him from the secure periphery of the war on terrorism into its morally charged nucleus.

Still watching Dupont across the room, Doyle realized she was looking back at him. He was stuck by the paradoxical quality of her grey-green eyes. Their penetrating sparkle reflected a youthful spirit, yet they appeared to be the eyes of an older woman, as though they had witnessed the good and evil of an entire lifetime. Meeting her gaze, he had the uncomfortable sensation that she had already judged him and found him to be at fault. As her eyes returned to whatever she was reading, he wondered if he had detected, beyond Dupont's cold judgment, a faint glimmer of compassion. But he realized that if she felt sympathy for him, he was beginning to doubt he deserved any.

CHAPTER 26

Ninth Day of the Investigation

It was not yet dawn when Doyle O'Gara took the taxi to *Hôpital de la Concepcion*. It contained the regional medical center for severe burns. A policeman was posted inside to keep out the reporters. Doyle showed his CIA contractor pass to prove he was not a reporter, but the officer said it was too early to disturb the patients, even for official interviews. Doyle asked if he could just observe the burn victims, promising he would ask no questions. The cop shrugged his shoulders and pointed down the corridor to the nurse's station. "Nine burn victims made it to the hospital," he called after Doyle. "But three were luckier than the others."

The nurse proved more difficult. Doyle flashed the CIA pass again, as though it were a police badge, but she refused to let him enter the burn ward. Doyle insisted he was conducting an urgent investigation for the United States government. The lie seemed to shake her resolve. She motioned for him to follow her into the ward, on condition that he say absolutely nothing to the patients.

There were six inside the ward. Doyle approached one of the beds and saw a young woman lying under a gauze tent. He could see her face and body were covered with burns. Some sort of ointment had been smeared over her skin and thick bandages had been placed over her eyes. She seemed to be unconscious, but as Doyle came near, her head turned toward him, as if she could see him through the bandages. The damage to her face was mostly obscured by the ointment, but from what Doyle could see, it was awfully red and swollen. Her lips and nose seemed to be wrenched to one side, as though her face had melted and then congealed back into a different form. "What are the tubes?" he whispered.

"Some are for fluid resuscitation," the nurse explained. "We are trying to irrigate the burned areas. The other tubes are for analgesics. We have them on morphine sulfate, so they are not feeling anything now. They will feel a lot when we have to reduce the dose." The nurse breathed deeply, as though she were anticipating the pain. "She has fourth-degree burns on her arms," she murmured, "so they will probably need to amputate." The girl's body shifted slightly and then seemed to stretch. "Don't worry," the nurse said, evidently reading his mind. "They sometimes move in their sleep, but she cannot hear us."

Doyle moved further into room. The next patient appeared to be in worse condition. They had finished the first round of emergency skin grafts, the nurse explained. It looked to Doyle as if the young woman had been butchered. "She has third-degree burns over a quarter of her body as well as some fourth-degree burns," the nurse said. "It is doubtful she will survive, but we are doing the best we can." Doyle regarded the girl's hideously swollen face smeared with ointment. After a few moments, he turned to look at the third bed.

Perhaps he should have been prepared for what he would see, should have anticipated that the victims would be arranged in ascending order of trauma. But he was not prepared, either for what he saw or for the awful thought that accompanied the sight. Later, he would wrack his brain to understand the origin and intention of the thought. Had it formed defensively around his mind, like a protective shell to block out the guilt that was starting to overcome him? Or had it sprung forth aggressively from some venomous recess of his soul that had never before erupted to the surface? Whatever its source or purpose, he regretted the thought instantly, but there it was. He could never erase it from his mind, any more than he could undo the devastation that lay before him on the third bed.

He turned his head and started walking out of the burn ward. "Don't you want to see the others?" the nurse asked with a sharp whisper that echoed down the corridor. No, he did not. He could not endure seeing the others. Was it because he found their condition too intolerable to regard, or did he fear that seeing them would bring back the same thought?

When he reached the end of the corridor, the cop looked up from a copy of *L'Equipe* and repeated the question the nurse had asked: "Do you want to see the others now?" He may have seen confusion in Doyle's face, because he added, "The other three are downstairs, in the morgue." *Three were luckier than the others.* The cop's earlier words came back to Doyle and he suddenly understood. "Like I said," the cop went on unnecessarily, "nine made it to the hospital alive but three of them died by the end of the afternoon. It was better for them, if you see what I mean." As the cop returned to *L'Equipe*, Doyle stared at the upside-down photos of the Marseille team defeating a Spanish rival the night before.

The cop must have thought he was waiting for more information, because he looked up again and began reciting figures. In total, nineteen people had been killed or severely burned. Thirteen of the victims were young women, plus the captain, three of his crew and the two men in the small boat. All of the deaths were caused by burning or drowning, but some of the drowned ones had been burned as well. The cop seemed well informed about the investigation. None of the passengers or crew had confessed, he said, but it was pretty clear what they were up to. They had been smuggling the girls into the country, maybe drugs, too. That accounted for the small skiff that had met the boat. The Americans had asked the French to examine everything for traces of radiation, including the corpses, but no radiation had been found. He asked Doyle what he thought of the six women still in the burn ward, of their chances of survival. Doyle said he had no idea.

The sun had risen over the hills east of the Marseille by the time Doyle left *Hôpital de la Concepcion*. Several taxis waited on the street, so he got into the first. The driver said something in French. "Where to, mister?" he asked again in English after Doyle failed to respond. Doyle said he wanted to go somewhere in the countryside, he didn't care where. The driver started the engine and headed the car toward the hills north of Marseille.

"You American?" he asked after they had driven a few kilometers.

"No, I'm Danish," Doyle lied.

"Good. They killing lots of people yesterday. On the radio." He drove on, still heading north toward the hills. "Americans," the driver added over his shoulder. After a few minutes he asked again where Doyle wanted to go. Doyle said he didn't know, just somewhere outside the city. "I taking you Aix-en-Provence. Not far, but tourists going there."

Doyle said nothing as he looked out the window and saw the Provence countryside for the first time. Fields of sunflower and lavender adorned both sides of the road ahead, their alternating colors blazing in the intense morning sunlight. Looking further ahead, Doyle saw dark clouds approaching from the north, their black bellies sliding slowly over the sunlit hills. As the clouds advanced, the illuminated hillsides seemed to grow brighter against the dark background, until the brightness appeared unreal to Doyle, as though the hills had become gaily painted plywood replicas intended to promote a residential development. He pressed his face against the window glass, trying to see if the hills were real or not, and heard himself shouting for the driver to stop.

"I thought you going Aix," the driver protested. "Twenty kilometers."

Doyle told him again to stop, he would walk the rest of the way.

The driver seemed angry when he saw Doyle had only dollars. He started to calculate the exchange rate, but Doyle threw a bunch of bills on the front seat and opened the door. He figured it was more than he owed, whatever the exchange rate, but he did not care about the money. Walking away, he heard the taxi door open and thought the driver was coming to argue for more, but then he heard the door slam shut and the tires rush against the gravel.

He continued walking away from the main highway, following a narrow road between two fields. He thought again about the hospital. Then he realized he had never stopped thinking about the hospital, not once since he had turned away from the third bed, not even while he had talked to the cop in the corridor. He had not stopped thinking about it during the taxi ride and he wondered if he would ever stop thinking about it. Then the awful thought came back to his mind, the same thought that had come when he saw the girl in the third bed. He fought to press it back, still wondering about its origin and its purpose, but he could not stop the thought from returning. *At least I saved her from becoming a whore.* It was true, he reassured himself, if they had not come along and blasted her boat, she would be getting her initiation right now from one of Ramadan's buddies in Marseille. He pictured her lying on her back under some two-hundred-pound sailor reeking of wine and sweat. How old was she anyway? It was hard to tell with her face so distorted. By the size of her body and what was left of her youthful skin, she was probably still a teenager. Then he started screaming. *At least I saved her from becoming a whore!* But he was not really screaming, not out loud—not yet, anyway—just screaming in his mind as he started walking faster down the narrow road. The word *whore* echoed in his silent scream as he saw the image of the girl's face melting away as if she were a deformed character in a sick cartoon. "But you knew!" he screamed. Now he was screaming out loud and running along the road. "You knew!" His words roared skyward before they fell into silence among the fields of lavender and sunflower.

He stopped running. Ahead of him on the narrow road, he saw the pavement darken where the approaching clouds were beginning to rain. His mind replayed the events in the Langley control room, frantically editing new versions. Like a child watching his bedroom go up in flames after playing with matches, he could still not believe he had caused the catastrophe. He imagined himself speaking up during the last fateful minutes before the Predator attack, saving the *Izmir Queen* passengers from death and agonizing burns. He watched the wet part of the road approach him, halting occasionally before it lurched forward, as though the clouds were hesitating in their stealthy advance toward him. He smelled the air grow humid as the first drops of rain hit the warm asphalt around him. Then he felt the rain on top of him. First a few heavy drops, then a swelling deluge. Now he was screaming again, screaming obscenities up into the pouring rain, imagining it might be possible with enough rain to wash away what had happened, if he just stood there long enough, and then he saw the girl in the third bed, saw her through the cleansing rain, and he realized her suffering was just beginning and would not end with the rain. Then he turned around and walked back down the narrow road toward the main highway, shivering but no longer screaming.

They were waiting for him at the end of the road where it rejoined the highway. Douglas Grebb rested his tall body against the car, holding an umbrella above his head. "Your cell phone," he explained as he motioned Doyle into the back seat. Ronnie Lapoint was behind the steering wheel. Doyle was surprised to see Stan Stebbins sitting on the passenger side. He must have flown to Marseille overnight, after they realized what a mess they had to clean up. As Lapoint started the car, Grebb came right to the point. "Why were you trying to flee?"

"I wasn't fleeing. I just wanted some time to think."

"You have a lot to think about, O'Gara. Have you thought about why you failed to tell us about the inaccurate translations?"

"I didn't realize they were inaccurate until yesterday."

Stebbins in the front seat turned and said, "You're lying, O'Gara. Your translator told you before." The words snapped out of his mouth like the barking of an excited dog.

"What do you mean?" Doyle asked, still shivering in his wet clothes.

"Jihan Ammar," Stebbins replied. "She told you that she could hardly understand the Ramadan intercepts."

"I explained to Howard Silver that there were ambiguities," Doyle shot back. "He exaggerated things during the meeting."

"If you thought he exaggerated why didn't you say something?" Grebb countered. "Silver says he put you in charge of the translations. He was relying on you. That's why he insisted you come to the meeting."

"And that's where you fucked up." It was Stebbins again from the front seat. "You never corrected Silver when he started talking about dirty bombs. All you had to do was raise your hand."

"I didn't think it was the right place to correct my boss. Besides, Ramadan's precise words seemed like minor details among all the other evidence you guys were discussing."

"Minor details?" Grebb repeated.

"Yes, at the time," Doyle said. "Ramadan was clearly linked to the Paris group and he was meeting the *Izmir Queen* to receive the stolen radioactive material. I still don't understand why you haven't recovered it. Do you?"

"We assume the stuff sunk to the bottom of the Mediterranean, but that's not the point, O'Gara. We never would have blown a hole in that boat if you had told us Ramadan was expecting a cargo of call girls."

"This is not the first time you've concealed information from the Agency," interjected Stebbins from the front. "We know you've had secret Internet messages and phone calls." Stebbins reached into his briefcase and removed a file. Doyle could see over the seat that it contained transcripts.

"He calls himself too, too excited," Stebbins continued with a derisive smile. "Would you care to tell us what you were doing with this guy, if it's not too personal?"

"I thought 22excited was a girl, at least most of the time. I was curious, so I responded. Nothing came of it and I never revealed anything about my work." Doyle saw Lapoint gazing at him skeptically in the rearview mirror.

"Why didn't you report the contact to the Agency?" Grebb demanded.

"I told you," Doyle said. "I thought it was a private matter."

"Have you ever seen the inside of a Turkish jail, O'Gara?"

"What?"

"I don't think you realize how much trouble you're in," Grebb said softly. "They're not very happy in Turkey about having so many of their people die on that boat." Doyle looked back at him steadily, but felt his heart pounding faster. The purplish blotches under Grebb's eyes looked sinister, as though he had donned an African war mask. "If you don't start cooperating, the Turks may ask us to turn you over for questioning. Believe me, their methods may not be as gentle as ours. It would be out of our control." Doyle glanced out the window and saw that the car was moving faster. The frightening scenario raced through his mind. When his parents inquired, the CIA would claim he had disappeared in France. The French would back them up, saying he was last seen walking into a lonely field in Provence visibly disturbed. A possible suicide?

As the car hurtled toward Marseille, Doyle began to tell them everything he could remember about his exchanges with 22excited. From their questions he could tell they'd recovered the messages, despite all the changes of computers, e-mails and chat rooms, but they wanted to hear everything again from him.

"Didn't you realize that this guy was a terrorist trying to recruit you?" Grebb asked.

"What? Absolutely not! Like I've told you a dozen times, I suspected it was a girl from work, maybe even Leslie, or some prankster like Suresh. The initial e-mails were flirtatious and the later ones seemed like outrageous jokes. It was only near the end that they seemed too nosy about my work, so I cut them off."

The corners of Grebb's lips twisted in disgust. "You are still lying to us, O'Gara. Your friend called you from Paris the day of the bombing. We have the phone records." Doyle had no idea what Grebb was talking about, but he recognized immediately the terrifying implications of his words. Stebbins passed another transcript over the seat. It was a billing record for Doyle's personal cell phone. A call received on September 1 was highlighted. Doyle let out an audible cry when he saw the caller had used the SIM card nicknamed *Fromage* by the Paris team. He knew the number by heart after so many days of investigation. His mind scrambled in several directions, trying to grasp how it could possibly be on his phone record. Was it a forgery or a high-tech prank? Was he being framed?

"I think I should speak to a lawyer."

No one spoke for several seconds. Grebb looked out the window as though he had spotted something interesting in the Provence countryside. Stebbins broke the silence. "Do they permit lawyers during interrogations in Turkey?"

"I'm not sure," Lapoint replied. "Maybe not until the trial."

Doyle realized his mistake and reversed course. He would continue to cooperate. They would get to the bottom of the mystery together, he was sure. The questioning continued in the car until they reached Marseille and then upstairs in the hotel room. Doyle clung to his defenses at first, unwilling to accept blame while so many questions remained unanswered. Grebb and his two lieutenants, a triple tag team of wrestlers, seemed to grow more energetic as the afternoon darkened into evening.

Oddly, in the midst of the questioning, Doyle's thoughts turned to his parents and, more precisely, to his boyhood on their farm in Northern Michigan. His mother and father, divorced for several years, had long ago drifted to the periphery of his life, but he sometimes missed certain spiritual qualities that he associated with his childhood, such as the certainty of following a well-worn path through the woods or the purity of plunging into an icy lake. Alone with his interrogators and their sinister theories, Doyle felt as never before how far he had traveled from such purity and certainty. He also thought of Leslie. Their romance was over, he realized, but she was perhaps the only friend he had left in the world. He had a few in Ann Arbor, mostly pals and girlfriends from his university days, but none had stayed in touch after he had moved to Washington to start his new life. If Leslie were with him now, he imagined, she would awaken him from this nightmare with an impudent pinch and spirit him away for the evening in one of her off-beat karaoke bars. His present companions from the CIA offered him no such escape. Under their relentless questions, Doyle at last admitted the guilt he had screamed out in the rainy Provence field. By the time they finished late that night, Doyle felt the cleansing relief of a penitent sinner after confession. The only thing he could still not wash from his conscience was the haunting memory of the burn ward.

CHAPTER 27

One Month after the Paris Attack

When Doyle saw his parents in the courtroom, they looked mismatched and out of place. It had been months since he had seen either of them and years since he had seen them together. His father bore a stoic expression, his habitual stance when faced with adversity, but also looked perplexed to see his only son being led to the defendant's table by a US marshal. His mother wore an elegant mauve suit that Doyle did not recognize. He felt touched and vaguely embarrassed that she might have bought a new outfit for the occasion. The judge began to speak, but Doyle was not listening closely. He was still wondering how he would explain to his parents the events that had led to this unsought reunion. They had not yet hired a lawyer, due to lack of time or disagreement over the choice, Doyle was not sure which, so a public defender sat next to him. As the judge read the charges, Doyle realized that telling his story would be as difficult as Dorothy explaining the Land of Oz to her folks back home in Kansas. No, it would be more like her describing how she had killed the Wicked Witch of the West, except that in Doyle's case there had been nineteen victims. The public defender whispered for Doyle to stop muttering to himself and then, after the judge had finished reading, prompted him to say not guilty. It was over in five minutes.

The prosecutor had filed the criminal complaint in the United States District Court for the Eastern District of Virginia. The courthouse was located in Alexandria, not far from the CIA. Doyle supposed they wanted to keep him within easy reach. Rising from the table to confront his parents, he felt strangely indifferent to what lay ahead. The government could not punish him any more than he already wanted to punish himself.

A few days after the arraignment, Doyle met Stuart Brons, the lawyer he had hired with the help of his parents. The law firm, which specialized in criminal defense, was located in a sleek, low-rise office block near Pennsylvania Avenue. Doyle's father had assured him the firm had considerable experience defending people accused of violating national security laws. Judging by the firm's offices, defending criminals was a good business. A receptionist led Doyle from the paneled lobby to the personal quarters of Stuart Brons. He was seated behind a massive desk of glass and chrome, studying Doyle's file. When he stood, Doyle wondered what kind of impression the middle-aged man would make upon a jury. His suit looked expensive but did not quite compensate for his short stature; his sparse red hair was combed neatly across his scalp yet only seemed to highlight the territory lost to baldness; his smile would have appeared hearty had it not been framed by the ruddy complexion of an alcoholic. As they shook hands, Brons placed his left arm firmly around Doyle's shoulder and drew him to the seat before his desk, a gesture apparently intended to inspire Doyle with confidence, or at least to prevent him from fleeing. After returning to his side of the desk, Brons cleared his throat and began a little speech about the conversation being privileged and nothing leaving the room without Doyle's consent, a speech he had evidently delivered often.

It took Doyle several hours to tell his story, interrupted frequently by Brons's probing questions. By the time Doyle finished, Brons seemed to have lost interest, as though he had heard the same story too many times before. He seemed more interested in the file now, flipping through it expertly with his thick index finger in search of information, the significance of which Doyle could only imagine. Then Brons appeared to lose interest in the file, turning his attention back to Doyle, still seated across the desk.

"I've spoken to the US Attorney," Brons disclosed. "His version of the story is pretty much in line with yours, except for some important details. Your translation errors clearly contributed to the *Izmir Queen* tragedy, but he will have trouble convincing a jury to convict you of homicide and bodily injury, even the negligent varieties. If the jury comes to understand your motives and the pressure you were under, they'll be inclined to cut you some slack. You were in the middle of a war; you thought the enemy was about to strike again; in the fog of battle you fired in the wrong direction. But your intention was always to protect your country." He paused as if he were already considering how his words would sound to the jury. "That's why I'm not too surprised the US Attorney is already offering us a deal. I think he's afraid to go to trial."

"What kind of deal?" Doyle asked.

"If you plead guilty to aiding terrorists, they will drop the current charges."

"Aiding terrorists? They can't prove any of that."

"Can you explain the guy who contacted you by Internet and phoned you from Paris?" Brons appeared to study Doyle's reaction. "The government seems more interested in that part of the case, even though the *Izmir Queen* homicide and bodily injury charges may be more serious." Doyle must have looked puzzled, because Brons came around the desk and sat next to him. "Look, Mr. O'Gara, let's go over the cards the prosecutor has in his hand. First, he has the big boss at Sentinel Systems, Howard Silver. He will say you misrepresented the translations of the telephone interceptions from the guy in Lyon, what's his name?" He pulled the file closer and searched his notes. "Oh yeah, Abdallah Ramadan." Brons picked up a pencil and underlined the name. "Mr. Silver makes a big point about how many times he told you to have the translations checked by multiple translators. According to Silver, you never complained about lack of resources." Brons flipped to another page. "Faced with the emergency, they had no time to recheck your work, but if you had said something, they certainly would have slowed things down." His finger moved further down the page. "He will say he relied on you during the critical meeting. He looked over to you several times and you nodded in confirmation. That is the story Mr. Silver will tell."

"Based on the testimony of the translator, Jihan Ammar, they think they can show you were aware of ambiguities in the translations. Miss Ammar even says you told her not to double check portions of the transcripts that would have clarified the ambiguities." Doyle's face evidently betrayed surprise. "Yeah, that is a damaging bit," Brons acknowledged. "She says there were jokes in the unchecked parts that revealed they were talking about hookers rather than explosives." He wrote something in the margin of his notes. "But that is only half their case. They will also make a big point about you not reporting the suspicious Internet contacts, in violation of your contract with Sentinel and your CIA security clearance. They have a CIA employee"—he looked down at his notes again—"Leslie Jumana, I believe, yes. She is expected to testify she told you to file such a report and you led her to believe you had done so." Brons gave Doyle a quizzical look, as if expecting him to explain the omission. "Those are their big cards. They think they can convince the jury that if you had disclosed the suspicious Internet contacts or the ambiguities in the transcripts, then the Agency would never have attacked the boat. Their theory conveniently allows them to blame you for the entire mess."

Brons smiled, turning his fleshy palms up and lifting his shoulders slightly. "If you take the deal on the table, they will drop the homicide and bodily injury charges, which carry heavy penalties, but they will still make you spend four years in prison for aiding terrorism."

"But that charge is absurd!" Doyle protested. "What do you think?"

"I would advise you to reject the offer. As I said before, I doubt they want to go to trial. That will raise too many embarrassing questions about the CIA's negligence. They have already achieved their main objective simply by indicting you. That's why they rushed to file charges; they like having your face in the media better than the smoking boat and young victims. If you reject the offer, there's a good chance they'll drop the case before trial. Even if they insist on going before a jury, we will still have a good chance to win. We may be able to keep out some of their evidence on the grounds they refused your request for a lawyer in France. It is not clear how Miranda applies to the CIA overseas, but it is worth a try. Of course, we'll need to come up with an explanation for those e-mails you failed to report." Brons raised his pencil to his rosy face and tapped his temple as though trying to dislodge some half-forgotten fact from his memory. "Also that phone call from Paris; that part is pretty weird. In any case, we should be able to show all the CIA's errors of judgment. They will try to block some of the evidence on national security grounds, but the jury will see that a lot of others were equally involved in the fiasco. They just picked you to blame."

"Maybe I deserve the blame," Doyle said quietly.

"How do you figure that?"

"I sat in the CIA control room and heard Howard Silver exaggerate the transcripts," Doyle said. "I don't recall nodding in confirmation, but I did remain silent. It wasn't because I was intimidated; it was because I really wanted them to destroy that boat."

"Because you believed it was filled with terrorists and stolen nuclear material."

"No," Doyle shot back. "I knew there were ambiguities in the translations, but I figured it was worth taking the risk. I should have said something. Innocent people are burned or dead because of me. Maybe *I am* guilty of homicide and bodily injury."

Brons grimaced and twisted slightly in his chair before responding. "Look, Mr. O'Gara, you're paying me to provide you a defense. This is not a confessional or a therapy session. It is not for you to decide whether you are guilty or not. Like everyone else involved in this case, you're confused because they never found any radioactive material on the *Izmir Queen*. That little mystery has caused you to doubt your judgment. Well you might be interested to know that the boat *was* carrying ingredients for a dirty bomb."

"What? I don't understand. You mean they found it after all?"

"Yes, but not where you expected. The details are classified, or so the US Attorney claims, but he told me the stuff was apparently taken off the boat in Turkey. The Turkish authorities recovered it last week south of the Port of Trabzon."

"In Turkey?" Doyle's mind raced, trying to understand how that location squared with all the evidence he had seen during the investigation.

"They think the Muslim Brotherhood of Syria cooked up a deal to sell the radioactive material to Kurdish terrorists in Turkey." Brons checked his notes. "Yes, to the PKK, the Kurdish separatists."

Doyle looked past Brons, through the window, into the clear autumn sky above Washington, considering how the new information fit with everything else he knew. "So our interpretation of the Syria intercept was correct; the guys from the local Muslim Brotherhood were talking about a dirty bomb attack."

"Yes, but an attack in Turkey, not in France. They think Istanbul was their target."

Doyle's heart sunk as he realized the errors they had made that night. Why had no one considered the possibility of a different destination for the radioactive material? If they had, then they might have interpreted the Ramadan intercepts correctly.

"Of course, you didn't know any of this back then," Brons added. "For you, the Syrian intercept confirmed the stuff on the *Izmir Queen* was to be used in a dirty bomb attack, so when you heard Ramadan was rushing to meet the boat in Marseille, you naturally jumped to the conclusion the attack would take place there."

Doyle continued to stare out the window, trying to reconstruct that night. After a long moment he asked if he could have a few days to think over the offer from the US Attorney.

Brons shrugged his bulky shoulders. "Sure, take all the time you want. They won't be in a hurry to settle until the public loses interest. Right now, you're their cover story."

CHAPTER 28

Two Months after the Paris Attack

Doyle O'Gara's legal problems were largely ignored in Paris, where Christine Dupont was swiftly wrapping up the largest terrorism case in recent French history. The first suspect to be arrested, a rotund Saudi immigrant named Hani al-Omari, had appeared incredulous when police interrupted the dinner he was enjoying with his parents and young wife at one of the family's apartments in Marseille. He denied all knowledge of the matter until Dupont mentioned a cooperative car thief named Abdallah Ramadan. Apparently believing he could gain leniency by disclosing a few bits of the truth, particularly those bits that implicated others, al-Omari revealed that the mastermind of the attack was a Syrian named Mohammed Jamal who had first appeared in Paris with his partner, Yusuf Ghamdi, only a week or two before the attack. Al-Omari claimed his only involvement had been to drive from Lyon to Paris one of the cars purchased from Ramadan. Like Ramadan, he'd had no idea how they intended to use the car.

Al-Omari did not mention his friends Waleed Yarkas and Zacarias Essabar, but his Saint-Denis neighbors soon identified them to the police. A few days later both men were arrested in the southern city of Toulouse where they had gone into hiding. They were reported by a shopkeeper who noticed they spent money too freely. He was among the millions of French Muslims who condemned the Paris attack.

To increase pressure on al-Omari, Dupont pointed out that several of the bombing victims were citizens of the United States, a country that still imposed the death penalty long banned in Europe. His continued cooperation, she implied, would be a factor in deciding how to handle American extradition requests. When she expressed disappointment that he had not helped them track down Yarkas and Essabar, neither of whom was talking yet, al-Omari raised his bid with one more bit of the truth: He had seen an Algerian youth named Ali Benhadj in the company of Jamal and Ghamdi. He believed this same youth might somehow be involved, as al-Omari had not seen him in the neighborhood since the bombing. They should check his Saint-Denis apartment for DNA traces, al-Omari suggested, as Benhadj had once visited him, although he barely knew the youth and had no idea what role, if any, he might have played in the horrible events in question.

Meanwhile, to satisfy calls for progress, Dupont fed more details to the media. Photographs of the Saint-Denis jihadists appeared for the first time: Hani al-Omari, his full lips pursed within a circular beard, attempting to smile for the police; the acne-rippled face of Zacarias Essabar with his earring shining brightly under the camera flash; the contemptuous stare of Waleed Yarkas, his livid scar partitioning his right cheek, a broken tooth visible in his half-smiling mouth. A few days later, pictures of the suicide bomber, Ali Benhadj, a/k/a Abu Salem, joined the others. His expression in the French visa photo appeared aloof and judgmental, oddly pretentious for a young man of nineteen years, even a bit comical. Another photo, taken at the Algiers airport, showed him in eclectic costume: a tight-fitting bomber jacket of brown leather, the parting gift from his mother, above baggy trousers of white cotton reminiscent of an Algerian peasant, topped off with a baseball cap over his short hair and a Marlboro hanging from his mouth. An article accompanying the photos contained brief quotes from his martyrdom video found on a jihadist website, although more space was devoted to a psychological profile provided by terrorism experts.

The following week Lebanese authorities arrested Sheik Musawi al Amin, the spiritual father of the Saint-Denis plotters, thanks to more leads supplied by al-Omari, who now seemed desperate to win leniency by providing information before police discovered it for themselves. Despite his increased cooperation, however, al-Omari was unable to shed any light on the whereabouts of the alleged leaders, Mohammed Jamal and Yusuf Ghamdi. Both had disappeared and presumably remained at large. Public interest in the mysterious foreign participants subsided when no further attacks ensued and attention turned to the upcoming trial of the Saint-Denis jihadists. Perhaps the government had even invented Jamal and Ghamdi, one of the new political bloggers argued, as part of its ceaseless campaign to increase defense spending and reduce civil liberties.

Preparing for the trial, Dupont followed reports about the case against Doyle O'Gara in the United States. She found it surprising that he had been singled out as the culprit behind the CIA's terrible decision to attack the *Izmir Queen*. She recalled his role in the botched translations, of course, but she wondered how such a marginal character, a techie working for a CIA contractor, could have managed to cause so much trouble. *That pudgy nerd.* She smiled to recall the charming American phrase that Douglas Grebb had used to describe him. Though he had been a minor player from her perspective, she felt she had done him one big favor: Her capture of the Saint-Denis gang and the publication of their photos had removed Mr. O'Gara from the front pages, at least in France where the public was more interested in the barbarous attack on the *Champs-Élysées* than in the unfortunate destruction of the *Izmir Queen*. As for the rest of his problems, she could do nothing more than wish him *bonne chance*.

— — —

".... the suspected terrorist accomplice, Doyle O'Gara of Tyson's Corner, Virginia ..."

Doyle heard his name on television with increasing frequency thanks to reliable sources close to the investigation, as they were described, who fed reporters details of Doyle's mysterious contacts with Islamic radicals and his sabotage of the CIA's investigation. Television commentators in brightly colored shirts and blouses debated degrees of culpability and penalties. The events they recounted sounded familiar to Doyle, yet they were strangely distorted, turned into bite-sized versions suitable for TV viewers to consume like appetizers with a glass of Pinot Noir while preparing dinner. After ten minutes of debate and a brief pause for commercials, the commentators generally concurred that the events off the coast of Marseille had been disgraceful and that someone needed to be held accountable. Doyle emerged as the leading candidate, although some advocated firing the Director of the CIA or impeaching the President. The country was justifiably outraged.

What to do? The question was constantly on Doyle's mind. He was inclined to follow his lawyer's advice to reject the plea bargain offer. He should not be asked to bear all the responsibility alone. Sentinel Systems, particularly Suresh Kumar, was negligent for accepting too much translation work without adequate translators. Doyle should never have been forced to depend upon a sole translator, herself exhausted at the time, to translate critical messages. More important, Howard Silver had exaggerated the translations, omitting ambiguities that Doyle was sure he had mentioned. Silver's distortions may have started out as mere puffery of Sentinel's services, the half truths of an inveterate salesman, but the master of corporate damage control was now deliberately lying to deflect responsibility for the disastrous consequences. Surely the jury would see through his mendacity. As for the CIA, Douglas Grebb had been negligent in rushing to conclusions before comparing notes with the French. That simple step would have revealed the translation discrepancies, as they later discovered in Marseille. Higher up the ladder, Burt Brown and Stephen Holbrook should have at least tried to have the *Izmir Queen* intercepted before ordering her destroyed by a Hellfire missile. It later came to light that a French customs boat could probably have reached her in time.

As Stuart Brons often said, there was plenty of blame to go around.

Blame for just about everyone except Christine Dupont, it seemed. She was basking in public acclaim for the quick roundup of the Saint-Denis jihadists. Journalists found the photogenic young woman to be the perfect heroine to personify society's triumph of over the new enemy. Adulatory articles recounted her successful investigation and speculated on her possible appointment as the next Minister of Justice. Looking at the accompanying pictures, Doyle saw that her stylish coiffure was now an inch or two longer, a few gray highlights lending her a sagacious look. He studied Dupont's eyes, the same eyes that had judged him so swiftly in Marseille, searching for the glimmer of compassion he thought he had seen in them. But if her eyes still contained any sympathy for him, Doyle could not detect it in the photos.

Doyle also studied the pictures of the Saint-Denis jihadists. He was surprised, even disappointed, to see that the opposing army in the war on terrorism looked like a troupe of motley clowns, but he was also seized by a desire to know more about them. He scrutinized the brief biographical sketches that emerged in the media, searching for telling details that might explain his adversaries. He was puzzled by the absence of information about the foreign participants, Jamal and Ghamdi. Not so much as a photo of them had appeared. Were they already captured and under interrogation in some secret CIA black site outside the United States? Or were they still at large, about to resurface with fresh *noms de guerre* upon some new battlefield? Their motives and fates seemed essential parts in his own story, but until more news came to light, they would remain incomplete characters, inhabiting unfinished chapters.

What to do? Doyle knew his career was over at Sentinel. He could probably not find a decent job anywhere for years. If Brons was right, he might avoid prison by rejecting the plea offer, but could he ever restart his career or overcome his guilt? No matter how many others were to blame, it was his own silence in the CIA control room that had caused the *Izmir Queen* catastrophe. The intense remorse he had experienced in Provence had subsided, but left in its place was a dull sense of shame and a growing desire to pay for the damage he had caused. The entire country was demanding that someone be held responsible. The crime was too ghastly to be ignored as just another case of collateral damage. Someone had to be punished, no matter how collective had been the decision to attack the boat and how unintended had been the tragic results. So, if the CIA needed someone to take the fall for the team, Doyle reasoned, then maybe that should be his mission.

But should he take responsibility *for the wrong crime*? He was certain he had never aided any terrorists, at least not intentionally, but by going to prison for a crime he had not committed, the public would feel that someone had been held accountable for the *Izmir Queen* tragedy. It was an elegantly twisted form of justice. As the demands for accountability grew more intense, Doyle became convinced that going to jail would serve a useful purpose for him, too. He knew they would not award him any medals for throwing himself under the bus, but no matter what people thought about him, the sacrifice would give some meaning to the next few years of his life. Besides, what else was there left for him to do?

Not surprisingly, Doyle's parents encouraged him to take his lawyer's advice; it was perhaps the only thing they agreed upon. His father, who had been drafted reluctantly into the Vietnam War and remained bitter about returning soldiers being treated like war criminals, was adamant that Doyle should not become a scapegoat in the latest war. His mother tearfully assured Doyle that the jury would understand he had been fighting for an honorable cause and would excuse the unintended casualties. Of course, his parents had not seen what Doyle had seen in the Marseille burn ward. He saw the face from the third bed every night in his dreams. Each morning, as he awoke, he shuddered to think what it would be like to meet her in reality. If such a meeting ever occurred, he hoped she would not recognize him from his pictures in the newspapers.

Doyle did not hear for several weeks from any of his former colleagues at Sentinel Systems or the Central Intelligence Agency. People he had regarded as friends a few weeks earlier now shunned him as though he were a wife beater walking into a singles bar. Of course, he understood they could not talk to him about the case. He was, after all, under criminal indictment and they were witnesses for the prosecution. But Doyle guessed that the total ostracism sprang from something deeper. The dreadful mistake off the coast of Marseille had made the entire team appear disgraceful to the public, no better than the enemy they fought. Doyle had let them down. What hurt most, Leslie Jumana had not returned any of his calls. He had accepted that their love affair was over, but now he realized their friendship had also ended without so much as a good-bye. Then, shortly before his third meeting with Stuart Brons, he received a call. He did not recognize the number that appeared on his cell phone, but he knew the voice. "What happened to your phone?" he asked her.

"They subpoenaed it for the investigation," she replied. He started to speak but she cut him off. "Listen, Doyle, I can't talk about what happened."

Her voice sounded friendly, but strangely formal. He pictured her in business attire.

"You never know who may be listening," Doyle said. He hoped for a chuckle but Leslie remained silent. He sensed coldness in the empty pause.

"Are you still avoiding desserts?" she asked. Before he could answer, she continued, "I just wanted you to know I've been thinking about you." Her voice conveyed concern, but also impatience, as though the call was a painful duty she felt anxious to complete.

"That means a lot."

"You know, Doyle, everyone regrets what happened that night." He remained silent, not knowing what to say. "I'm sorry you're the one who has to pay the price so it doesn't happen again." Before he could respond, she mumbled something about having to go and wanting to stay in touch, and then she hung up.

Doyle puzzled over her message. Evidently, she thought that if he went to jail, others at the CIA would be more careful. If that was the price she wanted him to pay, then why was not she offering to pay it with him? She and the others had all been there that night, cheering when the boat was struck, so why were not a few of them stepping forward now, front and center, to share responsibility when it turned out to have been such a horrible mistake?

CHAPTER 29

Three Months after the Paris Attack

When Stuart Brons next asked Doyle to return to his office, he had big news. "The FBI thinks they know who sent you those e-mails and called you from Paris on the first of September." His thick fingers combed back his fine red hair, either to distribute it more evenly over the baldness or simply to give Doyle time to react. "It is someone named Khalid Osman, a former employee of Sentinel Systems."

"Ozzie, the translator?" Doyle's tone expressed surprise.

"That's the guy. They decided to recheck his background when someone recalled he had left the company abruptly." Everything about Khalid Osman had checked out as before: his certificate of birth in Barsa, a Maronite Christian village in Northern Lebanon; his high school records from Tripoli Evangelical School, one of the country's oldest; his college records from American University of Beirut, where he had graduated in the fall of 2001 with a degree in Public Administration. Everything had checked out—that is, until they spoke to his parents, a step that had been omitted during the original background check in the rush to recruit qualified translators. It turned out that Khalid Osman had died in a car accident near Damascus, Syria, on New Year's Eve, just a few weeks before someone claiming to be Khalid Osman had applied for an Arabic translator position at Sentinel Systems.

The identity theft was impeccable. No death certificate was on file, although the emergency room physician swore one had been submitted. His passport and driver license—both allegedly lost—had been renewed with the photograph and fingerprints of a different person. Charges and payments had continued on his credit cards, although the billing address had been changed to a Beirut post-office box. "They've been running the biometric data through the big computers at the CIA," Brons explained. In fact, they were doing the same checking at the FBI, DST, INTERPOL and just about every other police agency on earth. But all without results. The photograph and fingerprints apparently belonged to someone who had never been arrested. The trail led down a blind alley that had been scrubbed so thoroughly one could eat off its pavement.

Doyle pictured Ozzie the day he had first sat down at lunchtime in the Sentinel atrium garden, looking so intelligent behind his round rimless glasses, like a visiting scholar. He had long suspected there was something concealed behind Ozzie's generosity, his little compliments and his feigned interest in baseball. Why had he reached out to Doyle, and what had he expected to gain? His concise lectures on Arabic translation were always interspersed with discreet questions about Doyle's work. Under his subtle interrogation, Doyle may have disclosed more than he learned. Had he disclosed too much? Once, Ozzie asked him if he had a girlfriend. The diffident tone caused Doyle to wonder if he were gay, but now he realized Ozzie was trying to learn what might turn him on, which buttons he should push. Was his erotic masquerade over the Internet a ploy to gain from Doyle a few intimate glimpses into Sentinel's work for the CIA?

"So Ozzie was somehow linked with the Paris plotters," Doyle said.

"It sure looks that way," Brons replied, his eyes resting on Doyle's as though waiting for him to offer more. "Remember, he called you on one of their phones. Fortunately for you, the FBI has concluded you never answered the call or listened to the message he left."

"What message?"

"That's further proof you never listened to it," said Brons, chuckling as he searched his notes. "All the caller said was, 'Hello, Doyle. It's 22excited. I'm phoning to thank you for your help. I have other friends there. You'll be hearing from us. Bye for now.' That's all he left, except for his Middle-East accent and some traffic noise in the background. Naturally, the FBI is combing the world to find the guy, but they've had no luck, yet. They've also gone crazy searching for ways you might have helped him, but they've found no evidence of that. They've been forced to conclude you were nothing more than a victim."

Yes, it was clear that Ozzie intended to harm him. The ingratiating smile, rather than expressing friendship or desire, concealed hatred and contempt. Did he simply want to claim Doyle as one more casualty in his war against the West? He certainly achieved that. Or perhaps he sought from Doyle some sort of dialogue with the enemy, some semi-official recognition for his cause, as unimportant as Doyle may have been as a CIA contractor. Doyle sometimes wondered why he had not reported his suspicions about Ozzie sooner.

Brons' voice returned Doyle to the present. "Which brings me to another piece of good news: the US Attorney is willing to cut the plea bargain down to two years if you cooperate."

"Cooperate how?"

"Tell them everything you know about Khalid Osman. They're paranoid he's infested the CIA. The usual fumigation is underway, but you're no longer the chief cockroach."

So now it was Ozzie they were after. Doyle wondered what they thought he had done. Surely the self-effacing translator was no more than a low-level mole, a simple gatherer of information, most of which was publicly available. Or, did they think he might be higher up in the organization? Whatever he was, Doyle realized, Ozzie had just done him the favor of knocking two years off his prison term. "I'll be glad to tell them whatever I can. What does this mean for my case?"

"My advice stands: reject the plea bargain offer. I still think they're terrified that a public trial will expose too many errors by the CIA. Their willingness to offer us a two-year deal this early shows how desperate they are. I expect they'll settle for just your cooperation." He fell silent, apparently to let Doyle absorb the advice. When Doyle did not respond, Brons pressed gently for a decision. "So, if you agree, I'll inform the US Attorney."

"No, I've decided to take the offer."

"Now wait a minute, Doyle. You realize that means two years in prison?"

"I understand."

"But that's crazy!" The lawyer's normally bloodshot complexion had darkened to wine red. "I'm confident you'll get off scot-free if you reject the deal." Doyle remained silent. Brons came around from behind his glass desk, his stout physique somehow magnified by his high-priced suit, and stopped behind Doyle's chair. "I know you feel guilty, but don't jump at the chance to do prison time. If you need to do penance, maybe you can pray or something." He began a vigorous massage of Doyle's shoulders with his meaty hands. "Let old God decide how to punish you."

"I can't do that, Stuart," Doyle said over his shoulder. "This is kind of between me and my conscience."

Brons returned to his chair, his color restored, but still looking troubled. He argued with Doyle for another half hour over the pros and cons, conceding that the decisions of the prosecutor or the jury could never be predicted with certainty, but insisting that the case was unlikely ever to reach a guilty verdict. Doyle should at least hold off accepting the prosecutor's current offer, Brons advised, because the terms would likely improve as the trial date approached. In the end, however, Doyle stuck to his decision to accept the deal on the table. With evident misgivings, Brons scribbled a few notes and picked up the telephone.

Listening to his lawyer negotiating with the US Attorney, Doyle thought again about the night in the CIA control room. Why had he not spoken up? He had come to believe that the answer had something to do with the truth motto carved into the wall of the CIA lobby, the spot where Leslie Jumana had met him for their impromptu first date. *And ye shall know the truth and the truth shall make you free.* At first glance, it seemed like a fitting motto for the nation's intelligence agency, until Doyle learned it was a quote from the New Testament. It was then that he realized that blind faith and allegiance, the two moral virtues demanded by every religion in history, had distorted his perception of the truth that night. *And the truth shall make you free.* However certain and loyal he may have felt, his silence in the control room had deprived his colleagues of part of the truth, so it was only right that he should sacrifice a bit of his freedom.

Reflecting on his own motivations, Doyle wondered what had driven Ali Benhadj to pursue martyrdom on the other side of the strange war. He could only speculate, but when he tried to imagine what ideas had gone through Benhadj's mind, what surprised Doyle was how familiar those ideas seemed. Echoing across every battlefield in history, he could hear the myriad shouts for God, king and country. The dying scream of Benhadj was just one more battle cry among the millions heard in the past and the millions to be heard in the future until the last battle had been fought. Measured against the endless history of human warfare, Benhadj's horrendous act of murder and suicide on the *Avenue des Champs-Élysées* seemed depressingly ordinary.

Not that Doyle saw any moral equivalency between himself and Benhadj. No, there were essential differences between his fatal silence in the control room and the bloody massacre committed by the young jihadist in the restaurant. But Doyle had come to believe they also had something in common. The more he thought about what motivated the adversaries on both sides of the war, the more Doyle worried about how it would all end.

By the time Stuart Brons hung up the phone, the next phase of Doyle O'Gara's life had been settled. As anticipated, he would spend the next two years as a guest of the Allenwood Federal Penitentiary in Pennsylvania. The US Attorney had insisted that the sentencing take place promptly and that the imprisonment begin immediately thereafter. Evidently, the Government was anxious to satisfy the televised demands for moral accountability so the war against terror could march forward under an unstained banner. The terms suited Doyle. A week would be long enough to vacate his apartment and say good-bye to his parents. He had no desk to clean out at Sentinel Systems, no farewell parties to attend.

Doyle felt oddly unconcerned about the prospect of going to prison as he walked along the Capitol Mall later that day. Freedom did not seem important when he had no idea what he would do with the rest of his life. He had arrived in Washington eight months earlier filled with lofty, noble intentions. He had plunged into his new post at Sentinel with all the gusto of a boy diving into a clear stream on a warm day. But now he felt soiled by shame and regret. It had all been such a comedown. He was not sure if the sacrifice he was about to make would restore anything to his diminished life, but as he surveyed the darkened landscape of his soul, he could see no other path that might lead him back out of the abyss into which he had fallen.

CHAPTER 30

Afternoon of the Paris Attack

When the first explosion occurred inside the restaurant, Mohammed Jamal felt the shock wave fifty meters away on the other side of the avenue. Smoke and debris rose high into the air and pieces of furniture, chunks of concrete and shards of glass fell crashing onto the street and the tops of cars. People around him seemed to rush in opposite directions at the same time, torn between the instinct to escape and the desire to witness the horror. Jamal remained standing beside his café table. He spotted the yellow Renault Clio, still parked illegally near the smoldering restaurant, but now covered with debris from the explosion.

After a few minutes, he heard the first sirens and saw the police cars and ambulances approach down the avenue, squeezing their way between the lines of paralyzed cars and along the sidewalks. Jamal removed the second radio transmitter from his aluminum briefcase and slipped it into his jacket pocket. Then he forced his way into the moving crowd until he found a place near the center of the ten-lane avenue where he could better observe the scene. From his new vantage point, he saw people pressing closer to the bombed restaurant even as uniformed officers tried to cordon off the area. He waited patiently until he could no longer see the Renault Clio behind the thickening crowd.

Feeling his heart beat faster, Jamal placed his hand into his jacket pocket. In that same instant, a large man carrying a child on his shoulders stepped in front of Jamal and blocked his view, but the radio signal passed through the man, across the broad avenue and into the Renault Clio, detonating the second explosion before Jamal's finger had fully depressed the button on the transmitter. The shock wave was even stronger than the first, unbalancing the man and causing the child to fall from his shoulders. Jamal stooped to help the crying child to his feet. When he rose, he saw through the rising smoke and dust the great space that had opened up before the restaurant. He sensed the swelling against his trousers, the familiar arousal, but he was astonished by the size of the space and wondered if Rashid Badawi had packed more explosives than they had agreed. *No, I carried the bags myself; I felt their weight.*

His heart was pounding now. He did not expect there would be so many bodies. Half that number would surely have been sufficient. This would be the last operation, he suddenly decided. This one would be enough. He lifted one hand to his chest to slow the pounding. But this was war, he reminded himself, so the bodies were inevitable. The West had waged war against Muslims for centuries with weapons far more horrific than car bombs. The bloodshed he had wreaked today was justified by self-defense and the great objectives he would achieve. He must proceed with the plan. Trying to concentrate on the next steps, he heard the two explosions again, this time in his mind, and he felt the dull thud of the shock waves. Turning away from the destruction, he walked slowly up the avenue toward the *Arc de Triomphe* trying to appear inconspicuous, weaving unhurriedly among the halted cars and twice-shocked drivers, fighting the desire to break into a run.

He seized upon a stray question to refocus his mind. How was it possible for a radio signal to pass through solid objects, such as the body of the man and the metal of the car, when light could not pass through them? *One of those miracles of physics we take for granted.* But his mind jumped back to the double explosions, the two excruciating stabs he had thrust into the heart of Paris, and he realized he was laughing out loud, not an expression of mirth but a triumphant release of emotion over the enormity of his accomplishment. He looked around to see if anyone heard the laughter he was trying to suppress. He was relieved to see that all attention remained on the smoking ruins behind him.

"What happened?" the driver asked as Jamal entered a taxi at the *Place de l'Etoile*. The sounds of sirens could be heard in the distance.

"I don't know, some kind of accident." His voice sounded a pitch higher than usual, but the driver would have no way of knowing. "Take me to *94 avenue Mozart.*" The driver took off without hesitation. The motion seemed to relieve Jamal's palpitating heart. "I will need just a few minutes there. Then you can take me to *Gare du Nord*. I'm booked on the Eurostar to London this afternoon."

"You said number 94, *n'est ce pas?*—Near the corner with *rue de la Source*, correct?" By his accent, Jamal judged the driver to be Moroccan, about the same age as Waleed Yarkas. *But what a mind!* Paris must contain a hundred thousand street corners, yet the driver's brain had raced through all that data instantaneously to locate a single address, all while asking about an accident on the *Champs-Élysées. The mind of an ordinary taxi driver, like a supercomputer.* Jamal started to laugh again, but caught himself in time. He saw the driver smiling at him in the rearview mirror. "I bet he was a foreigner," he said over his shoulder.

"Who?"

"The guy in the accident. They don't know how to drive in Paris like we do."

By the time they reached the *Avenue Mozart* apartment, Jamal's heartbeat had returned to normal. Minutes later, he was back inside the taxi with his travel bag, heading to the city's largest train station. Yusuf Ghamdi would finish scrubbing the apartment of fingerprints and personal effects, then a dummy company would terminate the lease; no trace would remain of their brief presence in Paris. Jamal turned his attention to the trip ahead, but his mind jumped back to the huge space before the restaurant. They had no choice, he reassured himself. Without such provocation, the complacent West would never provide the catalyst for the change required in the Middle East. It was an enormous gamble, he realized, but what great man in history had risen to power without rolling the iron dice of violence?

He thought about the documents in his aluminum briefcase. Better to play those cards later, he decided. If the conservative regimes survived the political earthquake, then he would use the bank instructions to undermine whatever support they still had in the West. An anonymous message to the CIA would provide them all the clues they needed to trace the money back to Joseph Morgan and his oil-rich clients. The trail led through closed bank accounts in half a dozen tax havens, but the road map in Jamal's briefcase would enable them to identify everyone behind the financing—everyone, that is, except him, because by then he would no longer be Mohammed Jamal.

He saw *Gare du Nord* just ahead. He had no intention of catching the Eurostar to London. Instead, he would check into a cheap *hôtel de passe* near the station long enough to dye his hair blond, including the mustache that was growing bushier each day, and replace his glasses with baby-blue contact lenses. Transformed into a Northern European, he would then walk two blocks to *Gare de l'Est* and rent a car. With a Dutch passport and driver's license prepared a year before to match his planned appearance and identity, he would join a million other motorists on the French roads, crossing two uncontrolled borders on his way to Amsterdam. From there he would take a flight to Istanbul. He had selected the ancient city as his next target for unleashing jihad in Western Europe to unsettle the Middle East, because Istanbul straddled the two affected continents. He wondered if others would appreciate the symbolism in his choice.

Driving the rental car northward from Paris, he spotted a shopping center, its immense parking lot nearly empty. *Closed Sundays*, he noted with a smile. Despite their supposed Enlightenment, the French were still enslaved by their quaint Christian traditions. He stopped behind the shopping center, next to a row of metal dumpsters, and stepped out of the car. He had one more use for the cell phones in his briefcase before he disposed of them. *Every great artist must sign his work.* He had left his first signature in Paris that morning. He assumed they would be smart enough to identify the phone carried by the boy into the restaurant, and then connect it with the one he now held in his hand. He did not underrate their abilities the way they misjudged his. Now he would leave a second signature, a clue he expected would enrage and distract them. He dialed the number in Washington D.C. and waited for the signal to connect. He recalled the months he had spent there studying the opposing team. *A postgraduate course*, he chuckled. Looking up at the position of the late-afternoon sun, he judged that the US capital must lay somewhere on the other side of the metal dumpsters. This time, the phone signal would have to penetrate two thick walls of steel, he thought with fresh wonder.

He heard the recorded greeting of Doyle O'Gara. *It could have been anyone,* he thought, *but you happened to be sitting alone that day. You played your insignificant little role surprisingly well, my friend.* When the greeting ended, he left his brief message. Thinking of the consternation it would cause, he let loose a burst of laughter. The sound of his exultation died quickly in the vast emptiness of the parking lot, but the pleasure remained. He felt happy that his adversaries would come to know he was the man behind the Paris attack and realize how far he had gotten inside them.

But who was *he*, exactly? He knew his voice-mail would lead them to his imposture of Khalid Osman. Searching their all-knowing databases, they would eventually match the photographs and fingerprints to some of his many passports, but all his passports contained false identities. Since joining the Islamic Brotherhood, he had never used his real name on any official document. All his papers were forgeries, including the Dutch passport that would get him through Amsterdam emigration and onward into Turkey, where yet another false identity awaited him. Even among his Islamist associates, no one knew his real name.

He buried the phones deep inside the dumpsters, together with the Egyptian passport he had used for his recent travels. Within a day or two, he supposed, they would be buried still deeper in a rural French landfill, unlikely to be unearthed until the next Ice Age. He was not so arrogant as to believe they would never find him. No, they would eventually link one of his false identities to his physical person, but with his new name and appearance that would take time—several months, if he were lucky. By then, his operations would be complete and the Middle East would be convulsing with Western reprisals and popular uprisings. The West would be only too happy to bargain with the new masters in order to restore peace and keep the oil flowing. He expected to be part of those negotiations. Then the entire world would come to know who he was, if things went as planned.

The unsettling question did not occur to him until he had rejoined the highway and accelerated into the northbound traffic: *What if things don't go as planned?* A premonition of his own death flashed through his mind with terrifying clarity. *What if God or Fate or Quantum Mechanics— whoever or whatever controls things—suddenly swerves events in a different direction?* If they found his body on the side of a highway far from home, they would never determine who he really was. All they would have was an unknown driver carrying a false Dutch passport. His fingerprints and DNA would lead them nowhere except to another dozen false identities. They would never know it was *him*. Frowning, he turned on the radio. The angry shriek of a heavy metal band jolted the car, until he fumbled the volume down and switched through the stations, hoping to hear the latest news reports from Paris.

THE END

ABOUT THE AUTHOR

Marc McGuire is an American-born international lawyer who has lived much of his career in Europe, first in Zurich, Switzerland, and later in Paris, France.

NOTE FROM THE AUTHOR

Word-of-mouth is crucial for any author to succeed. If you enjoyed *Missions*, please leave a review online—anywhere you are able. Even if it's just a sentence or two. It would make all the difference and would be very much appreciated.

Thanks!
Marc

Thank you so much for reading one of our **Crime Fiction** novels.
If you enjoyed the experience, please check out our recommended
title for your next great read!

Caught in a Web by Joseph Lewis

"This important, nail-biting crime thriller about MS-13 sets the
bar very high. One of the year's best thrillers."
–BEST THRILLERS

www.ingramcontent.com/pod-product-compliance
Lightning Source LLC
Chambersburg PA
CBHW011136100726
47898CB00009B/3000